irresistible

REFRAIN

Edited by Pam Berehulke
Cover design by Michelle Preast at Indie Book Covers
Formatting by Elaine York at Allusion Publishing
www.allusionpublishing.com

irresistible REFRAIN

MICHELLE MANKIN

ABOUT THE BOOK

Two years ago everything changed for the remaining members of the Seattle rock band Tempest.

Two years is a long time.

Too long to keep on remembering.

Not nearly long enough to forget.

In trouble with nowhere else to go, songstress Lace Lowell seeks refuge with the band during their stop in New York City. It's a risky move for her because they are both there, two impossibly good looking men whose lives are inseparably entwined with hers. One who bruised her heart and one who smashed it into pieces.

Warren "War" Jinkins, the mercurial lead singer of Tempest, has always had a thing for Lace. But then again so does his best friend and bandmate.

Bryan "Bullet" Jackson, the sinfully handsome tat-sleeved lead guitarist, has a bad boy reputation befitting his nickname. For the past two years Bullet's had a rule with the groupies: one time, never twice, leave 'em satisfied, but always leave 'em.

Two guys, one woman, and a host of dark secrets all together within the tight confines of a tour bus as the group travels cross country.

Can the past be forgotten and buried?

Will friendships prevail?

Or will the three of them succumb to seductive impulses too addictive to resist?

IMPORTANT AUTHOR NOTE

A prequel novel is available. For the best reading experience, I recommend reading *Southside High* before reading *Irresistible Refrain*.

REFRAIN:

To keep from doing, feeling, or indulging in something; a recurring phrase or line, especially at the end of each stanza or division of a poem or song; a chorus; or the musical setting of a refrain.

Bryan

Six years ago

"**Y**our old man's an asshole."

"Tell me something I don't already know," I mumbled.

With my chin on the arms I'd crossed on top of my upturned knees, I turned my head to look at War as he lowered himself to the curb beside me. He mirrored my frown, his expression sympathetic. I reached back and pulled the hood of my jacket onto my head while he zipped up his. Southside Seattle in the summertime was still chilly, especially late at night.

"He shouldn't put down your mom like that." War stretched out his long legs. He and I had both recently grown several inches, just in time to start high school.

I nodded, my hands clenched into fists. *I hate the bastard.*

War looked over at me. "Better to have one that's not even around, huh?"

My eyes held his for a long moment, and the bravado he usually wore momentarily slipped away.

Though I'd known War since the beginning of middle school, he was one of those guys who kept his emotions light and near the surface—until three months ago, when he told me the truth about his father. Or more accurately, when he confided that his mom refused to tell him who his old man was. The identity of his father was a secret that I now knew gnawed at him constantly. War's outward *in your face* attitude was more of a defense mechanism, a shield he put up to keep most everyone else at arm's length.

"Yeah, fuck 'em." I bumped my shoulder to his. "I don't know why my mom lets that asshole in the door. It's the same damn thing every time he shows up."

I dug my hands into the front pockets of my jeans. War was better off with just him and his mom. No fake father pretending he cared.

"He comes back all nice and shit for a couple of weeks. Then he disappears again."

I glanced away, hated how my father always made me feel, as if I didn't measure up somehow. The first couple of times he'd come back around, I worked my ass off trying to be the perfect son, so desperate for his approval, so badly wanting him to stay.

Not anymore.

When I glanced back at War, his chin was down, his brow furrowed in concentration as he peeled the label off a discarded soda bottle.

This summer, our friendship had moved up to another level. Sure, we'd hung out a lot before. We both loved rock music—fast, heavy, and loud. We both dreamed of forming our own band one day, but there was more that kept us together now.

I knew about his old man, and he knew about mine. That knowledge cemented our bond.

And since neither of us had a brother, that's what we became to each other. If we weren't at each other's houses, we were prowling the streets together, looking for trouble. We did all kinds of crazy shit. I covered for him with his mom, and he covered for me with mine. Neither of us really wanted to be at home.

In the rare times that we weren't together, War scoured his house, looking for clues to his dad's identity. And I did my best to pretend to get along with mine, if only for my mom's sake.

Truthfully, I fucking hated my dad. He lounged around on the couch, drinking beer and doing nothing all day while my mom slaved away. She worked, cooked, cleaned, and went to school at night. Like doing all that would somehow change him. I promised myself I was never going to be that hung up over anyone.

Irritation spiked in me, just thinking about it. I couldn't stand to sit around and stew out here anymore. I needed an outlet. Our friend Kyle had a dirt bike he'd been letting me ride.

I turned to War. "Kyle still having that party tonight?"

"Yeah, you know Kyle. He's always having a party."

"I changed my mind. I wanna go."

Kyle's unofficial hobby was dealing dope. Mainly, he pedaled soft stuff like weed and pills. His way of bringing in new customers was to hand out free samples at his parties.

But I didn't really care about that. I just wanted a turn on the bike. I needed to feel the wind on my face, and put a little physical distance between my old man and me. Pretend that he didn't exist for a while.

"Fair enough." War held out his hand as I stood.

I clasped it and pulled him up. He didn't question me about why I'd changed my mind, but I didn't miss his knowing glance.

"Cut through to Fifty-Second?" he asked.

"I guess," I said with a shrug. It would be faster but would take us through La Rasa Prima territory. That didn't really

3

bother War since the leader of the gang's sister had a thing for him, like a lot of the older chicks did.

We cut quickly across the adjacent vacant lot and slipped through a break in the chain-link fence on the other side. A couple of gangbangers turned to watch us dart across the busy street, but they left us alone. *Thank God.* A confrontation with guys like that never ended well.

We kept our heads down and passed by several closed businesses, their windows boarded up and spray painted with graffiti, before we finally arrived at Kyle's apartment complex. Broken glass crunched beneath my shoes as War and I walked up the front sidewalk to his unit. I didn't know how Kyle was able to have, let alone afford an apartment, but I suspected it had something to do with who he dealt drugs for.

Loud bass boomed from the music being played inside, and I set aside speculation. However Kyle came to have the apartment, it was as good a place to be as any.

Kyle answered the door and slurred out a greeting to War. Glassy-eyed and swaying, he led us inside the apartment. I scraped the hood off my head, pushed my hair out of my eyes, and waved off an offer of a drag from his joint.

"Wasn't expecting you to bring your wingman," he said to War, his red-rimmed eyes glancing in my direction.

"Bryan's cool." War threw an arm around my shoulder.

Warmth spread through my chilled limbs. War and I had had an unwritten understanding since our first meeting in middle school. He took care of me, and I had his back. No one was ever going to come between us. It was as simple as that.

We stood in the living room for a while, War and Kyle smoking pot and me goofing around, until War wandered off upstairs with a woman who looked to be in her twenties. It wasn't the first time I'd seen him hook up with someone that much older, but so far, there hadn't been any fallout. There didn't seem to be any consequences for War, no matter what or who he did.

From day one, I'd decided that Warren Jinkins was the absolute shit. Worrying about the way I looked up to him was the reason my mom had enrolled me in a teen leadership class. When I told War the teacher's slogan was to *do what's right and your peers will follow*, War had laughed.

"More like do what's wrong," he'd joked. "And you'll always have enough people for a party."

I'd already taken a spin on the bike and was just getting bored when War came back downstairs, finger combing his brown hair with one hand and tucking in his T-shirt with the other.

He steered me toward the door. "Let's get out of here."

We ended up hitting our favorite convenience store on the Ave for snacks and then went to his place, a small foursquare house two streets over from my apartment. I pulled out the secondhand Epiphone I kept stored in his closet, and we worked on a couple of songs, me on guitar, and War on vocals. They weren't original tunes, just covers. When we were done practicing, we crashed hard.

• • •

I blinked slowly when War shook me awake around dawn.

"What?" I muttered, wiping drool off my cheek.

"Get up."

I pushed up from the worn couch I usually slept on in his room. My eyes narrowed as I studied his face. He looked really upset about something. "What's going on?"

He waved a piece of paper in front of my face, and I pushed his hand back so I could actually read what it said. It appeared to be a brush-off letter addressed to his mom. Before I could finish reading it, he yanked it away.

5

"She'd hidden it in her jewelry box, folded up under a false bottom. It's from my dad, Peter fucking Frangella." War's earnest eyes met mine. "I looked him up. He's some kind of big shot with his own law firm."

He was so worked up, his hands shaking as he bent over to pull his shoes out from under his bed.

"And he's married," War mumbled. "With two kids."

Shit.

With War determined to confront his dad immediately, we rode the train to Bellevue. It took forty-five minutes and two transfers. The squalor of Southside gave way to tree-lined streets, landscaped yards, and thriving businesses. Once we got inside his dad's office building, War bullshitted his way past the security guard while I waited in the lobby, my stomach knotted up with anxiety for him.

It didn't take long.

A flurry of F-bombs echoed off the walls as soon as War exited the elevator, his expression darker than I'd ever seen it. He slapped a hand against the glass entry door to fling it open, and I followed him out of the building. I glanced behind us, half afraid by the way he was acting that someone would come chasing after us. War pulled me into the building's adjacent parking garage.

"What happened?" I asked, a little out of breath.

"First, he tried to pretend the letter wasn't his." War raked a hand through his hair. "When he realized I wasn't buying that shit, he flat-out told me to get out. He even threatened to call security if I didn't go."

Seeing War so upset, I got mad right along with him, furious that we both had such fucked-up fathers. That's when I happened to notice the name on the assigned parking spot to our left. *Frangella.*

I pointed it out. "That must be your dad's car, right?"

Scowling, War glanced at it and nodded.

"Fucking asshole has a brand-new BMW. Still has the dealer tags on it. Doesn't seem right." I rubbed my chin. That shiny paint job seemed to be taunting me, as fake and false as both our old men were. I glanced at War, raising a brow in question. "You know, Kyle showed me how to hotwire and cut the alarm on one of these."

"Fuck yeah," War said without hesitation, his lips curving into a wicked grin.

Within minutes, I had the alarm disabled and the car started. War took shotgun. We both wore crazy-ass grins on our faces as I steered the BMW out of Eastside and took the entrance ramp onto the 405. We rolled down the windows. It was fucking awesome.

I didn't have much of a plan. I just remembered a field trip we'd taken several years ago, so I exited on Southeast Eighth Street with a vague idea of heading to Kelsey Creek Park and hanging out.

But we never made it there.

With the music up loud, I wasn't paying enough attention to the road. I was fifteen, and I found out quickly that a car was a lot more difficult to negotiate than a dirt bike. Long story short, our fucking good time came to an abrupt end when we rammed into a train trestle at a good thirty-five-mile-an-hour clip.

My face stinging, I wrinkled my nose at the unpleasant chemical odor that came from the deployed airbag I was buried in. After disentangling myself from the sticky material that didn't seem to want to let me go, I glanced to the side. War's face was bright red like someone had bitch-slapped him. I probably looked exactly the same.

"I'm okay," War said, his wide-open brown eyes meeting mine. "Just kinda woozy and sore."

That's exactly how I felt. Without saying any more, we released our seat belts and unlatched our doors. As I got out, I noticed there weren't even any skid marks on the road because I hadn't reacted in time to apply the brakes.

I looked at War over the roof of the car. "We'd better get out of here, dude."

"And fast," he added unnecessarily, looking more than a little freaked out.

We hit the ground running flat-out, our adrenaline high and breathing hard. But we weren't fast enough. A couple of cops in a squad car passed by us, did a double-take, and swung a U-turn.

Shit.

"Let me take care of this, Bry," War said under his breath.

"What are you going to do?" I asked, my eyes huge and my heart pounding hard as the cops pulled up beside us.

War gave me a serious-as-shit look. "I think it's been established that I take care of my friends, right?"

I nodded. He certainly had. War had pulled my ass out of the fire plenty of times. Most recently, by taking the blame when I'd spray painted some choice obscenities on a bathroom wall at school.

It went without saying that I'd had a lot of anger issues since my old man came back.

War spoke quickly as the cops climbed out of the squad car. "You know that's just me. But more important is that my mom won't give a shit if I get in trouble. Hell, she probably won't even notice, but yours will. You've got a good thing going with your mom," he said, and I nodded. "We both know that if she found out you did something like this, it would wreck all that. So, bro, let me handle this."

As we stood there together side by side on the rain-slickened pavement and watched the cops approach, my fritzed-out thoughts were all over the place. But above the static, what hit me hardest was what War hadn't said, yet I understood, especially after the deal with his father today.

I was the only real family Warren Jinkins had.

Bryan

Present day

I woke with my head pounding out a heavy bass throb and glanced at my watch. Four fucking a.m. *Damn.* I'd only been asleep for a couple of hours.

The bottle of tequila had obviously been a big mistake, but not the worst one I'd ever made. I'd have to go back to my senior year in high school for that one.

Before the memories could surface, I slammed a lid on them.

My mouth tasted like sand. I needed a bottle of water and at least two extra-strength Tylenol.

I rolled out of my bunk, cursing when my toes met the freezing-cold floor of the tour bus. A forceful winter storm wind rocked the forty-five-foot-long structure from side to side and howled beneath the undercarriage.

Pulling on yesterday's jeans, I grabbed a pack of cigarettes and my lighter before pushing the button to open the pocket door to the front lounge. A woman sat at the banquette with her back to me, a woman I'd recognize anywhere. She was my costliest mistake and the best of everything all wrapped up in one.

Lace.

I froze, wondering when she'd come on board. It must have been last night while I'd been preoccupied with the twins.

Quickly running back over the previous evening's events, I realized that War had been conspicuously absent from the meet and greet. He must have been with her. The familiar jealous burn seared the inside of my chest like battery acid.

Hundreds of memories rushed to fill my mind.

Walking with Lace. Talking to her. Sharing, connecting, wanting her. Having her . . . once. Hesitating a moment too long afterward and losing her. That wasn't just any wall between us now; it was an unbreachable one.

Her face was as captivatingly beautiful as I remembered, framed by honey-blond hair that was much longer than it had been the last time I'd seen her. She was thinner too. Too thin. Her cheekbones were more prominent, her complexion pale, and even her wide lips seemed drained of their usual apricot color.

Her head turned slightly, and eyes the color of expensive whiskey met mine. "Bryan."

That breathy voice of hers shot right to my groin. Even with me being hung over and recently satiated, my dick came right to attention, clamoring after what it could never have. What *I* could never have.

The woman War loved.

"Lace." I took my time taking her in. The long-sleeved black Tempest T-shirt War had worn onstage last night hung to mid-thigh on her.

I knew damn well what was underneath that shirt. As I remembered the shape, the texture, and the taste of her, my hands shook so badly, I had to shove them into the back pockets of my jeans so she wouldn't notice.

Lace gave me a darting sidelong glance while bringing her long, shapely legs closer together, and tucked a strand of hair behind her ear.

She looked nervous. I didn't get it. So what if I was shirtless with my jeans half-buttoned? It wasn't like she hadn't seen me this way before. I wasn't going to cover up for her.

She licked her lips. "Nipple ring's new," she said quietly.

"Yeah, nice of you to notice." I got my legs going and moved toward her, motioning to the banquette. "Scoot over."

Holding the hem of the shirt in place over her ass and thighs, she slid toward the window to make room for me. I flopped down on the padded two-person bench seat and stared at her profile.

"You get in last night?"

"Yeah." She shifted away from me, just a tad but enough that I noticed, twisting her hands so tightly together that her fingertips turned red.

"What the hell are you doing here?" My tone was harsh and demanding, even though I was secretly glad to see her. I drank her in from her head to bare toes in a greedy gulp, cataloguing every line and curve.

It had been too long. Two and a half years. My memories didn't do her justice.

"I thought you were with Martin now."

Lace had started up with him right before the band had signed our first record deal, and she couldn't have chosen a more dangerous man. War had been apoplectic. Me, I'd hidden how I felt, just like I'd been doing for as long as I could remember. My friendship with War left me with no other choice.

"He'd kick your ass if he knew you were here," I said. "War's too."

I'd been joking around, but when she turned her head, I sucked in a sharp breath, wishing I hadn't been so flippant.

The left side of her face was covered with a collage of faded purple and yellow bruises. It was obvious she'd been hit hard, multiple times.

I gripped the side of the table with both hands, wishing I could squeeze Martin's neck instead.

I'm going to kill that motherfucker. I didn't care that he was armed and had a bodyguard.

A spark of defiance brightened Lace's eyes, giving me a glimpse of the vibrant woman I remembered. "Yeah, well, as you can see, he already took care of that. I didn't stick around to give him a chance to make both sides match."

"What the hell happened?"

Her shoulders sagged, the momentary flash of sass disappearing quickly. She was quiet for so long that I didn't think she planned to answer.

Finally, she said, "It's not important. Not anymore. It's over between us."

Lace had that stubborn tilt to her jaw that I recognized. I wasn't going to get any more information out of her than she wanted to give.

I was overjoyed by that news, ecstatic, but . . . "Does Martin know it's over?"

"Oh yeah. I think his fists made that perfectly clear."

"You mean to tell me that *he* broke it off with *you*?" I couldn't hide the disbelief in my tone. The guy was an idiot as well as an asshole. What man in his right mind would give up Lace if he had her?

"Yes, he did. It was terrible. It had been bad for a long time, but I just chose to ignore it." Her gaze dropped to her lap, her sexy lips pressing into a tight line. "I pawned the engagement ring he gave me for a bus ticket out here. What's left over from that is all I have."

Most women I knew would have teared up after all this, but not Lace. She never cried. *Strike that.* She never cried anymore. When we'd been kids, she'd cried a hell of a lot. But the last time had been the night of the Metallica concert.

"I'm sorry." I reached over and covered her delicate hand with mine.

"Don't be," she said, slowly pulling her hand away. "Martin was just another mistake in a long line of them."

Lace watched me for a moment through a gap in the curtain of her gold hair.

"What about you, Bullet?" Her eyes took on a mischievous glint. "Or should I say,"—she paused and added an orgasmic-sounding breathless moan—"Oh, Bullet! Faster! Harder!"

The corners of her mouth lifted with amusement at my expense, and I winced.

Shit. She'd heard me in the back bedroom with the twins. I didn't usually go for multiples. It was too much work, but after getting the brush-off from Avery Jones, the beautiful lead guitarist of Brutal Strength, I'd felt like I had something to prove.

"You know me, Lace." I watched her face carefully. "I don't do relationships. I told you once why." I got up and snagged a couple of bottled waters from the refrigerator.

"Yeah, that's not something I'm likely to forget," she said softly, her voice sounding strained.

Sensing the undercurrent of meaning just beneath the surface of the words we were saying to each other, I swung back around. But her eyes didn't give anything away.

"I'm sorry. I was just messing with you," she said with a dismissive wave of her hand that I didn't buy. "What you do with your personal life is none of my business. No offense, okay?"

"None taken," I said, but I still felt uneasy.

I handed her one of the bottles of water, and she took it before turning away to look out the window. Holding back a groan of relief, I grabbed the Tylenol bottle from the table and knocked back a couple of tablets while watching her.

We were silent for a while, both lost in our own thoughts. Tension hung between us, but it was familiar and not entirely uncomfortable. I'd known Lace Lowell practically all my life.

I'd never forget our first meeting at the apartment my family had lived in at the University House. I was seven and she was five . . .

· · ·

Fourteen years ago

"Get the door, Bry."

My mom was cooking in the open galley kitchen, but her voice carried easily across the small space separating it from the living room where I'd been sitting, playing my video game.

"Sure, Mom." The sizzle of cooking meat and the aroma of garlic and cheese from my favorite flavor of Hamburger Helper filled the apartment, making my stomach grumble.

I dropped the game controller onto the soft throw my mom used to make the old couch from Goodwill look nicer, and stomped over to the door.

"Who is it?" I asked before opening it, just like she'd taught me to do.

"Dizzy Lowell," was the muffled reply.

I grinned. Dizzy was my new best friend, and yeah, that was his real name. He sat in the desk in front of me in Miss Harper's second-grade class. We traded Pokémon cards at recess, and played this really fun game at lunch where we tried to gross each other out by mixing different items from our lunch trays. Today, Dizzy won. He'd stuffed his bread roll into his chocolate milk carton and added ketchup. I'd laughed so hard at the face he'd made that milk had spurted from my nose.

"Hey," he said when I opened the door. His long blond hair was all messed up. My mom wouldn't have let me out of the apartment with my hair like that. But Dizzy looked like that all the time. His clothes were usually dirty too. "I had to bring my little sister with me. Is that okay?"

"Sure." I opened the door wider and watched a little girl follow him inside. Her hair and eyes were the same color as his, and her small hand was fisted in his worn-out shirt.

Dizzy stopped in front of our TV, and his mouth dropped open. "You have Pokémon!"

I nodded. "I told you. My mom says we can play until dinner is ready."

Dizzy spun around and squatted down in front of his sister to put his hands on her shoulders. Her bottom lip stuck out, and she looked like she wanted to cry.

"Lace, don't be afraid, okay? Bryan's cool." He tugged on one of her braids and helped her up on the couch. "Sit here, right next to me."

She watched me with her golden eyes, but she didn't move or make a sound the entire time we played. That was weird, not at all like my younger sisters. When they were awake, they were a royal pain in the rear. They got into all my stuff, and they never shut up.

"Bry," my mom called out after we'd been playing for a while.

Beside me, Lace squeaked and tried to climb behind her brother's back.

Shoot. We were just getting to the good part.

"Time to stop."

My mom came in, drying her hands on a kitchen towel, and Lace started shaking. Mom frowned as she looked at her.

16

"I'm going to wake your sisters from their nap," she said to me in a soft voice. "I'll be right back."

"Why's she so scared?" I whispered to Dizzy after my mom left the room.

"Lace is afraid of grown-ups." He turned around and touched her back. "Come on. Stop hiding. It's time to go."

"Wait," I said. "Maybe you can stay a little longer. Let me ask my mom." When she returned to the living room, I gave her my best puppy-dog eyes. "Can we have five more minutes? Please? We're almost done."

She leaned over the couch and ruffled my hair. I knew her answer before she said it. Puppy-dog eyes worked every time. "Dizzy," she said, using a soft voice. "Would you and your sister like to stay and eat dinner with us?"

"We can't." Dizzy stuck his hands in his pockets and stared down at his dirty sneakers. "My mom wants us in our apartment by six."

"Maybe Saturday for lunch then?"

"Sure." Dizzy gave her a big smile before asking to use the restroom. He went to the back and my mom returned to the kitchen.

I sneaked a peek at Lace. She'd pulled her legs up under her chin and wrapped her arms around them.

I was the man of the house, and my mom told me my job was to take care of the girls. It made me sad to see Lace looking so scared.

Wanting to make her smile, I scooted closer to her. She put her cheek on her knee and watched me. When I stuck my tongue out at her and rolled my eyes, her lips twitched. I put my hand under my armpit and made the farting sound a couple of times.

Lace giggled.

Yes! I slid right beside her, happy when she didn't move away.

"I like your eyes," I said in a soft voice like my mom had used. "They're pretty."

Lace gave me a smile so big, I could see that her top two front teeth were missing. "Are you Printh Charming?" she asked me with a lisp.

"Huh-uh." *As if.*

Dizzy came back in the room and grinned at me as he flopped back on the sofa. He must have heard that last bit.

"I'm going to marry you someday," Lace said, nodding like it was a done deal. "When I'm all growed up and pretty like Cinderella."

I started to laugh, but choked it back when I saw how serious she looked. It seemed so important to her that I found myself agreeing. Even though I knew Dizzy would never let me hear the end of it.

• • •

Present day

Here we were, all these years later, and Lace Lowell still had the ability to tie me up in knots. I still wanted to protect and please her, but I was powerless to do either.

Some fucked-up fairy tale I'm living.

She stared out the one-way windows of the bus. There was nothing to see. It was dark, and we were parked between two buildings with only an occasional flicker of white from blowing snow to break up the monotony of the view.

"What's Avery Jones like?" Lace asked quietly, turning to face me.

Tense, I gave that some thought, choosing my words carefully. "She's a hell of a guitarist."

Lace swallowed. "And?"

"And nothing." I shrugged. "She's back with Marcus Anthony now, if that's what you're asking."

"Sorry. I saw some pictures of you two." There was an edge to her voice that hadn't been there before. "It seemed like she might be important to you."

I was seriously contemplating telling Lace right then and there that she was the only woman who had ever been important to me, when I heard the door to the bus's sleeping compartment slide open behind us.

"Guys, it's four fucking a.m." His voice gruff with disapproval, War brought our intimate predawn reunion to an end. Looking wan and strung out, the lead singer of Tempest shuffled into view, wearing only a pair of red boxers and scratching his bare chest. "Come on back to bed, babe."

Shooting me an irritated glance, he held out his hand to her. She patted my knee, and I took the cue to scoot out of the booth ahead of her so she could exit.

War threw a proprietary arm around her shoulders as soon as her bare feet hit the floor, then grinned at me. "Night, loser."

"Night, asshole."

He gave me the middle finger before he closed the door.

I stared at the door for a long time.

Nothing had fucking changed. I had twenty thousand people screaming my name during my guitar solo at Madison Square Garden, plus twins in my bed afterward, but none of that mattered to me.

Not when my best friend had the woman I'd always wanted.

chapter 2

Lace

My mind remembered how badly Bryan Jackson had hurt me, but my traitorous body wanted me to forget. It wanted me to go back to the front lounge, wrap my legs around that washboard waist of his, curl my fingers into his tattooed biceps, fuse my mouth to his, and beg him to make *me* moan instead of those twins.

Fortunately for me, my mind overruled, and the nail prints in my palms were the only casualty I sustained after this particular run-in with Bryan.

I followed War past the triple stack of bunks where my brother and the other band members slept. The dotted line of emergency lighting on the floor our guide, War ducked his head to enter the small, dark bedroom in the back of the tour bus.

He was tall, a half inch taller than Bryan, and his lean frame dwarfed the full-size bed as he crawled into it and held the covers out for me. Knee to the mattress, I slid underneath the covers with him and shimmied close. An errant light brown strand tickled my nose as I laid my cheek against his smooth chest, right over his solid-black heart tattoo.

I tried to make myself relax while he stroked my hair. But relaxing after being around Bryan wasn't easy. In fact, I knew from experience that it was nearly an impossible task.

"You okay, babe?" War's deep voice rumbled near my ear. It was dark, but I imagined his brown eyes were probably crinkled at the corners with concern.

"Yeah," I lied. "I'm okay." The truth was too depressing for anybody to want to hear.

"Why were you up?" he asked.

"Couldn't sleep."

"Need another hit?"

"No."

Drugs didn't work anymore. No matter how much shit I did, my mind still raced around in pointless circles.

In the wreckage of my life, there were no easy answers. I'd gotten myself so far off course that I didn't see any way to make it right. It seemed like I'd suddenly woken up one day to find myself here, but the reality was that by making one poor decision after another, I'd slid further and further away from my goals and the person I wanted to be.

War shifted, the sheets rustling softly as he turned on his side, facing away from me. Being alone in the dark with my thoughts was something I'd grown accustomed to. He fell asleep quickly, the sound of his breathing evening out. As the lonely minutes of the night ticked slowly toward morning, I remained awake.

My thoughts drifted to Bryan, as they often did, even while I'd been with Martin.

If possible, Bryan had gotten even better-looking since I'd seen him last. His light brown hair was trimmed short into a faux hawk. Long on top, short on the sides, it was the perfect style to set off his gorgeous gray-green eyes and that shadowed square jaw of his. It was disheartening to discover that the years apart hadn't lessened the hold he had over me.

Why couldn't I accept the way things were? Bryan was never going to be mine, no matter how much I wished things were different.

My mind drifted to the past.

I remembered when Bryan, his mom, and his younger sisters had moved into the apartment below ours. I'd been five, and he was seven. Bryan, Dizzy, and I had become the best of friends, an inseparable trio, using our imagination to escape the harsh reality around us.

Our favorite game had been pretending we were rich-and-famous rock stars. When I was in charge, I was Britney Spears, and the boys were my roadies. When it was their turn, Guns N' Roses or Metallica was the band, which left me with only one choice . . . to be the band manager, of course.

I'd idolized Bryan Jackson for as long as I could remember. He treated me with the same respect he did his own sisters, and I loved him for that. He and my brother were the only protectors I had in a neighborhood where drug deals and drive-by shootings were commonplace, in a world where even my own apartment wasn't safe.

• • •

Eight years ago

"Hi, Lace." Mrs. Jackson looked up at me as I entered the apartment with the key she'd given Dizzy and me to use years before. She wanted to be sure we had somewhere safe to go whenever our mom was strung out.

"Bryan ready?" I asked, wondering where he was.

"He's in the shower. He should be out any minute." She laid aside the pants she'd been mending, an old pair of mine. She'd been adding material to the cuffs so I could wear them longer. "I can't believe he won Metallica tickets. Are you as excited as he is about going?"

I nodded.

"Come and sit with me." Mrs. Jackson patted the cushion beside her.

Though it had a new slipcover, it was the same old couch I'd buried my head in the first time I met Bryan, the time I told him I was going to marry him someday. That was still my plan. Only now I was eleven, I was mature enough that I didn't speak every thought out loud.

I took a seat next to my future mother-in-law and plucked at the loose threads in the knees of my frayed jeans. Grown-ups still made me nervous.

She touched my hand and gave me a smile just like his that made her eyes sparkle. His mom was really nice, nothing at all like mine. Bryan's mom was always doing things to help Dizzy and me out without making it seem like charity.

"How's school?" she asked.

"Fine."

"Bry says you made the top grades in your class again."

I shrugged, but inside I was always pleased by Bryan's praise. "In everything but math. I hate it."

There was a long silent pause. Finally, I heard the shower shut off.

The one-bedroom apartments at the University House high-rise were small, even by public-housing standards. All had the same layout. The kitchen, dining, and living areas were in one room, with the bedroom and bathroom down a short hallway in the back. Bryan's family of four was cramped inside the tight space. His sisters and mom shared the only bedroom, while he slept on the couch.

Despite being the same floor plan, Bryan's apartment and ours couldn't have been more different. Bryan's mom was always adding little decorative touches like the slipcover that transformed their place from an apartment to a home. Our apartment was a disaster zone, littered with trash, dirty laundry, and our mom's pipes and needles.

Whenever she was on a long binge, like her current one, it got even worse. Dangerous, paranoid, and unpredictable, Mom would hole up in her room for days and didn't even bathe. It was a relief to be able to escape and come downstairs, even if it was only for a little while.

"Hey, Lace." Bryan walked around the couch, running a brush through his wet hair. "Where's Dizzy?"

"Should be here soon," I said. "He's changing clothes."

Dizzy had a weekend job bussing tables and washing dishes at Mr. Spinelli's Greek restaurant on the Ave. At thirteen, he was way too young to officially hold a job, but Mr. Spinelli overlooked that and paid Dizzy in cash. That money helped us purchase the basic things we needed like food, toiletries, and school supplies.

Suddenly, a loud thump came from the apartment above. *Our apartment.* Worried, I froze, staring at the ceiling and listening intently. Muffled yelling followed and then an ominous crash.

I jumped up, my heart racing. "I'd better check and see what's going on."

Hurrying to the door, I threw a quick glance at Bryan. His worried expression matched mine. He was the only one who really knew how bad things were up there.

"Lace, wait." Mrs. Jackson's voice followed me out into the hall, but I ignored her.

I flew up the stairwell and burst through the door of our apartment. Fear transformed into full-blown terror as I took in the scene. Two drug dealers I recognized stood at opposite sides of the living room, one near my mother, the other holding Dizzy, who was struggling to break free.

"Lace, get out of here quick!" my brother yelled.

I bolted for the door, but I wasn't fast enough. Two meaty hands landed on my shoulders, and I found myself spun around.

"She's a pretty one, Mama," the pusher with long stringy hair said to my mother.

His rancid breath nearly made me puke as he leered down at me, and I started to shake.

"Leave her alone!" Dizzy shouted while twisting violently in the arms of the large man restraining him. "She's just a kid."

"Sean likes 'em young," the heavyset dealer said. His fat lips curled into a sneer.

His fingers digging painfully into the sensitive flesh of my upper arms, Sean backed me up against the wall. Bile burned the back of my throat as he let go of one arm to touch my cheek. Warm tears leaked out of the corners of my eyes.

"Mama." Sean threw a meaningful glance our mother's way. "If you want your candy, I get your daughter. That's the deal."

"No!" Dizzy struggled in the heavyset guy's hold. "Let her go, you piece of shit!"

"Shut him the fuck up, Trace," Sean said harshly.

With a sharp metallic click, Trace opened a switchblade and brought it to my brother's throat. My eyes widened and my chest got so tight, I could barely breathe. I shook my head, but no one paid attention to me.

"You heard him, little man," Trace said to my brother, and a volcano of ineffectual anger erupted inside Dizzy's eyes. "Be quiet."

I looked to my mother for help. "Please, Momma. Tell them no. Make them go away."

Her eyes dull and lifeless, my mother stared right through me as if I didn't even exist. Sean yanked my arm and pulled me toward the bedroom.

"No," I shouted, trying to slow him down by dragging my feet. "I'll scream."

"You better not, or I'll have Trace carve up that brother of yours." Sean gripped me tighter, his fingernails digging into my arms, and more tears stung my eyes. "And stop your bawling. Tears don't change a damn thing in this shitty world. You're old enough to know better."

Inside the bedroom, he kicked the door closed and had me pinned to the bed within seconds. I struggled at first, but stopped when I realized he grinned even wider at that. His body was so heavy on top of mine that I found it difficult to breathe, and when his hands slithered up under my shirt, I stopped wanting to try.

I turned my head toward the door and curled up inside myself, pretending I wasn't even there. Just as a welcome blackness was taking me away, a heavy pounding and loud voices came from outside the apartment.

"Police!"

That one word was my lifeline. It gave me the strength to renew my struggle.

Sean threw a furtive glance at the window, but our apartment was on the eleventh floor, so that wasn't going to work out very well for him. Evidently reaching the same conclusion, he gave me a hard shake before he jumped off me.

"Keep your mouth shut, or I'll come back for you and your brother. I know a guy who likes little boys. Understand?"

Scrambling off the bed, I nodded and went to the far corner of the room, wanting as much distance between him and me as I could possibly get. My back against the wall, I slid to the floor. I pulled my knees to my chest as he threw open the door and froze in front of a cop's drawn gun.

"Turn around. Hands up on the wall, Evans," the uniformed officer said. "I should have known slime balls like you and Carson would be involved in something like this."

Behind him, another officer had already restrained Trace. My mother stood listlessly beside them, her eyes vacant, and made no effort to come to me.

"Detective Shannon. So nice to see you," Sean said, his voice dripping with sarcasm.

"I suggest you exercise your right to remain silent." Detective Shannon's gaze swept over me as he cuffed Sean, then glanced over his shoulder. "You can come in. The girl's in here. Looks pretty shaken up."

Dizzy came in first, tearing up when he saw me, and Mrs. Jackson was right behind him. My brother crossed the room and knelt on the floor, reaching out for me.

"No." Cowering, I shook my head. "Don't touch me."

Dizzy withdrew, looking hurt. When I noticed Bryan hovering in the doorway, watching us with a worried frown, shame burned my cheeks. I laid my head on my crossed arms and closed my eyes, trying to block everything out.

"Let me talk to her," Mrs. Jackson said. "I think she'll respond better to a woman right now."

I felt the warmth from her body as she sank down beside me and gently stroked my hair.

"You did nothing wrong, Lace," she said in her soft voice. "But you need to tell the police the truth. You and Dizzy can't stay here anymore with your mom. It's not safe."

After that, Dizzy and I had moved in with our uncle Bruce. He was a mean son of a bitch, but he didn't knock us around, and at least we were off the Ave.

I didn't see Bryan again until high school. By then, I was so full of myself, my ego had inflated along with my cup size. I'd believed my good looks and curves would be my salvation, my way out from under the shameful shadow my mother had cast over me. I was so certain that I could make good grades, play my music, and make something out of my life.

But I was so very wrong.

chapter 3

Bryan

Present day

I paced inside the cramped backstage area, waiting for my family to arrive for the show. They were coming in from Seattle to catch our second performance at Madison Square Garden.

Over in the corner, War, the lucky bastard, had his arms wrapped around Lace. She wasn't smiling but looked rocker sexy, having knotted a tour T-shirt underneath her breasts in a way that accentuated them and exposed a great deal of skin above a pair of dark jeans that fit her like a glove.

Watching the two of them together made me even edgier. I looked away, spinning the leather cuff on my watchband around to check the time again. Thirty more minutes before we went on. *Shit.* Since we were the opening band for the mega-group Brutal Strength, there was no way Tempest could go on late.

Where was my family? Their plane landed hours ago, and they should have been here by now. I wondered if last night's winter storm had something to do with them being delayed.

"Bry!"

Relief rolling through me, I turned at the sound of a trio of familiar feminine voices calling my name, and had only seconds to brace myself before being enveloped in a group hug.

"Mom." I kissed the top of her head, which only came to the center of my chest now. My mom might be tiny, but a more resilient woman I'd never met, except perhaps for one other.

The crappy hand life had dealt my mom hadn't made her bitter. She'd only become more determined to succeed, sacrificing everything over the years to take care of my sisters and me. I could never repay her for all she'd done for us, but that sure as hell wasn't going to stop me from trying.

I rocked back on the heels of my favorite pair of motorcycle boots and looked at my younger sisters.

Miriam was the oldest, a senior now, and the one I worried about the most. Although as driven as my mom to succeed, Miriam had a talent for getting into trouble. She acted first and thought things through later . . . if at all.

Recently, it had taken quite a bit of finesse on my mom's part to keep the school from suspending Miriam when she'd been caught on the roof having an impromptu snowball fight with her friends from the drama department. Her vivacious personality and good looks were ideal for the career she wanted as an actress. If only she could stay out of trouble.

"What the hell are you wearing?" I whispered in Miriam's ear. "It's freezing outside, and you're practically coming out of that blouse."

"Lighten up, Bry." She smiled and flipped a lock of black hair over her shoulder. Eyes the same gray-green as mine twinkled mischievously. "It's a rock concert, not Mass."

Before I could pursue the matter with her further, my sister Ann, a book tucked under her arm, threw one arm around me and hugged me pretty damn tight. My heart warmed, and I returned her hug with equal enthusiasm.

Ann, I didn't worry about. She was as studious as Miriam, but had a gentle soul and a level head. I tucked a strand of her straight brown hair behind her ear, and she peered up at me over the top of her glasses.

"Still enjoying working weekends at the veterinary clinic?" I asked her.

The enthusiastic smile on her face broadened. "I have two shifts now. Mom says when I'm a junior, I can add one day during the week too."

"That's great, Ann."

Animals were her passion, and always had been. Though we'd never been able to have a real pet, she'd collected the stuffed version since she was three. She wouldn't give any of them away, and had so many now that they filled all the built-in shelves in her bedroom. I planned to get her a real live Labrador puppy to go along with the house I was saving up to buy for the three of them.

"We're on in five," King said from his side of the backstage area.

I nodded and turned back to my family, frowning when I caught the long look that passed between our drummer and Miriam.

What the hell?

King was totally checking her out. I was going to kill him. And fuck if Miriam wasn't returning the favor. She was even arching her back to make her boobs look bigger.

I grabbed her arm, and Miriam hissed under her breath at me.

"Bry! You're hurting me."

I ignored her, guiding all three of my girls to one of the roadies I trusted. "Mark, can you take my mom and sisters to their seats?"

"Sure thing, Bullet."

"Thanks." I laid a palm against my mom's soft cheek. "Mark will bring you backstage after the show. I want to introduce you to all the tour personnel."

"Can we meet Avery Jones?" Miriam asked, her face bright with anticipation.

My smile flattened. It had been a bit of work, but I'd managed to avoid Red since she dumped me. But it would be far better to spend the evening with her than endure another night watching Lace with War.

"Sure," I said with a sigh.

chapter

4

Lace

I sat on top of a stack of amps, watching the Jackson family reunion. On the outside, way, way on the outside now looking in, I extinguished the desire to be included. That was never happening. My chin dropped to my chest, my long hair sliding forward to effectively conceal the longing on my face.

Stop it, Lace. That kind of family love and loyalty in all its Hallmark loveliness wasn't for me. Once upon a time, maybe, but not anymore.

My gaze followed Bryan after his mom and sisters left, and he moved to take the stage. I hopped down from my perch and wandered closer as he and the guys got ready to perform. I'd arrived too late in New York the night before to see last night's show.

King took off his shirt as he climbed up onto the drum riser, and my eyes widened.

When had King gotten those guns? He used to be the chubby one, but he wasn't even remotely so now. He was as cut as an Abercrombie and Fitch model, a sexy Latino version with his square jaw, bronze skin, and closely cropped dark hair.

My gaze drifted to Sager, the other half of Tempest's comic duo. He and King had been best friends as long as Bryan and War. Everyone in the band knew their constant joking was really a coping mechanism, their way of dealing with the crap they'd been through.

Their humor was as much a part of who they were as the clothes they wore, although Sager wasn't wearing much right now, just faded jeans. The lanky bassist had recently dyed his wavy brown hair jet black. Long uneven wisps of it framed his angular face.

Bryan came over and said something to him that I couldn't hear. Sager nodded, pulled a newsboy cap down lower over his brown eyes, and pointed his hawkish nose to the floor as he tuned his Fender.

Bryan's gaze flicked to me, and I couldn't force myself to look away. I'd stare for hours at those mesmerizing eyes of his, if the rest of him weren't equally as enthralling.

The deep black ink of his tattoos scrolled over the bulges of his biceps down to his wrists, where an assortment of black leather and silver bracelets were stacked together. Just like the other guys, he was shirtless, and I found myself lusting after the sexy lead guitarist of Tempest. His chest was smooth, his abdomen flat, and his narrow hips were laced into a pair of tight black leather pants.

When War called to Bryan, he turned away, giving me a view of his backside. Even his ass was perfection. I swallowed to moisten my dry throat as Bryan sauntered in heavy biker boots to meet War at center stage.

War clapped him on the shoulder before plucking the mic out of its stand. Giving me a wink, he faced the audience and draped his hands lazily over the mic stand, waiting while a man in wire-rimmed glasses finished the band's introduction.

His spiky black-and-platinum hair gleaming beneath the stage lights, my brother plugged in his favorite Gibson

Plaintop, made an adjustment on his footboard, gave Bryan a thumbs-up, and flashed me his infamous double-dimpled smile.

I smiled proudly back at my brother.

I didn't envy Dizzy his success. Not really. He deserved to be out on that stage, unencumbered by the burden of me. He was one of the best rhythm guitarists I'd ever heard, though I was a little biased, for sure. His steady, reliable pacing gave Bryan the freedom he needed to go crazy on lead guitar.

My heart squeezed. I'd missed my easygoing brother so much. Maybe if Dizzy had been around, I would have had the guts to leave Martin sooner, instead of just a couple of weeks ago.

$$\bullet \bullet \bullet$$

Two weeks ago

"Go ahead and leave, bitch," Martin said to me in that same disaffected voice he always used whenever I threatened to leave. Which wasn't often anymore.

What other choice did I have except to remain with him?

I had no money of my own, and I wasn't welcome to return to my uncle's house. When I'd tried to go back there the first time Martin had hit me, I'd gotten the reception I anticipated. My uncle had refused to shelter me, while making me feel like more than a failure than I already did.

"You're just like your mother," he'd predictably said.

Turned out, he was right.

I pressed my lips together, my vision blurring as I stared at my arms. Just looking at them made me sadder, while at the same time I longed to shoot up again to forget. I hated what I'd become, and I hated Martin, but I loved the drugs more. I craved that next high more than food or water, more than oxygen, more than life, more than love.

And that's what gave Martin the power he had over me.

My gaze returned to him as he slipped the Glock into his shoulder holster and pulled on a jacket. Eyes as hard and dark as flint met mine. He was handsome, except for his eyes. If the eyes really were windows to the soul, I should have realized much sooner than I did that Martin didn't have one.

His gaze was cold, emotionless, and calculating as he studied me.

A growing sense of unease flooded me, making my pulse pound and my respiration increase. There had been thinly veiled statements from him lately, pressure to do things that I'd been able to deflect so far, but I didn't know for how much longer.

When we first met, he'd been kind at a time that I'd desperately needed kindness, and I'd believed there had been something worth having between us. But now I was just as certain it had been wishful thinking. Wishes so often deceived me. I'd been wrong about Bryan, War, and so many other things.

One thing I was sure of—guys just wanted a piece of me. They would say or do what they needed to until they got it, and then they were gone.

Bryan was the first to teach me that lesson. I didn't know how much I needed and took his approval for granted until it was withdrawn. Two years later, and my throat still clogged at the memory of his callous dismissal of what I'd thought we shared.

What a stupid little girl I've been.

Never welcome.

Never wanted.

My mother had been right in her assessment of me all along. I no longer fought it.

A part of me—the part with dreams, the beautiful part—had been snuffed out by darkness. Fear had replaced hope, and apathy had replaced fear, until all that remained was this empty frame, a place card for the woman I'd once been. Still pretty to look at, but hollow inside.

"Still want to leave?" Martin asked, grabbing my shoulders and squeezing just hard enough to hurt.

"No." Gritting my teeth, I looked up at him, keeping my expression as neutral as possible. I'd had to adapt quickly to survive his sadistic streak.

"You usually change your mind after thinking it through for a moment." He grinned darkly. He enjoyed breaking me down so he could control me, and I wasn't the only one. Most of the time, he didn't get physical if I didn't show weakness. It was strength he admired, my backbone that he respected. What remained of it, anyway.

"I've got some China White coming in tonight." His coal-black eyes searched mine. "I'll bring you a bindle."

"All right." My lips curved up into a thin caricature of a smile.

His dark grin was a travesty as well, feral and predatory. He didn't even try to hide his disdain for me as he gave me a last glance before going out the door.

Why should he hide it? He had me. I had nowhere else to go, and he knew that. He always seemed to know everything, just like he'd known how susceptible I'd be to him and his brand of fake charm the first night we'd hooked up together a couple of years ago.

I'd had an idea who Martin Skellin was before that night. His reputation should have scared me away, but after being tossed aside by everyone I trusted, I hadn't really cared what happened to me.

But I should have.

Because although Martin was attentive in the beginning, letting me continue my friendship with Chad and using his influence to get me a job singing at a local club, his true colors began to bleed through shortly afterward.

Martin was into some seriously illegal shit. I woke up nights, seeing and hearing things that I wished I hadn't. Suspicion became a reality that I tried but couldn't ignore.

Then Tempest hit it big, and Martin had a new terrible game to control me with. He showed me articles and pictures of the guys, enjoying pointing out what a big success they were without me. I tried pretending it didn't matter, thinking eventually he would give up torturing me and move on to something else, something less painful, but he hadn't.

Instead, he homed in on my weakness. *Bryan.*

An explicit YouTube video of the infamous bad-boy guitarist of Tempest became the final wrecking ball that demolished what remained of my heart.

Not that I shouldn't have been accustomed to Bryan being with anyone but me. But loving him, longing for him, it was all I had left to cling to.

I gave in after watching that video, and regularly took whatever Martin offered. Why shouldn't I? Forgotten and abandoned by those I'd loved, it was inevitable where I would end up. Better to get it over with and fast-track the trip.

I learned to compartmentalize my life, sticking the bad stuff into a box and pretending it didn't exist. And when the needle was under my skin, when the drugs hit my bloodstream, everything else faded away. I lost the will to care about anything. I stopped dreaming about the future and settled for shuffling like the living dead through the lucid times until the next time I could get high.

That night, I waited up for Martin. He came back as promised, but he didn't come alone. Strader was with him.

Tall and thin with a pockmarked face, Strader embraced a brand of evil made Martin's seem angelic.

Slowly, I rose from the couch, pulling my robe tightly closed with one hand fisted over my chest. Outwardly, I tried to project confidence, but inside, my nerves were all over the place. It wasn't lost on me that both men tracked my movements with an anticipatory gleam.

This isn't good.

"I'll just leave you two alone to discuss business," I said. Keeping my chin down, I skirted the couch and hurried toward the back bedroom.

"I'll go with you." Strader leered at me, practically drooling with lascivious intent.

What? No!

My eyes wide, I looked to Martin for help.

"No, wait." Martin held up his hand. "Let me talk to her first."

Strader looked like he was going to refuse, but then his expression changed. He gave me a lurid grin, his gaze raking me from head to toe in a way that made my flesh crawl. "Sure. But just so you know, it's going to happen, willing or not."

And there it was. There was no longer any doubt what he wanted, what he'd come to get.

Me.

My heart beat so fast, it felt like my chest was going to explode. It was unlikely I would be able to convince Martin to change his mind. I knew he owed Strader a lot of money.

Being under Martin's thumb had been one thing, but becoming a disposable plaything for a man like Strader was entirely another. I'd reached the end of the road, and I refused to go further, deciding right then and there that I'd rather die than endure whatever torment Strader had planned for me.

But I wasn't going down easy.

A deadly calm fell over me as Strader give Martin a tight nod, saying, "I'm going out to the car. I'll be back in ten minutes."

As soon as the door shut after him, I turned to Martin, my chin lifted and my hands balled into fists at my sides. "I won't go with him," I said firmly, so proud that my voice didn't quiver. My heart might be wrecked, but inside me were remnants of the person I'd been before.

Martin laughed, not a trace of mercy in his eyes. "Like you have any choice."

What a fool I'd been to believe a man like Martin Skellin had ever cared for me.

"Come here." He reached for me.

"No." I croaked out the word, even though fear had sucked the air from my lungs. Shaking my head vigorously, I took a step back.

That was a mistake.

"You strung-out bitch." Martin's eyes flared. He grabbed me by the shoulders and shook me so hard, my teeth clacked together and my thoughts became rattled. "You'll do whatever I say."

"No." My eyes burned, but I didn't cry and I didn't back down.

That's when he lost it.

I didn't even see the blow coming, but the force of the impact knocked me back on my heels. I tasted coppery blood in my mouth, and my vision wavered.

Through it, I could see him glaring at me. I glared back, never hating anyone more than I did him in that moment. I went after him, pounding my fists ineffectually against his solid chest.

Martin easily knocked my hands away and smacked my face again with his open hand.

I backed away, covering my burning cheek with my hand. He'd hit me before, but never so hard, and he'd never looked at me with such malice. The entire left side of my face felt like it was ablaze.

Frantic, I retreated, looking around the room for something to defend myself with.

Then he rocked me with another blow, his fist like a brick as it blasted into the side of my skull. I reeled into a side table, knocking it over, and everything went black for a moment. When I blinked away the haze, I found myself on the floor with Martin looming over me.

"Okay," I mumbled. "I'll go. I'll go."

Those lips I'd once thought handsome widened into a smile as dark as death. "Knew you'd see things my way."

He extended his hand to help me up. I offered him my left, but the fingers of my right hand closed tightly around the base of the broken lamp beside me. It was self-defense, me or him.

As he leaned down, I swung the lamp at his head with all I had in me, and brass met bone with a sickening crack. He lurched face-first onto the carpet and didn't get back up.

Seeing Martin's chest moving, I knew he was breathing so I didn't stop to check on him. I fled down the hall and out into the night with just the clothes on my back and an engagement ring to pawn.

• • •

Present day

Shaken by the memory, I shoved my trembling hands into my jeans pockets and stuffed those dark thoughts back into the box. Leaning back against a column, I forced myself to refocus on Tempest's performance.

The guys were well into their set now, polished and confident. Sadly, there was no awkward empty space where I'd once stood.

Not needed.

Not wanted.

As that disheartening reality sank in, my gaze stalled dispassionately on War. His brown hair looked almost black, wet and plastered to his head. Grinning, he threw the tail end of his long lavender scarf behind his sweaty back as he strutted confidently across the width of the stage.

He'd made it so easy to resume our old relationship. I didn't know why he wanted me back, but he did, and I was grateful. He seemed to want to pretend that the past two years—with the RCA deal for Tempest, and my time with Martin—had never happened.

That was fine by me. We were on the same page in that regard, though our reasons were undoubtedly different.

With Bryan, on the other hand, I was afraid there was never going to be a way back to the close friendship we'd had before. We'd never talked about the night we spent together, but it was always there, an awkward and unbridgeable gap between us.

My gaze followed Bryan as he prowled dangerously around the stage with his guitar, by far the sexiest guy I'd ever seen.

As his fingers flew over his Les Paul, his lids lowered, and his face became an intense mask of concentration. His instrument screamed like a complex climax above the rhythm of the current song. My blood heated at the memory of those nimble fingers and the effortless way he'd employed them to play my body with strikingly similar results.

Long after the music ended, my gaze lingered on Bryan and the puzzle he represented. The handsome, playful, tender boy I remembered was still there, but he seemed older, changed somehow. I wondered at the faint lines around his mouth and the guardedness in his manner that seemed more permanent than before.

Apparently, the past two years had put some hard mileage on all of us.

chapter 5

Bryan

"Where have you been all day?" Dizzy asked, every spike of his black-and-platinum hair gelled into place when I arrived for sound check the next afternoon in Boston.

"Working out in the hotel exercise room." I set my iPhone in the dock and began tuning my guitar.

"Long workout." Dizzy's barbell piercing rose as he lifted his brow. "Did your mom and the girls go back to Seattle last night?"

I nodded. "Yeah."

I hated saying good-bye to my family, but I also hated dealing with Lace and War playing house within the tight confines of the bus. It was seriously pushing the limit of what I could take. I tried not to, but imagining what they did in that back bedroom with the door closed made me almost physically ill.

Wanting but never having her was just as bad as it had ever been. I didn't know how I was going to get a handle on it.

"You must've hit the weights really early. You were gone before I got up." Eyes the same whiskey color as his sister's narrowed suspiciously.

"So what if I was." I slanted a brow. I'd been at it for hours, but it hadn't been nearly long enough.

"Trying to avoid War and my sister, huh?"

My head snapped up.

"Wish I could." Dizzy shrugged out of his black leather jacket and lowered his head over his Ibanez RG, completely oblivious to my telling response. "When I left, they were already arguing at the top of their lungs. It was just like old times."

"She tell you anything about what happened with Martin?"

"No." Dizzy ran his tongue over the silver loop in his lip. "She doesn't do heart-to-heart chats with me anymore. Besides, that always used to be your territory."

I grunted noncommittally. Those heart-to-hearts ended abruptly two years ago. "I'd like to kill that son of a bitch Martin for what he did to her." I stomped down on my pedalboard so violently that it bounced off the black hardwood surface.

"Me too, man. I wish she would've steered clear of him in the first place. But the way I hear it, the dude's days are numbered, anyway. Word is he's gotten himself into a real tight spot. Owes a lot of money to higher-ups and doesn't have the funds to cover it."

Before I could pump him for more information, the sound of War's raised voice reached us.

"What'd I tell you?" Dizzy's chin lifted as War and Lace came into view. "They're still going at it."

Lace looked beautiful with her hair pulled back from her face in a messy bun, loose tendrils curling around her neck, but her blond brows were drawn together.

"No, Warren Andrew Jinkins. I don't want to. I haven't sung anything in over a year." Her sexy lips pressed flat into a tight line. "Not in public, anyway, and your label sure as hell won't like it if I get up onstage during your set."

"Come on, Lacey. Just do a number here at sound check." War blocked her path, his tone coaxing. "I wanna hear that sexy voice of yours over the speakers."

Shaking her head, she stepped around him and dropped into an abandoned folding chair, then threw her coat on the floor.

His hands on his hips, War continued to glare daggers in her direction as King and Sager came strolling in side by side. They were the same height, though King weighed about twenty pounds more than Sager now, all of it muscle. He'd taken to drinking protein shakes and lifting weights with a religious fervor since his dad's heart attack.

King had his cell held out in front of Sager, the screen turned sideways. Sager bent his head to watch, his brown eyes hidden beneath unruly strands of inky hair. The bassist snickered at whatever King was showing him. Probably some College Humor Production, King's current favorite. Whenever he found something funny, he couldn't wait to share it with Sager and then the rest of us.

Smiling big, Sager clapped King on the shoulder before they separated to set up.

"War, come on, dude, let's get started," I said, pulling his attention away from Lace. "We gotta get outta here by one, so they can change the setup for Brutal Strength."

"All right," War muttered after throwing one more loaded glower at Lace. "We're not through discussing this."

"Yeah, yeah." She shot him the finger, and I hid my smile.

"You guys haven't changed a bit. Two of the most stubborn people I know," Dizzy said. "Can't you compromise?"

"Not when I'm right and she's wrong," War said with his usual arrogance, grabbing the center mic and turning to look back at me. "Let's do 'Truth.'" He dipped his chin. "Hit it, Bullet."

I fingered the three-string riff repeatedly to set the pace for the frenetic opening. Hips swaying back and forth to the beat, War began the opening lyrics at the same time as King came crashing in with the drums, Dizzy with the rhythm, and Sager with his steady bass line.

I moved to stand between Sager and Dizzy, all three of us leaning back as a choreographed unit, our instruments held at pelvic level as we jammed away together.

Since you were born, you wanted life a certain way
Not quite buying all the lies that you've been told
But some things shouldn't ever see the light of day
'Cause before you know, your innocence is sold

I'm the truth
You say you wanted some
Well, brother, here I come
You ain't gonna like me
I'm the truth
I'll flip you upside down
And burn you to the ground
Now how do you like me?

With trembling hands, you open up that second box
But the truth never really wanted you at all
And now you wish you'd never tried to pick her locks
'Cause what you found just led you to a fall

I'm the truth
You say you wanted some
Well, brother, here I come
You ain't gonna like me
I'm the truth

I'll flip you upside down
And burn you to the ground
Now how do you like me?

I'm staring right through you
Just like I never even knew you
But now I think you realize
You've seen me with your own two eyes

I'm the truth
I'm lying underneath
I'll kick you in the teeth
Let's see if you like me
I'm the truth
I'll rip your world to shreds
Until all hope is dead
Now how do you like me?

Except for a couple of interjected echoes by me during the chorus, "Truth" was a vocal showpiece for our lead singer from beginning to end.

"Holy shit!" Lace exclaimed after War let out the last primal yell. "Why didn't you guys do that one in New York? It sounds even better live than it does on the recording."

She stood, smoothing the wrinkles from her black tunic top, and walked over to me, gesturing at my Les Paul. "How the hell do you do that?"

Sager chuckled. "Bullet's pretty fast with his fingers."

"Ah, so that's how you got the nickname." Lace smiled. "Faster than a bullet on the frets, huh?"

"Uh, sort of." King shoved Sager. "Even faster to get a woman off. One time, he even—"

"Shut it," I said quickly, glaring at King.

Lace's smile wobbled, but she managed to right it.

"What?" King shrugged. "It's Lace. It ain't like she never heard that shit."

"If you bitches are done joking around," War said, "I wanna have a serious word with you, Lacey."

"Stop pushing me," she said firmly, her hands fisting on her narrow jean-clad hips. "Leave me the hell alone. I'm not changing my mind about it."

"I'm thinking you will." War edged closer. "Babe, you wasted way too much time and talent when you were with that asshole Martin."

Lace's eyes narrowed under the criticism. "Yeah, well, I'm not wasting any more of my time with you today when you're acting like such an authoritative jerk." She scooped her coat off the floor and stomped down the stage-right stairs.

"Lacey, come back. Don't be that way," War called out after her, but she didn't stop.

Her angry strides took her quickly up the aisle past the rows of empty seats. She finished buttoning her coat before she disappeared through the double doors at the top.

"Bry." War turned to me. "Go keep an eye on her for me, will you? You know she won't talk to me when she gets like this."

"All right," I said, realizing that Dizzy was right. The way War and Lace argued was just like old times.

I unstrapped my guitar and placed it in the stand, then jogged after her, catching up to her at the other end of the mezzanine.

"Lace. Hold up." I grabbed her arm, feeling the same electrical spark I always did whenever I touched her.

"Leave me alone, Bryan." Jerking her arm free, she whirled around, her back as straight as a board, her chin lifted and eyes flashing.

When she got all worked up like this, she could be a handful. I also thought it was cute as hell, but I knew better than to mention that.

"Don't take it out on me, Lace, just because you're pissed at him," I said, and when she continued to scowl, I grinned. "You know I've got more than a few inches on you." I cocked a brow and took a step closer to demonstrate. "I'll use that to my advantage if I have to."

"Promise?" Her lips twitched. Planting her hand in the center of my chest, she pushed me back.

Hell yes. I'd meant my height, but she'd obviously taken my comment in a whole other direction.

It had been too long since Lace had flirted with me like this. I missed it. Missed her. So damn much.

I leaned into her hand, my eyes focused on hers, my nostrils flaring as my lungs drew in her familiar scent. In the past, she'd carried a tube of vanilla-scented lotion around in her purse. It had pissed War off when she got the slippery stuff on the equipment. For the past couple of years, I could never smell vanilla without remembering her and our night together.

I lowered my voice, pouring on the persuasion. I wanted to spend time with her today—for myself, not for War.

"C'mon, I haven't seen you in years. We used to be really good friends. I miss that. Miss you," I said truthfully, speaking my thoughts out loud as I reached in my pocket for cigarettes. "There's nothing exciting going on around here until seven. Why don't we go hang? Explore Boston?"

"I'd like that," she said, and then graced me with an all-out, eyes-sparkling, rock-my-world Lace smile.

My fingers tightened around the plastic wrapping of the cigarette pack. She was so fucking beautiful when she smiled. I'd forgotten how it could affect me.

A hundred memories of her smiles came rushing back as I basked in the radiant glow of the one she now gave me. I still wanted to do whatever it took to make Lace happy. Nothing had changed in that regard since we were kids.

Nothing had changed at all for me with her, and I wasn't sure it ever would.

chapter 6

Lace

I sat on a bench in Boston Common with Bryan, the sun heating my back. Picnickers crowded the park, and children dashed back and forth between outspread blankets. Bostonians were out in droves enjoying the atypically warm January day.

Staring at Bryan, I noticed his shades were pointed in the direction of a young girl with braids being chased in circles by a couple of boys.

"I remember when you used to have braids like that," he said. "Before your insanely annoying Britney Spears phase." He shifted, angling his long jean-clad legs toward me.

He was so handsome with his light brown hair peeking out from underneath his black knit cap. Unfortunately, the mirrored aviators he wore, though sexy, shielded his dark eyebrows and his gorgeous gray-green eyes from view. My gaze traced the strong line of his jaw and lingered on the sensual lips I continually fantasized about kissing.

I cleared my throat. "Do you remember the time we built that stage in front of University House? And how we got the other kids to pay fifty cents each just to see us perform?"

Giving me an amused smile, he nodded. "Sheet for a curtain. Glass bottles for microphones. You had a stuffed snake for a prop."

"You wore a top hat like Slash's." My lips tipped up as I remembered. "Where on earth did you find that ratty thing?"

"A dumpster behind the Tuxedo Warehouse." He reached over and gently removed a strand of hair that the breeze had blown across my lips.

I pulled the edges of my worn pea coat together, pretending that my shiver was caused by the cold and not the feel of his rough fingertips against my mouth. "We had some good times."

"Some, yeah." The little girl zipped by again, giggling, and his head turned to follow. "My mom asked about you last night. She wondered why you and War didn't go out with all the rest of us."

Swallowing hard, I said, "Tell her I'm sorry."

I couldn't tell him the truth, that what War and I had been doing, his mother wouldn't approve of. That I wasn't the good little girl his mom remembered. I wasn't even a semi-acceptable high schooler anymore. I didn't deserve to be around Bryan's family, so I gave him a near truth instead.

"War and I had some stuff to do. Tell her I'll try to drop by to visit the next time I'm in Seattle."

I could feel Bryan's gaze on me, boring into my soul from behind those dark lenses. Not moving, I kept my own gaze straight ahead, my throat tight.

Don't push me. Please. I didn't want to explain, didn't want him to know how far I'd fallen.

"Okay," he said softly. "I'll tell her." He was quiet for a moment, and I concentrated on breathing, needing every bit of that moment to compose myself. "I remember lots of things about you."

"Like what?" I asked, tilting my head.

"How you used to go from sweet one minute to all-out sassy the next." He snapped his fingers. "Just like that."

His teasing tone lightened my mood considerably.

"I still do." I managed to look at him. "It's a woman's prerogative."

"You're unpredictable, Lace." His lips curved up. "It's one of many things about you that's impossible to resist."

"Yeah, right. More like one of the many things about me that's annoying."

I studied him, wondering if there was a mischievous twinkle in his eyes behind those shades. But I couldn't allow myself to read more into what he said. He was just being Bryan, flattering and a little flirty, the guy I'd known and crushed on since I was a little girl.

I regretted making the suggestive quip earlier, regretted agreeing to come with him. I couldn't deal with this, the easiness of being with him one on one. The reminiscing, the playful banter we'd once done so easily, it all hurt too much. It was dangerous for me to be around him at all anymore.

But dangerous or not, I craved him.

"I'm hungry." I slapped my hands against my thighs and stood. Unacceptable craving aside, there were other ones I could indulge in. Plus, I needed to put distance between us. "I want some popcorn. I saw a vendor on the way into the park. It smelled delicious."

"Still an addict, huh?" he asked, falling into step beside me.

I winced at his choice of words and glanced at him sharply, but his expression gave no indication that he knew about me or meant anything deeper.

I was addicted to him, to a lot of things that weren't good for me.

After we each got a bag of popcorn, we strolled toward Beacon Hill, where there were supposed to be some unique shops and restaurants.

"Do you think there might be a vintage store around here?" I asked, bouncing eagerly on the balls of my feet in my ballet flats.

Bryan groaned. "Warning you now, I'm not up to a marathon shopping spree." He studied me for a moment. "Sixties fashion still your favorite?"

"Yeah. Anything from then. The short skirts, the platform shoes, the hair and makeup, the music."

"I'll take that as a yes," he said, amusement in his voice and the ghost of a smile on his sexy lips.

"A *hell* yes."

I nodded enthusiastically, chewing on another blissful mouthful of salty buttery goodness rather than allowing myself to think about his mouth, how his kisses felt, or how he tasted.

"How about you?" I asked, attempting to redirect my own thoughts. "You still a big Metallica fan?"

"Oh yeah. They're practically my entire playlist when I work out." He shrugged. "But I don't get as much time to work out or just to kick back and listen to music anymore as I'd like."

"Yeah, I can imagine."

From sound check to meet and greets late at night, the tour schedule was rigorous.

I stopped as we turned the corner. An enchanting narrow cobblestone street lined with Federal-style row houses stretched out in front of us with their red brick facades, black-shuttered windows, and wrought-iron gates.

"This is nice."

"One of the roadies is from around here." Bryan threw his half-full popcorn bag in a trash receptacle. He'd just had a small sampling, and yet he tossed it aside. I tried and failed not to draw parallels to our one night together. "When he described the area, I thought it sounded like a cool place."

"It is cool," I said, though with my thoughts mired in the past, my enthusiasm waned in the present.

"You ever take any of those classes you wanted to in fashion design?"

"No." I shook my head, more regret pulling my lips down into a frown.

"Why not?" he asked, sliding out a crumpled cigarette pack from his jeans.

"Do you really think Martin and I had the type of relationship where he was supportive of me and my silly schoolgirl dreams?"

"I guess not." Bryan cringed at the sharpness of my tone. He tapped out a cigarette and lit it, then his gaze narrowed as he exhaled smoke through his nostrils. "But it wasn't silly. It was a cool idea."

"It was unrealistic." I sighed. One dream among many that were never going to come true.

No address of my own. No credit record. I could go on and on, but why bother? Excuses wouldn't change anything, any more than wishes would.

I crushed my empty popcorn bag, wiped my greasy hands on a napkin, and tossed everything into the same trash can he had. The window display in the shop behind us caught my eye. It had a mannequin wearing a fringed jacket and bell-bottom jeans.

"I'm going in here," I said. *Translation: I needed a moment to regroup.*

A bell rang as I entered the tiny shop jam-packed with racks and racks of colorful vintage clothing. Hats and accessories hung from pegs on the wall, and heavy incense saturated the musty air. By the time Bryan wandered in a few minutes later, his cigarette extinguished and his cap off, I already had several things laid over my arm.

"Is there somewhere to sit in here?" he asked with an exaggerated sigh.

"Sure," the shop girl with blue-dyed hair said. "Over there." She pointed to a small velvet tufted chair against the back wall.

Bryan dropped into the chair and scrubbed a quick hand through his already messy hair. The disarrayed look worked for him. I didn't think there was any look that wouldn't.

Frustrated with myself and the fascination with him that I couldn't seem to put to rest, I pulled a couple more dresses off the rack with a little more force than necessary.

When my gaze drifted back to him, his shades were resting on top of his head. He wasn't even looking at me. He was typing into his cell.

"Do you have a dressing room?" I asked the shop girl.

"Yeah." She pointed to the velvet curtain near Bryan's chair.

"Thanks," I murmured and swept past him into a small two-foot-square space. While changing, I heard the shop girl complimenting Bryan on his ink. He must have taken off his hoodie.

I'll bet that's not all she's admiring, I thought as I shimmied into a lemon-colored dress.

"Hey, wait a minute," the girl said to Bryan just as I stepped out of the dressing room. "Aren't you the guitarist from Tempest?"

"Yeah." Bryan nodded.

"You're playing at the Orpheum tonight."

"I am." He tossed a sheepish look my way.

"The show sold out before I could get tickets. Could I get an autograph and a picture with you?"

"Sure." Bryan posed with her while I took their picture with the girl's cell.

Once more, I was relegated to the duty of photographer, only now I was officially out of the band. My stomach churned.

"What's your name?" Bryan asked the girl as he prepared to sign a blank piece of cash register receipt.

"Janie," she said.

"Here you go, Janie." He handed it back to her when he'd finished. "Would you do me a favor?"

"Absolutely." Janie nodded.

"Use my cell to take a picture of Lace and me. She's an old friend, and I've missed her."

"Oh no, Bry," I said, though a little needed warmth filled my chest. "I look terrible." I covered the bruised side of my face with my hand.

"Bullshit. You're gorgeous as usual."

Bryan pulled my hand away and tucked me in front of him, wrapping both his arms around me from behind. His chest against my back, enveloped in his heat, I inhaled the familiar crisp undertones of his cologne. A wave of memories washing over me, I acknowledged now, just like I had back then, that there was no place else that I felt as safe. I laid my hands on his inked arms and melted into his embrace.

"You two make a beautiful couple," Janie said as she snapped the picture.

If only . . .

I stared at the picture when Janie handed his phone to me. No way did I want Bryan to see it. The look of longing on my face was as obvious as it was pathetic.

He didn't want you, Lace. Well, not longer than one night, anyway. Don't forget that.

"Hey." Bryan leaned over my shoulder. "Give me my phone back. I wanna see the picture."

"Oops." I slid my finger in a deliberate motion over the screen. "I accidentally deleted it."

"You're such a liar, Lace Lowell." He frowned at me when I handed him his phone.

"Right back at ya, *Bullet*," I said airily, returning to the dressing room and snapping the curtain shut.

After the third outfit I modeled, I noticed Bryan getting fidgety. He'd lasted a lot longer than I'd anticipated, but I heard him mutter under his breath, "War owes me big-time for this."

"Spending time today with me was all War's idea, huh?" I asked, my lips turning down.

"Yeah," Bryan said hesitantly, picking up on my vibe. "You know how he worries about you."

Even though I suspected Bryan had been ordered to watch me, disappointment stabbed my chest.

Stupid, Lace, as if Bryan "Bullet" Jackson, famous Tempest guitarist, would choose to spend the day with you if War hadn't put him up to it.

Bryan probably had scores of groupies lined up and waiting for him to get them off back at the venue. I shouldn't have let down my guard with him today. It was too easy, though. It always had been.

I thrust my arms violently back inside the sleeves of my top and my legs back into my jeans. When was I going to learn to stop reading more into Bryan's attention than there was?

"You done in there?"

His sudden question startled me.

"Give me just one more minute." I leaned my forehead against the cold glass of the mirror and closed my eyes tightly, willing my emotions back under wraps.

"Okay, but heads-up. War just texted. I gave him the address here earlier, and he's on his way over. Wants to grab something to eat with us before the show."

"Great," I muttered, not bothering to hold in a curse.

"You're not still pissed at him, are you?"

"I just hate being pushed around," I grumbled, throwing open the curtain, dresses rehung and lying across my arm.

War was stubborn and possessive. Grandiose heart-warming gestures aside, the day-to-day getting along, the necessity of breathing room, and compromise seemed to escape him.

"He means well." Bryan stood and lazily stretched his arms over his head.

"Really?" I snapped, mad at War and irritated with myself that just a tiny glimpse of Bryan's abdomen made my pulse leap. "Did he mean well negotiating a deal with RCA that didn't include me?"

Bryan's eyes widened, but he didn't respond. There was no getting around that horrible truth. I could feel his gaze on my back as I stomped across the store, returning the clothes I'd tried on.

"You didn't want any of them?" Janie asked me with a puzzled look.

"No. They're beautiful, but I can't." I shook my head, hiding my disappointment.

I would have really liked to have bought the hot-pink dress with the geometric design, but I couldn't afford it. I needed to be careful with the money I had left, which wasn't much after buying the bus ticket. I shouldn't have tortured myself by trying on any of the clothes.

After thanking Janie, I exited the shop with Bryan on my heels.

He immediately spun me around as soon as we were outside. "The way the whole thing went down with RCA was bullshit."

"It's okay," I said, only it wasn't, not even close. War had been my boyfriend, Dizzy and Tempest my family. I'd depended on them, and they'd left me behind. "Dizzy's explained about all the pressure you guys were under. About all the other offers you'd already turned down because no one wanted a woman in the group."

"You need to know I told War not to accept that deal," he said, and that part was news to me. His fingers tightened on my arms and his gray-green eyes stared intently into mine. "But he was so sure that once we were signed, he'd be able to convince RCA to give you a deal of your own."

I knew that was one of War's excuses. "What's done is done." I buttoned up my jacket with sharp movements. "Like a lot of other things, it wasn't meant to be. I shouldn't have brought it up."

It hurt. It would always hurt, but I couldn't hold grudges. At least I was back with my brother and Tempest, the only family I'd ever really known.

Bryan's gaze moved across my face as if he was working something out in his mind.

"Yeah? Well, I'm sure we all would've handled things differently in the past if we could." His brow creased, and his voice lowered to that intimate tone that never failed to make my insides quiver. "What happened to you, Lace? One minute you were with War, and then Martin the next?"

I shrugged. "I did what I had to do."

How dare he stand there judging me? What other option had there been? Bryan had rejected me. War had betrayed me. I had to move out of my uncle's house. Chad had problems of his own, and he couldn't take me in, anyway. Martin had been my only option.

A rush of anger swept over me. "But that's what girls like me usually do, right, *Bry*?" The emphasis I put on his nickname made his eyes narrow. That was what his family and closest friends called him. What I'd called him too until after prom night.

"What the hell does that mean?" His eyes flared, and he flicked the unlit cigarette he'd just pulled out to the ground.

"Girls that put out. Girls like you're used to. Girls you sleep with one time, then toss aside in favor of the next one."

"You're not a slut, Lace." He grabbed hold of my shoulders, his nostrils flaring as he glared down at me.

"I know that's what you think. Why keep up the pretense?" I shrugged out of his grasp, stifling the urge to yell at him, or even worse, to cry. "I heard what you said to Dizzy right outside my bedroom door after we slept together."

The old wound ripped open, but I didn't want to keep it covered anymore. It was time we got it all out, even if it was raw and gaping.

A shocked gasp came out of Bryan as if my words had knocked the air out of his lungs.

So what if he was shocked that I'd finally brought it up after all this time? I turned away. It was good he knew that I knew. This was what I wanted, wasn't it? But I couldn't bear to hear him lie or see the pity in his eyes as he made up an excuse.

"Lace, listen." He moved in front of me, stopping my forward progress.

I saw the regret on his face before a cold gust of wind whipped a strand of hair into my eyes. They watered instantly, and I blinked, reaching to pull it away, but he beat me to it. Under the spell of tenderness I read in his gaze, I froze while his fingertips skimmed my cheek, gently brushing the tendril of hair aside.

Softly, he said, "I didn't—"

"Hey, you guys ready for dinner?"

The familiar voice broke the spell, and I turned to find a taxi idling at the curb beside us, War leaning out the window. I must have given him a blank stare, because his confused gaze moved to Bryan.

"What's going on? You didn't what?"

chapter

7

Bryan

After the concert at the Orpheum, we were required to attend the meet and greet with Brutal Strength. At the Mantra restaurant next door, candles flickered, crystal glasses clinked together, and soft music played in the background as the band members from both groups mingled with the few Bostonians fortunate enough to get VIP passes.

I'd been nursing a rum and Coke while trying to keep a low profile all evening. I definitely didn't feel like talking to anyone, except for Lace. My stomach was a mess of churning acid after the bombshell she'd dropped on me earlier.

Frustrated, I yanked a fistful of hair through my fingers. All this time, I thought she'd changed her mind. After all, she'd gone right back with War afterward. I never knew that she'd heard me say those things to her brother that I didn't mean. This was so fucked up. I needed to talk to her and explain, but I hadn't been able to catch her alone.

"Hey, Bullet." A young woman heavy on the makeup brushed her breasts against my arm. Her nipples were clearly visible through the tight white T-shirt she wore.

Oh hell. I took a step back when just days earlier, I would have been full-steam ahead.

Confusion creasing her brow, the woman glanced back across the crowded room. War tipped his shot glass in our direction. "War told me you'd take me to the bus," she said, her lips rounding into a pout.

"Not tonight, babe." I wasn't pleased that War had sent this girl over like an appetizer to sample while Lace was watching. "Why don't you go try Dizzy? I'd bet he wouldn't mind giving you a tour."

"Fine," she whispered.

As she walked away, I returned my focus to across the room. Lace was perched in War's lap. Her beautiful whiskey-colored gaze connected with mine briefly before flitting away. I sighed, my chest burning with regret. No wonder her attitude had changed so dramatically toward me.

At least she'd worn the dress tonight, the pink one from the vintage shop, which was my attempt at a peace offering. I'd placed a call to the shop, and Janie had helped me arrange delivery to the hotel. It looked wonderful on Lace. The material clung to her figure like it had been made for her, just as it had when she'd tried it on in the shop.

Her wearing it tonight has to mean something. She can forgive me, can't she?

The long sleeves flared at the elbows, and sitting as she was now, the bottom hem lay just on this side of decency. But where War's hand rested on her thigh beneath the hem of her dress wasn't decent. It was crass, sending the wrong message about the kind of woman Lace was. I could tell by her downcast expression that it reinforced the erroneous low opinion she had of herself.

I now knew I shouldered some of the blame for that, but dammit, War was treating her like one of the groupies.

As if he sensed my interest, he shifted in front of her, blocking my view. *Access denied.*

If I hadn't panicked that morning, if I hadn't made those stupid comments to Dizzy, could it have been us together right now, her eyes shining up at me, her face tilted up to mine?

I should let it go. I should let *her* go. But that's what I'd done two years ago, and I didn't know if I had it in me to do again.

Even for War.

I swallowed and moved to stare out the windows, my gaze unfocused as my mind rewound to high school. That day when Lace had first walked back into my life again, no longer a child but a beautiful woman, one who turned out to be far beyond my reach . . .

• • •

Nearly four years ago

"Bryan Jackson!"

Hearing my name, I slammed my locker door closed and turned around. "Dizzy!" I grinned, dropped my backpack on the floor, and clapped my old friend on the back. "Since when did you start going to Southside High?"

"Since today. My uncle took a new job, so we had to move. Now we're here."

"Ah. Well, that's great. My mom has a new job too. She finished nursing school and works at Seattle General. We live at the Grammercy Apartments on Rosedale now."

"That's nice."

"It is." I studied Dizzy. He looked the same but a little older, his spiked hair a two-tone color now. "How have things been since you moved out of University House?" I asked, turning away from my locker.

"Okay, I guess." Dizzy fell into step beside me like we'd never been apart. We headed out of the building together. "It sure as hell's better living with him than it was with our mother."

"How's Lace?" I asked, pushing the bar to open the heavy outside door.

"She's all right," he said, stepping outside with me. "Mostly, she goes her own way now, and I go mine. She has a huge attitude," he muttered, zipping up his hoodie. "Way smart. Her head's so big, it practically needs its own zip code."

"I can see that happening. She always made good grades. And she sure used to crave a lot of attention."

"You don't know the half of it. She's such a center-stage hog. You should come by and see for yourself," Dizzy said with an exaggerated eyebrow wiggle. "Why don't you come by the house later, around nine? My uncle works the night shift, and a group of us are gonna hang out, maybe jam some in the garage. I have a used amp and a sweet Fender I'd like to show you. It doesn't sound too bad."

"No shit. You really taking the idea of a career in music seriously?"

"Yeah." He shrugged. "I'm working on it."

"Me too. And I sure as hell would like to try out your Fender." I ran a hand through my hair. "I have a beat-up Epiphone I could bring over."

"Sounds great. If you need an amp to plug into, I could hook you up with one."

"Cool." I adjusted the strap on my backpack. "You mind if I bring along a friend? He actually sings pretty good."

"Sure, man. Whatever," Dizzy said as an Oldsmobile that was more Bondo than metal pulled up alongside us. "That's my ride." He motioned, then turned to give me a fist bump. "I gotta go back inside and find Lace. But I'll catch you later."

Later that evening, War and I sauntered up the short driveway to the detached garage, met by loud music and a pack of teens. Dizzy handed us a couple of red Solo cups filled with beer. We sat down to get acquainted, but before long, I noticed that War had lost focus on the conversation. His gaze was riveted on something over my shoulder.

"Dude." War grabbed Dizzy's arm and pointed. "Who's that smoking babe?"

Dizzy turned around, groaning as he rolled his eyes. "My sister."

Holy shit.

Hair that used to lean more toward dark gold had lightened. It was long and straight now, and the curled ends brushed across the top of a really nice pair of tits. She was practically falling out of the tight camisole and sweater set she wore. Her narrow hips and long slender legs were sexy as hell in a pair of tight jeans. No wonder War was distracted.

Lace Lowell had grown up into a total knockout.

The guy she was talking to touched her arm, and a primal urge rose inside me. I wanted to push that guy the fuck away from her.

Evidently feeling the weight of our stares, Lace turned in our direction. Those familiar amber eyes met mine in a collision that left me reeling. She blinked slowly before her lips curved up and she glided over, her hips drawing my attention as they swayed.

Before I had a chance to make my move, War intercepted her. Grabbing her by the arms, he pulled her into him, even rocking his hips suggestively near hers.

"Hey, beautiful," he said, using the same line I'd heard him use a hundred times before. "Name's Warren. Friends call me War, but you can call me whatever the fuck you want." He eased back, looked her over, and shook his head in disbelief. "Damn, you're hot, baby."

Her cheeks turned as pink as her sweater set.

As War intertwined his fingers with hers and led her over, my stomach took a crashing nosedive into the pavement. She wasn't likely to notice me with War around. Girls took to War even more readily now than they had when we'd been in middle school. To my dismay, it appeared that Lace was no exception.

"We were just talking about our band with your brother. I'm the lead singer," War told her.

Seriously? We didn't have a band. We'd only just discussed the idea a couple of minutes ago. But that was just like War. He'd shoot off his mouth and throw out a grandiose idea, even if most of the time nothing ever came of it.

"Lace," I said, my tongue suddenly too thick for my mouth. "It's good to see you."

Damn, she was even more gorgeous up close. The garage spotlights made her hair shine, and her amber eyes sparkled with laughter. Her smile was sexy as hell, and her lips practically begged to be kissed.

"Bry," she said, her voice low and flirty as she checked me out from my button-down to my boots. "You grew up nice."

"You too, Lace." I shoved my hands into the front pockets of my jeans, hoping she couldn't tell that there was a lot more *up* at the moment than just my height. I'd never been so tongue-tied or so undone by a girl.

"A band, huh?" Her smile widened, and she turned toward War. "You've certainly got the arrogance to be a lead singer." She reached out and touched his face, tilting his chin one way and then the other as she studied him. "You're definitely handsome enough to pull it off." Her voice had lowered to a sexy purr that sizzled like an electrical current beneath my skin.

Then she turned to me. "So, if he's the lead, you'd be . . ."

When she paused, I filled in. "The guitarist."

"Ah, Slash. I should have guessed. Just like when we were kids."

I nodded, my heart thundering inside my chest. I wanted her to touch me like she'd touched War. Instead, she trailed her gaze over me, giving me a lingering half-lidded appraisal.

"Yeah," she said huskily. "You could totally rock the brooding guitarist role. I'd throw my panties at you."

"Would you now?" Playing along, I leaned in and cocked a brow.

"Uh-huh." She leaned in too, her face tilted up as she whispered, "If I were wearing any."

Holy hell! I reached for her arm, but War pulled me away.

"I need a beer," he said.

"What?" My mind was still turning over the panties thing.

"You thirsty, babe?" War asked Lace over his shoulder.

"I could use a beer, Mr. McMoves."

"All right." War laughed. "We'll be right back."

Reluctantly, I followed War. While he filled a cup from the keg, my mind reeled with thoughts of Lace.

"Bryan." War shook my arm.

"Huh?" I asked.

"I've gotta have her."

"Lace?" I laughed. "You only just met her."

"I'm fucking serious, man." War ran a hand over his face while holding his beer steady in the other. "I mean it. I've never felt this way around a chick."

My eyes narrowed. War was never serious about any woman.

"Come on, War. She's just fifteen. You'll be bored with her in no time." I cast a quick glance around. "Let me ask

Dizzy if he knows anyone." I lowered my voice. "Someone older, more interesting and experienced. You know, like you usually go for."

War frowned, his head cocked to the side. "What's your problem?" Tension crackled in the air between us, and he straightened. "You think Lace is too good for me?"

"Of course not. I'm not saying anything. I just don't think she's your type."

"You gotta be kidding. She sure the fuck is. Bold, sassy, sexy as hell." He raised his brows, looking at me like I'd lost my mind. "How's that not my type?"

"Okay." I shrugged, trying to be casual about it. Maybe he'd let it go. I prayed he would.

"Bryan." War put his hand on my arm. "We've been through a lot of shit together, haven't we?"

I nodded.

"And I've always had your back, haven't I?"

"Yeah, but I really don't see what this has to do with—"

"Took that stint in juvie when *you* wrecked my old man's car," he said quickly. "Still doing the community service hours." A shadow fell across War's face, giving him a sinister look.

Grimly, I nodded. He'd done all that for me and more. I owed him.

"I saw how you looked at her, man," he said, deadly serious. "But I don't want you coming between me and this chick, understand? This one's mine."

That night, I made a promise based on our friendship. I figured War would get tired of Lace in a week or so, like he always had with all the other girls before. Then I'd be free to make my move.

Unfortunately, it didn't work out that way. And that promise ended up costing me more over the years than I ever could have imagined.

chapter

8

Lace

Present day

As I sat next to War, my gaze followed the attractive brunette Bryan had just shot down. As she pulled herself unsteadily onto a bar stool, her shoulders sagged. The weight of Bryan's rejection had obviously hit her hard.

I can so relate.

Bryan hadn't been the first Tempest guy she'd approached during the meet and greet. She'd made overtures to all of them, except for my brother.

I watched her knock back another shot before she swiveled around on her chair and scanned the room. She stood, swayed a bit, and crossed the room toward Dizzy. He already had two girls with him, one on his lap and another one beside him. The brunette stood in front of him at least five minutes before he finally acknowledged her.

"Whatcha staring at, babe?" War asked me.

"Nothing," I muttered distractedly. I wasn't about to share. I didn't know why I found myself so interested in the girl, or why the dismissive way the guys were treating her disturbed me so much. Or maybe I just didn't want to examine my reasons too closely.

Dizzy waved her off too.

Shit. I stiffened when she rushed past me with tears in her eyes. "I'll be right back."

I slid War's hand off my thigh and went to look for her. I found her in the restroom, her hands braced on the edges of the porcelain sink. Telltale trails of mascara ran down her cheeks. In the mirror, eyes flooded with pain met mine before looking away. I obviously wasn't the one she hoped to see.

I moved beside her and said softly, "Listen. They're not all that."

"Who?" she asked, though I think we both knew who I was talking about.

"Tempest." I hooked a thumb over my shoulder. "Those jerks who just blew you off."

She nodded somberly.

"Listen, I grew up with those guys. They're no better than you are. They put their pants on one leg at a time."

Watching the desperate way she'd thrown herself at the guys made me sad for her. Third night on the tour, and I was already sick of this groupie bullshit. It turned my stomach.

I touched her arm. "I don't know when they started being such pompous asses, but I wanted to apologize. For my brother, Dizzy, in particular."

Her eyes widened.

"What's your name?" I asked.

"Lily."

"Well, Lily, let me tell you a few eye-opening things about Dizzy."

I pulled a paper towel out of the dispenser, wet it, and dabbed at the mascara on her cheeks. Without the makeup, she was much younger than I'd assumed, probably not more than seventeen. A hard age, a vulnerable age, the age I was when I lost everything.

"The guy's personal hygiene sucks. He literally stinks. I'm sure you noticed. He's been re-wearing the same clothes for the past two days. Then there's his eating habits. He thinks just because Milk Duds have the word *milk* in them that they're nutritious and therefore make an acceptable breakfast."

Her lips twitched.

"Oh yeah." I nodded. "He's a junk-food junkie. Eats Cheez Whiz straight from the jar. And even though he's twenty-one, he still acts like he's twelve. He watches SpongeBob. All. The. Time. He's got every single episode memorized. This from a guy who half the time can't be bothered to remember the words to the songs from his own band."

Lily smiled. "Why are you telling me all this?"

"Because I want you to get that he and the rest of the Tempest guys are just like the guys you probably go to school with. I saw the way they treated you out there, and I didn't like it. So they're in a band, and they look really sexy when they're up onstage under the lights? Big deal."

Her face clean now, I threw away the towel.

"Don't idolize them. Don't let them get to you." I took her hand and led her out of the restroom. "You deserve better than the disrespect that's being dished out there."

Back in the main party room, I stopped to study Lily again. Her eyes glittered way too much to have just been the result of my pep talk. Wondering what she was doing besides those shots, I scrambled for something to say that might help keep her from making the same mistakes I had.

Just as I was getting ready to speak, another girl walked up and joined us. She was blond, and her four-inch heels made her taller than me.

She gave me a hard look before turning to Lily. "This chick bothering you?" she asked, squeezing her shoulder.

"No." Lily shook her head. "She's cool. She's Dizzy's sister."

"You're really lucky to have someone looking out for you," I told Lily while I glanced around for the friend I'd once been able to count on.

Earlier in the evening, Bryan had been hard to miss in a charcoal-gray button-down that did amazing things for his eyes. He'd been standing over by the window before I'd followed Lily into the bathroom. But I couldn't find him now, and I wondered where he'd gone.

Turning back to the girls, I finished my thought. "Hold on tight to that. To each other. Just having one person who believes in you can make all the difference in the world." I pulled in a deep breath through my nose, suddenly feeling really old and worn out. "You two should get out of here. I love these guys, but you know as well as I do that they're not looking for a relationship. They're just looking to get laid."

"She's right." Lily's friend tugged on her hand and pulled her toward the door. "See? That's what I told you."

"What about you?" Lily asked, giving me a concerned look.

"I'm good," I lied. But I wasn't. In that moment, I realized why the stuff with Lily bothered me.

I wasn't really much more than a groupie myself. No remedy for it. I was a lost cause. Had blown my chance for anything better.

But those two hadn't.

After they left, I went back to War. He talked me into doing another line of coke in the coat closet. After that, he got really amorous, his tongue trailing up my neck, and his lips stopping below my ear.

"Lacey." He groaned, his hands framing my face. "Let's go back to the bus. I want you now."

"All right," I said.

Taking my hand, he guided me through the crowded room. As we entered the lobby, I slid on a pair of sunglasses. The lights were too bright for my dilated eyes.

The bus was deserted when we boarded.

War's mouth immediately descended, his tongue delving deep while his hands groped my ass in a way that was just short of being painful. War was an aggressive lover, a trait I knew from experience was magnified whenever he was high.

Tossing his sunglasses aside, he walked me all the way to the back of the bus without breaking the kiss. I removed my own shades, and they slid through my fingers as he pushed the button to open the door to the sleeping section.

He hefted me up. "Wrap those beautiful legs around me, babe."

I did as he asked, folding my legs around his waist as he stalked us to the back bedroom. He set me down on the window ledge and leaned back to look at me. My pink dress was hiked up around my hips, giving him an eyeful.

"Damn," he whispered, his voice thick and his eyes dark. "I need more of that mouth of yours."

War plunged his hands into my hair. The back of my head banged against the cold glass as his warm lips covered mine. My heart hammering against my ribs, I took in short shallow breaths through my nose as his tongue speared repeatedly, possessively, into my mouth. I threaded my fingers into his silky hair and scraped my nails against his scalp the way I remembered he'd always liked.

He groaned into my mouth, breaking the embrace just long enough to reach back between his shoulder blades to tug off his shirt.

My gaze trailed over his smooth, lean torso. He was just as sexy as he'd ever been, the irreverent black heart inked over the spot where his real heart lay. But my mind conjured up a vision of another.

"Gotta see you," War growled.

Pulling my head forward, he yanked down the zipper of my dress and unclasped my bra. Cold air hit my skin as my dress parted, then my bra. War peeled the material down my shoulders and off my arms. As he stared at my bared breasts, my nipples tightened.

"Feed me, baby." His voice was low and demanding.

I cupped my breasts in my hands while he spread my legs wide enough to step between them. His fingers dug deep into my upper thighs. He rocked his arousal against me before lowering his head to trace my breasts with his tongue, in and around my splayed fingers.

I moaned, and my head started to fall back when I heard a sound and looked up. Only a couple of feet away, Bryan stood beside his bunk, his eyes dark and hooded as he returned my gaze. At first, my cheeks flushed with embarrassment, but then I narrowed my eyes at him in defiance.

Go ahead and look, my expression told him. *You might not want me, but War sure as hell does.*

Bryan averted his gaze. "Shut the door next time, asshole," he said irritably before leaning forward to slap his hand against the door switch.

"Sorry, babe." War's lust-glazed eyes went from the closed door and then to me.

I dipped my head in acknowledgment but wasn't interested after that.

War didn't seem to notice. He removed my panties, lowered his jeans, and fucked me. Within moments, he finished. Tossing the condom aside, he moved away. Abandoned on the ledge and feeling used and shaky inside, I climbed down and readjusted my dress.

They're just looking to get laid.

"I'm going to get cleaned up," I said softly, tiny tremors shaking my hands as I grabbed my toiletry bag from the closet.

Oblivious to my distress, War grunted a response and flopped back on the bed with a magazine.

I padded out the door on tiptoes. King and Sager were laughing at something in the front lounge, their faces glowing from the reflection of the television. Hopefully, Bryan had already closed his curtain and gone to bed. I risked a peek at his bunk.

He was awake. His hands were clasped behind his head, his earbuds were in, and his piercing gray-green eyes met mine.

I couldn't move. Couldn't breathe. I'd only thought he looked dangerous onstage the other night, but that was an act. This was real danger. *He* was.

Dark energy radiated off Bryan in waves. Anger, disappointment, and something else that I couldn't pinpoint flickered across his face before his lids lowered and he shut me out.

Released, I shuffled into the closet-sized bathroom and locked myself inside. Free from his unsettling perusal, I leaned back against the door, and my breath came out in a rush. I put my hand over my mouth, trying not to be sick.

What was Bryan's problem? What right did he have to look at me like that? I shouldn't let him get to me, but he did. It seemed I was always a hot tangled mess of emotions wherever he was concerned.

Damn him, I thought, turning on the shower.

I should never have slept with Bryan. I gambled and lost everything that night, including my closest friend. And having sex tonight with War while Bryan watched just brought the stark contrasts between the two men into sharp focus.

The deep emotional connection, the heart-melting tenderness, the intense pleasure I'd experienced in just the one night of lovemaking with Bryan, was something I'd never come close to duplicating with War. And no matter how many times I reminded myself how badly hurt I'd been afterward, or tried to convince myself that the passage of time had exaggerated the experience, it didn't stop me from wanting to be with Bryan again.

After a quick shower, I wrapped my kimono around myself and exited, relieved to see the curtain to Bryan's bunk was closed. I reentered the bedroom and found War beside the nightstand with a tourniquet, a spoon, some cotton, a glass of water, and a couple of syringes lying on top of it like an illicit banquet.

My gaze met his.

"I know you said you were trying to cut back, babe. But it's been a couple of days, and I figured you might need a little something. It's just a small dose, but it'll probably help you relax. I know my heart's still racing from the lines we did earlier."

War was right. I'd never sleep tonight without it.

"Okay," I said. Though shame burned my cheeks, I knew this was who I was now, and what I needed.

Sinking onto the edge of the mattress, I held out my arm and let him do me up.

chapter

9

Lace

The bus was parked when I rejoined the land of the living. War snored softly, sprawled on his stomach in the bed beside me. Sunlight seeped in through the heavily tinted windows.

Groggy, I sat up slowly, more than a little nauseated. I put my head in my hands, and tears I swore never to shed burned behind my eyes.

I'm such a failure.

I tried, but I couldn't make it more than a few days without needing another hit.

With a heavy sigh, I picked up War's cell from the nightstand. It was eleven already. I'd been out for ten hours. Outside, roadies were moving in and around the tour buses parked beside us.

Ah, so we're already in Philly.

Quietly, I pulled on a distressed pair of jeans and drew a purple Henley with long lace sleeves over my head. As soon as I opened the door, the smell of coffee and doughnuts hit me, and my stomach lurched.

"Morning," my brother mumbled, wearing yesterday's clothes, of course. His gaze slid over me. "You look like shit."

"You don't look much better." I gave him the finger. "Who's in the bathroom?"

"King," he said.

My chin dropped. I'd been on the bus enough days to know what that meant.

"Yeah, it'll be a while." Dizzy banged on the door. "King, how many times I gotta tell you, brother? Shit, shower, and shave. That shouldn't take more than fifteen minutes. Get your sorry ass out already!"

Even through my nausea, I had to smile at my brother. "The three s's, huh?"

Dizzy chuckled. "King's a total diva with his morning routine. He even has moisturizer."

King's muffled voice drifted out. "I hear you, *pendejo*." *Dumbass.*

I shook my head and shuffled down the aisle to the front of the bus, swiping my sunglasses off the floor as Dizzy shut the door to the fridge.

He handed me a bottled water. "You should try and stay hydrated."

"Sure," I mumbled, taking a seat at the banquette.

Dizzy sat on the bench opposite me. "Lace," he said, rubbing his hands on his jeans. "You sure you're doing the right thing getting back with War so soon after Martin?"

"Are you seriously giving me grief about my love life?" I arched a brow in disbelief. "That's just wrong on so many levels."

My brother had the decency to look ashamed, but his gaze remained steady. "I should've been more outspoken how I felt about Martin. I hate what he did to you, Lace. All those times I called, you never let on how bad things were. And now I see the shit you're doing with War. I—"

"Don't," I said quickly. "No lecturing, okay? You've got no right. It's not like you're some kind of Boy Scout yourself."

"That's different. You're my sister." He sighed, his eyes searching mine. "I'm worried about you."

"Don't be. I'm all right, Diz. I'm all grown up now. You're not responsible for me anymore." Covering his hand with mine, I said, "I just need to level off some. Then I'll be fine." But I didn't get the sense that he was buying any of it.

"What's the deal for today?" I asked, trying to inject some enthusiasm into my voice before I took a small sip of water.

"Same as Boston. Room keys are at the front desk, if you wanna unwind inside the hotel. The whole tenth floor's exclusive for the tour. Catered breakfast and lunch. Sound check at noon. Band has to be at the venue by seven."

"Okay." I nodded. "I'm going to go get one of those hotel keys since King's commandeered the commode."

I stood and patted him on the back before heading out for the hotel.

. . .

After I got my key, I had a wonderfully long hot shower in a decent-sized bathroom. When I was done, I felt a lot better. Following my nose, I wandered down the hall to an open area where an elaborate breakfast buffet was laid out. It was so late, I really expected to dine alone.

Wrong.

My stomach flipped when I saw her.

Avery Jones was even more beautiful in person. Her red hair was shiny, her green eyes were striking, and her leather vest and merino-wool cowl sweater were obviously designer grade. I felt shabby and self-conscious by comparison in my no-name faded shirt and worn jeans.

"Morning," she said.

Well, Miss High and Mighty actually graced me with a greeting. What's the protocol? Should I bow?

81

Deciding to ignore her, I selected a banana, a yogurt, and a muffin, and poured myself a cup of coffee. Balancing my bounty, I turned. Brutal Strength's celebrity guitarist was appraising me with a speculative expression.

My spine straightened. *Bring it.* She was just a person, same as me.

"This seat taken?" I asked haughtily, indicating the chair across from her.

"No. Have a seat." Her full lips lifted into a friendly smile. "I'm Avery."

"Lace Lowell."

I wasn't buying the nice act. I made up my mind right then that I wasn't going to like her. For one thing, she'd probably slept with Bryan. Just the thought of his hands or lips on her was reason enough by itself. I worried that all she would have to do to get him running back to her was to crook her expensively manicured finger. Besides, she seemed like she had her shit together, when my life was a complete and utter mess, and that just pissed me off.

"I saw you the other night at the meet and greet in Boston," Avery said as I peered at her over the steam from my coffee. "You come down to Philly on the Tempest bus?"

"Uh-huh."

"Lowell." Avery's brow creased slightly. "You related to Dizzy?"

I nodded. "He's my brother."

"So, you're War's . . . girlfriend?"

"Yeah," I said, my spine snapping straight. "Who'd you think I was? Some random groupie?"

"No." Avery's auburn brows lifted at my sharp tone. "Only I've never seen Tempest bring a woman from one stop to the next. So I just didn't know—"

"I'm no whore, if that's what you're trying to imply."

"I didn't mean any offense." Avery's lips pressed into a frown. "I'm sorry. We seem to have started off on the wrong foot somehow."

Damn straight. I'd like to stomp on those Vince Camuto suede wedges of yours.

"What's going on, Ace?" a deep voice rumbled behind us.

I turned to see who that gorgeous voice belonged to. *Holy fucking shit.*

It was the lead singer of Brutal Strength, Marcus Anthony. The guy was definitely nice to look at with his dark, wet hair dripping into the collar of his T-shirt, ripped bod, and killer blue eyes. But at the moment, he looked kind of pissed.

"Nothing's going on." Avery glanced at me. "Just a little misunderstanding with Dizzy's sister."

"I gotta go." My chair clattered with the force I used pushing it back. "Later," I mumbled.

Hurrying out into the hall, I ran right into Bryan. He must have just gotten out of the shower too. His hair was wet, spiky, and he smelled really, really good.

My heart pounded hard.

The black Tempest T-shirt he wore fit his sculpted chest nicely, and the color made his eyes appear more gray than green in the low-lit corridor. He hadn't toweled off well, leaving a fine sheen of moisture glistening across the dark tattoos on his corded arms.

I glanced away, my cheeks burning as I recalled how I'd looked when he saw me last.

"Where's War?" he asked without any hint of embarrassment in his tone. Guess he'd already moved on from what happened last night.

"Back on the bus, would be my guess. He was still sleeping when I left."

"It's eleven fucking thirty," Bryan grumbled, drawing out his phone. His long masculine fingers moved quickly and efficiently across the screen.

"War. Asshole," he said into his cell. "Do you know what time it is? Get the fuck ready . . . Yeah, yeah . . . She's with me." A sigh. "Okay. We'll see you there."

Bryan slipped the phone back in his pocket. "Come on, Cinderella," he said, guiding me toward the elevator. "Prince Charming wants me to escort you to the ball."

chapter

10

Bryan

As soon as the elevator door closed, I turned and put my hands on her delicate shoulders. I could feel the warmth of her skin through the gossamer material.

I lowered my voice, even though we were alone. "Lace, I've been trying to tell you since yesterday. What you overheard me say to Dizzy that morning, you've got it all wrong."

She shook her head, and the silky ends of her hair brushed across the tops of my hands.

Like it happened just yesterday, I remembered how soft it had felt against my bare chest. All the blood in my body rushed south in response to the memory.

I took in a lungful of air, trying to get myself under control. Last night had been a test of willpower too, a toss-up between wanting to kill my best friend for having his hands on her, and wanting to be in his place.

I'd bought her that pink dress that had been bunched up around her waist. *I'd* wanted to be the one between her legs. *I'd* wanted her head thrown back in pleasure because *my* mouth, not War's, was on her breasts.

My heart rate jumped into overdrive at the memory. I lost the battle of mind over body, and my hold on her turned into a caress.

"What was it I got wrong?" Lace's shoulders tensed, and her angry tone penetrated my sex-hazed brain. "Was it our whole relationship, or was it just one of the two times you *fucked* me that night? Maybe it was my inexperience," she said, her expression as harsh as her voice. "Though the way I hear it, most guys get off knowing they're the first."

"Stop it." My fingers dug into her arms. "Don't make it into something ugly."

"I don't need to do that. You did that all on your own with what you said." Her eyes narrowed, and the pain I saw in them left me feeling cut up inside.

I had to fix this.

"Listen, Lace Lowell, and listen good." I lifted my hands to gently frame her face. "What I said to your brother was the *only* part about that night that wasn't real. Stop twisting my words. That night with you was beyond incredible. What you gave me was the most beautiful gift I've ever been given."

"Bryan . . ." She softly breathed out my name, looking unsure and shaken.

I put a finger over her smooth, satiny lips. What I intended as a silencing gesture became something else entirely as soon as her lips parted, and I felt her warm breath against my skin.

I stared into her mesmerizing eyes. "When Dizzy showed up, I admit I panicked. I didn't know what to do about War. Plus, there was all that pressure back then about the RCA deal. I was worried about how that would affect everyone, including you. I was just trying to buy some time so we could sort it all out. But I *never* meant to hurt you. I—"

The elevator dinged, and the door slid open. Dizzy, Sager, and King stared at us with their mouths open.

86

I dropped my hands, and Lace took a step back. She wobbled a bit as she stepped out and moved past her brother.

Dizzy frowned, then gave me a meaningful glance. "War's up. He's meeting us at the venue."

Silent as a funeral procession, we all piled into the chauffeured Suburban. Conversation was subdued.

Sager slurped on a coffee in the back row. In the passenger seat, King drummed on the dash, earning a couple of warning glares from the driver. Dizzy stared out the window, and I watched Lace out of the corner of my eye.

Looking pensive, she was perched on the edge of the middle bench seat between Dizzy and me. She kept her head down, picking at the threads on her jeans the entire fifteen-minute ride. I desperately wanted to know what she was thinking.

As always, I was hyperaware of her presence. The air between us was charged. My nerve endings sparked with heat each time we turned a corner and my leg brushed against hers.

Once we reached the venue, we all climbed out, passed through security, and then were escorted to the stage.

"Wow!" Her eyes big and round, Lace turned in a circle, taking it all in. "This place is huge."

"Yeah. With nineteen thousand capacity, it's a lot bigger than the Orpheum." Dizzy dropped his leather jacket on the floor and lifted his guitar from its stand. "That was more of a historic vanity stop. This is the real deal, a proper rock venue."

Sager whooped, his yell echoing in the empty, cavernous arena.

I continued to watch Lace. She still seemed unsettled from earlier, or maybe I was just projecting because I certainly was. Tugging on the lacy cuffs of her purple Henley, she looked uncomfortable and out of place as we got ready to play.

It wasn't so long ago that she would have been getting ready right alongside us. As I plugged in my Les Paul, she wandered over to the edge of the stage, and my mind drifted back in time to high school . . .

• • •

Four years ago

"Where is he, Bry?" Lace asked me again for the third time.

"I don't know," I said, but the truth was I did know.

War was at the courthouse, doing a little extra credit to reduce the sentence he'd served that should have been mine. But I wasn't at liberty to tell her that. I'd made a promise. And God knows I kept those, especially for him.

I blew on my frozen fingers. The temperature in her uncle's garage wasn't much warmer than it was outside, and the damp night air seemed to seep into my bones.

Sager scowled. "I've got to go to work soon. Can't we just go ahead and rehearse, crank out a few songs without him?"

"Yeah. This is bullshit." King punctuated his statement with a drum roll on his snare.

"Lace," Dizzy said. "Why don't you teach us that ballad you showed me the other day?"

She shook her head at his suggestion, her long blond ponytail swishing between her shoulder blades.

"C'mon," Dizzy said. "I told you it's really good."

"We could use a ballad," I said, throwing in my support for her.

She glanced at me, trying to communicate something. A warning or a plea? I didn't know which.

"I agree," Sager said with a nod. "We need something couples can slow dance to in the clubs."

All eyes turned to Lace.

"All right." She sighed and moved to her keyboard. "I'll play it through one time, but I'm stopping if anyone laughs."

Her jeans tugged tight across her ass as she took a seat. I swallowed and looked away, my gaze colliding with Dizzy's narrowed, knowing eyes.

I ran a hand through my hair, remembering his sobering warning to me. *"Unless you plan to tell War, you need to put a lid on those feelings, bro. If I've noticed how things are between you two, it won't be long before War figures it out too."*

I couldn't bottle it up. My feelings were way too strong to deny. Maybe I could have put a lid on them if War wasn't always sending me in his place to smooth things over with her whenever they fought, which was all the time. But I knew that was unlikely. From the moment Lace had stepped back into my life, I'd wanted her to be mine.

The first few notes of a somber cascade of sound reached my ears, demanding my attention. I turned to look at her.

Lace's eyes were closed. Her contralto voice was hesitant, but soft and powerful. It got under your skin and tunneled straight to your heart, just like she did.

Watching her, listening to her, I felt chill bumps break out all over my skin. Vaguely, I noted that everyone else was stock-still and staring at her too.

As soon as she started the chorus, I realized why she'd given me that look earlier. This song was about us. About hidden passion and desire that couldn't be denied.

• • •

Present day

"Lace, do 'Forbidden,' please."

Sager's annoyingly whiny voice brought my mind back to the present. His bass was strapped on and thrown over his back, his elbows resting on the piano where Lace had taken a seat.

"Please," he said again, putting his hand over his heart and acting like a complete dork. "I love that song. It always gets to me."

"No." Lace shook her head, glancing at me.

"Please, Lace." King begged, copying Sager's dorky gesture as he moved over next to him.

"Oh, all right, just for you two." Lace ran her fingers over the keys and tapped on the mic. "Test. Test." Then she sat back, poised her fingers over the keys, and began to play.

Her contralto voice sounded amazing in the empty arena, magnified by the tour sound system. Her face registered surprise when she heard it like the rest of us did. As we'd all already discovered, there was a world of difference between singing in a garage and hearing your voice pumped out through concert-voltage amps.

Straightening her shoulders, she continued without missing a beat. Her beautiful amber eyes took on a faraway look, and her voice . . .

Holy fucking shit.

It was strong, confident, and seductive as hell. She had a talent that was meant for center stage. *She* was meant to be where she was, only with a spotlight shining on her, nineteen thousand people leaning forward in their seats to listen.

For me, it was like no time had passed, and we were right back in high school when the emotions between us had reached their crescendo. During our first walk on the beach, I'd reached the tipping point. By the time we took our second one, she'd reached the same point.

If I ask you to begin
Would you make me all brand new?
I would never let it end
Build a world for me and you

My forbidden love
Do you feel the same?

I come all undone
When you breathe my name
Am I just wishing things
That can never be?

My forbidden love
Will you ever be with me?

If I lay my soul down here
Would you take it up from me?
It's yours to own, you know
If you could only see

My forbidden love
Do you feel the same?
I come all undone
When you breathe my name
Am I just wishing things
That can never be?

My forbidden love
Will you ever be with me?

If I beg to cross that line
Would you erase it now?

I know it would be so fine
If you were mine somehow

My forbidden love
Do you feel the same?
I come all undone
When you breathe my name
Am I just wishing things
That can never be?

My forbidden love
Will you ever be with me?

chapter 11

Lace

Four years ago

I peeked over at Bryan as he walked on the beach beside me. His hoodie was pulled back from his head, allowing the breeze to ruffle his hair, sifting through the silky light brown strands like I wanted to. He stared at the ocean, which sparkled like his gray-green eyes reflecting the last rays of the sunset. Waves rolled rhythmically onto the shore like gentle breaths.

I tried to focus on the soothing sound as I watched him.

What would he say when I told him? I wasn't sure. That's why I'd kept silent for so long, so I decided to ease into it.

"Have you given any more thought to my idea about adding my ballad to our set list?"

"Yeah, I think it's a good idea." Bryan turned, his eyes meeting mine. "I think the other guys are on board. But have you and War talked about it?"

"He was less than enthusiastic." I puffed out my chest and lowered my voice, mimicking him. "If you want a ballad in our set list, come stand at center mic and sing it." I completed my impersonation with one hand on my hip and a finger wag near Bryan's face.

"Yeah. That sounds about right." Bryan raised a brow. "I have to say, you're the only one with a voice to pull off singing 'Forbidden.'"

"Maybe you're right about that one." I gave him a long look, waiting to see if he would say or do something like he had on our last walk.

When he didn't, I was disappointed. But maybe he'd already made his move and was uncertain about my response. I realized that it was going to have to be me, all me this time, and not him.

"But we have other ballads," I said, "and you have to admit that ballads are some of the biggest hits for your favorite bands. 'Sweet Child of Mine' is Guns N' Roses' only number-one hit. And what about 'Nothing Else Matters' for Metallica, or 'Home Sweet Home' for Mötley Crüe, or—"

"Okay, okay, Lace," he said. "You made your point."

"It's what sells," I said, pressing my point. "More women buy music than men."

"Write another one then that War can sing, and I promise I'll back you up about it with the band and with War. Maybe together, we can win everyone over."

Together. Oh yeah. I liked that idea. A lot.

My heart pounded hard, and my palms got sweaty. No more stalling. Time to tell him how I felt. That I was in love with him . . .

Hopelessly.

Helplessly.

Heedlessly.

But I was terrified to say the words out loud.

Because although sometimes I thought Bryan might feel the same when he looked at me with warmth in his eyes, or when his touch lingered, there were plenty of other times like right now when I just couldn't read him.

And then there was War.

He and Bryan were so close. The bond they'd forged during their years together in middle school was real, strong, and obvious to everyone.

And I loved War too, but it was so different with him. He didn't make my heart pound out of my chest like Bryan did. Sure, War listened to me, but Bryan seemed to really hear me, and made me feel like my opinions were valuable.

With War, and the other guys I'd dated before him, I held a part of myself back. War never pushed to get past that barrier. More often, he just ran over me to get what he wanted.

Deep down, that made me wonder how much he really cared.

The longer I was with War, the more I found myself opening up to Bryan instead. Recognizing this, I pulled back from going all the way with War.

I wanted Bryan to be *the one*.

"Bry," I said, putting my hand on his arm at the same time he said, "Lace . . ."

"You first," I said with a teasing ghost of a smile. I was still afraid. Still unsure.

"All right." He sighed and stared back at the ocean. "I have feelings for you."

I froze. My heart racing, I held my breath.

"Feelings I have no right to have." He shoved his hands deep into the front pockets of his jeans and finally looked at me.

My heart stopped. This wasn't right. This wasn't the way I wanted the unfinished business between us to go.

"War's my best friend," Bryan said softly. "We've gotta stop hanging out together, Lace. It's wrong. I shouldn't have let it go this far. We can't do this anymore."

Shaking my head, I blinked back the tears that filled and burned my eyes. *No!*

I turned and ran back the way we'd come, too proud to cry in front of him. Hearing his footsteps behind me, I sped up, glad to be wearing lace-ups instead of slip-ons. I couldn't let him see me like this, so I ran faster. Thinking I was going to be able to get away when I made it to the stairs, I had my hand on the railing when he caught me. Stupid, stupid sand had slowed me down.

"Lace." Breathing hard, he grabbed my arm and spun me around.

My long hair slapped against my face, stinging like his words had.

"Let me go, Bry. I heard you. Message received, loud and clear. I get it." My voice sounded as raw and exposed as I felt.

"No, you don't, Lace. How could you? You didn't give me a chance to finish." He raked a hand through his windblown hair.

"So finish," I said harshly.

"You're only seventeen—"

"Oh, and you're such a man of the world because you just turned nineteen," I said, sticking my chin out. "I love you. I'm old enough to know that much. And I'll be graduating early, at the same time as you. I'm *not* a child."

He tenderly framed my face with his hands. "I know that. Believe me, I'm very aware of that fact."

I melted when he brushed his thumbs softly across my cheeks. The roar of the ocean and the cries of the seagulls receded, giving way to the thundering sound of my heartbeat in my ears. As we stared at each other, I could see myself reflected in his gorgeous eyes.

Bryan swallowed, breathed my name in a whisper, and then his lips touched mine. My body erupted with sensation— warmth at the point of contact, tingling across the surface of my skin, and molten heat inside that all but consumed me.

It was just as I'd always dreamed it would be with him, only better.

My fingers fisted in his shirt. I suddenly needed something to hold on to, to keep my balance in a world that felt like it was shifting beneath my feet. In a world that had suddenly been reduced to just the two of us.

His lips moved, a gentle persuasion, coaxing mine to open. The shaking escalated into a seismic explosion the instant his tongue rubbed softly against mine.

I tasted him. He was the dream. My hope. My chance to be the woman I'd always wanted to be.

He moaned, and I whimpered for more.

Suddenly, he pulled away, creating a separation I knew neither of us really wanted. When I heard War's voice, I stepped back too.

But if I had it to do over again, if I'd known at the time just how wide that gulf between Bryan and me would become, I would have never let him go.

chapter

12

Bryan

Present day

I watched as the guys congratulated Lace on her performance during sound check in Philadelphia. I was just about to go over and do the same when War showed up, the tail end of a long black scarf trailing behind him as he stalked toward her.

I stopped, tension holding me fisted in its grip. The realization hit me hard that I could wish all I wanted, but War would always be a wedge between Lace and me.

"What the fuck, Lacey?" War's expression was livid. "Why the hell didn't you sing that yesterday when I asked you to?"

She didn't answer, but her chin rose.

"You're doing it just like that tomorrow night in Atlanta," he said loudly, avoiding looking at me.

"No, War. I'm not." Her eyes flashed, and her hands balled angrily at her sides. "I was just messing around for King and Sager."

"I'm not taking no for an answer," War bellowed, and she jumped up from her seat at the piano. They faced off like two opponents in a ring.

"I'm my own person, Warren Jinkins!" she yelled, leaning in toward him, her hands moving to her hips. "Stop riding me. I'll decide what I will and won't do."

"War, hey." I walked over to him with my hands spread out. "Maybe you should—"

"Stay the fuck out of it, Bry," he shouted, his anger veering toward me like I wanted it to.

Lace took advantage of the distraction I provided and spun around, her footsteps echoing as she stomped off the stage.

War's gaze cut back to me. "Bullet, go—"

"Not this time," I said, cutting him and that shit off. "I'm done being the peacemaker. You want her, then you go after her. But I'd suggest you let her cool down first if you want to get anywhere."

"Hey, guys," a voice said, and we both turned as Marcus Anthony strutted up to us like he owned the place. "BS is up."

Was this asshole totally oblivious? His timing certainly sucked.

"Back the fuck off, chief." War pointed to his watch, and Marcus frowned. "Tempest still has five more minutes."

I grinned. Couldn't help it. Shit like this reminded me why War and I were so tight.

I was tempted to give War a congratulatory fist bump right there in front of Marcus's arrogant face.

Just because Brutal Strength was headlining, and Marcus got to fly around in a big jet while we rode on tour buses with the roadies, didn't mean his shit didn't stink. It hadn't been that long ago that Brutal Strength had been an opening band just like us. And it hadn't been that long ago that Marcus's fist had made a little contact with *my* face.

Granted, I'd punched him first. But still.

In a blatantly dismissive move, War turned his back on Marcus and stepped up to the center mic. He tapped it once and looked over his shoulder at King. "'My Way or the Highway.' Count it out."

King's sticks tapped out a beat, and War began to sing.

Speeding through the intersection
Crowding the yellow line
I'm not about to change direction
Close your eyes, we'll be fine

'Cause it's my way or the highway
Just so you know
My way or the highway
I'll show you where to go

I bet you think that I've gone crazy
Maybe I'm a bit disturbed
But you better quit with all your bitchin'
Or I'll kick you to the curb

'Cause it's my way or the highway
Just so you know
My way or the highway
I'll tell you where to go

Don't wag that finger at me
Act like you got a choice
'Cause I got a different finger for ya
I'm through with all your noise

'Cause it's my way or the highway
Don't say I didn't tell ya so
My way or the highway, baby
It's over now, just fuckin' go

You've been a sweet ride, honey

When we got back to the hotel, War jogged up beside me. "Got a minute?"

"Sure. What's up?"

When I stopped, he threw an arm around my shoulders and steered me to the right. "Come get a drink with me in the bar."

As soon as we entered the low-lit lounge, its every available surface covered with the Philadelphia Eagles motif, War excused himself. "Order me a beer. I'll be right back."

I grabbed a seat and was already nursing a Kinsinger, munching on some peanuts and watching the game on the wall-mounted television, when War returned from the restroom. He sniffed a couple of times and I frowned, not fooled for a minute.

"You told me you'd stopped doing that shit." I glared at him, my voice just loud enough to be heard over the television.

"Shhh." War cast a nervous glance around the half-empty room.

A prickle of unease tingled its way along my scalp as a disturbing thought occurred to me. *What if Lace is doing drugs with him?*

No way. She wouldn't.

She'd only been drunk the other night. After the crap we'd seen with her mother that Lace had lived through, not just seen, I totally ruled out anything more.

I leaned in closer. "Seriously, War, I don't want a repeat of the RCA tour. It took me six months to pay off my part of RCA's advance using Black Cat funds, and this long to rebuild enough savings to get my mom into a house. Don't fuck this up for us again with drugs and bullshit, man."

We all went a little too crazy on that tour. Too much booze, too many strippers, too many hotel rooms trashed. RCA cut us, leaving us to repay the advance money we'd already spent. We were just lucky Black Cat was standing in the wings, willing to take a chance on us with a contract containing a lot of behavior-clause modifications.

"I'm not gonna fuck up shit, Mama Jackson." He gave me an arrogant look that didn't eliminate my unease. "I just need a little help to be on for tonight's show. Don't go all narc on me just because you don't do 'em. I have it under control."

"Really?" My brows rose. "You almost slept past sound check today."

"Now that you mentioned band stuff . . ."

War frowned and reached for the beer bottle the bartender placed on a coaster in front of him. Tipping it back between his fingers, he took a long swig while watching me. This was his version of a dramatic pause. I was well acquainted with his shit.

Setting down his bottle, he frowned. "Gotta say, I didn't like the way you countermanded me in front of everyone, especially when it comes to Lace."

"Now wait a minute." I tensed, ready for a fight.

"Don't get all defensive. I realize it's been difficult having her on the bus with us." War propped his elbows on the bar.

He has no fucking idea.

"You need to chill, Bry. Tempest has a real good thing going right now." Straightening, he threw the scarf's end over his shoulder and leaned back in his bar stool. "Have you seen the press stuff that PR chick from Black Cat keeps emailing over?"

I nodded. "I've seen it."

"Right. So you know 'We're Through' is top ten on the Billboard. That's fucking huge." War pulled his sunglasses off his head and tossed them onto the bar before taking another swig of beer.

"Yeah, so? What does that have to do with anything?"

"So, I know you weren't happy when I insisted that we take the deal that excluded Lace. I know her being here is bringing back all that shit. It was a real tough time with the group, but that's in the past. She's back where she should be, in my bed, right beside me." He narrowed his eyes, and I clenched my fingers into fists in response to that statement. "And the fact that we're about to hit it big, bigger even than before, just proves that I made the right decision."

Deep down, I might agree that Tempest functioned best as an all-guy band. But I didn't agree with his methods. If it had been up to me, I would have left that RCA deal on the table. I never would have left her behind.

"If you believe that," I said, "then why are you pushing so hard to get Lace to perform with us?"

"Same reason I wanted her to come out with us on the road when we were with RCA. Visibility. Exposure. You heard her today. She's the shit. All it's gonna take is the right person to hear her. She has the potential to be a bigger deal than that British chick who came out of nowhere last year and won a Grammy."

War stared at me, his eyes so narrowed now, they were slivers of dark without any light as he continued.

"Lace doesn't know what's good for her. If left up to her, she makes piss-poor decisions, one after the other. Like putting me off so long before we went all the way. Like wasting all that time on school and the SAT. Like hooking up with Martin to spite me. If it weren't for that stupid two-year detour with that loser, she'd probably already be a huge star."

"War," I said low. Not agreeing with any of that shit except the part about Martin, I swiped a thumb across the condensation on my glass, choosing my words carefully. "Did you ever stop to think maybe singing isn't what she wants?

This lifestyle, being in the business, it's hard. It's not for everyone. She's really into fashion. She could still go back to school."

War snorted. "Bullshit. That would be a fucking waste of her time *and* her talent." He slammed his beer down so hard, the glass clattered on the granite surface of the bar. "Lace *is* going to be up on that stage in Atlanta. *Rolling Stone* is coming to do a feature on us, and it's the perfect opportunity for her to show everyone what she's got. And I want you to back me up on this. I expect you to, with the band and with her. You're way too soft on her. You always have been."

War then clapped me on the back as if he thought that would make his words easier to accept. "Don't take this the wrong way. I love that bitch. You know I do."

Yeah, I knew. Though I was beginning to think more and more that he didn't love her enough, and certainly not the way she deserved.

I scrubbed a hand over my face, feeling stretched to the snapping point.

Just like I'd been back in high school.

chapter 13

Lace

All by myself in the front lounge of the bus, I stared out the window, watching snowflakes drift down one after another, adding to the already foot-and-a-half-high berm along I-95. We were headed south on our way to the Atlanta show.

War was passed out in the back, just like he'd been since I returned to the bus. He'd made me so mad earlier that I skipped the show, wandered around Philly until it got dark, and then camped out in a local bookstore, thumbing through fashion magazines until the store closed.

It was nearing dawn now, and I still hadn't slept any. I rested my head in my hands. Pine trees stood along the roadside, lonely sentinels, tall and dark except for their adornment of white. A similar winter wonderland scene had been the picture on the front of our prom invitations. Prom and Bryan had been on my mind nonstop since our conversation in the elevator.

Was it possible that prom had meant to him what it meant to me?

Four years ago

I set the vellum prom invitation on my comforter and crossed to the dresser, looking at myself in the mirror.

I was in love with this dress. So what if it didn't fit the winter theme? It was a genuine vintage sixties dress with spaghetti straps, a straight bodice, and a black lace skirt over a blush-pink underlayer. I'd added a black silk ribbon around my neck instead of jewelry—I couldn't afford jewelry—and let my hair cascade long and straight around my bare shoulders.

I practiced a smile. I needed the practice, since I hadn't been doing much smiling lately. Not since I'd told Bryan how I felt. Not since that kiss on the beach. Not since I'd seen him with Missy at Kyle's.

I'd been so naive, thinking that our kiss had been special, that it had meant something, that *I* meant something to him.

War had been right. What it meant was that Bryan was a guy like any other, taking what was thrown at him, and not the honor-bound knight on a white steed that I'd made him out to be since I was a little girl.

Bryan didn't want my love, or even the action.

Get over him, Lace Lowell. He's not who you thought he was. He's not worth it.

I pressed my lips together and turned away from my reflection. Tonight wasn't about Bryan. It wasn't about the SAT. It wasn't even about school anymore either. That was all over. It was just War and me and going forward.

War loved me. War wanted me, and I was lucky to have him. Most of the girls at Southside High wished they were in my shoes. It was time to show him how much I cared.

Pep talk over.

Pushing aside my trepidation at my decision, I glanced at the bedside clock and frowned. My handsome guy was late, over an hour now. I hadn't realized. *Why hasn't War called?*

"Lace," Dizzy shouted from the stairwell.

Finally, I thought as I opened my bedroom door.

Out in the hallway, Dizzy's eyebrows rose. "Where'd you get that dress?"

"The consignment shop. Took it in a little bit," I said with a shrug.

"You look really beautiful." He took my hand and placed it on his arm, escorting me toward the stairs.

"Why aren't you dressed, Diz?" I asked as we descended the stairs. "I thought you were going with Elaine."

"There's been a change in plans. I'm running to the drugstore for War, then going over to his place. He's sick off his ass. Told me he's been retching his guts out for the past couple of hours."

"Oh no! Why'd you let me get all dressed up?" Annoyed, I stopped on the stairs, then froze when I saw Bryan standing at the bottom.

"Hey, Lace." Bryan gazed intently at me. "You look incredible."

Not as incredible as him. Bryan looked amazing in a traditional tux with a black bow tie, layers of his brown hair practically tangling in his long lashes.

"Hope it's okay if I take you instead."

"Sure," I managed to say, practically drowning in his sexy hooded eyes.

He stepped forward, a dream fulfilled from the storybook pages of my mind. I met him at the bottom of the stairs, and when he slid a white rose wrist corsage on my arm, I inhaled sharply. Chill bumps broke out all over me as his fingertips brushed across the delicate skin of my inner wrist.

Dizzy's brow creased as he looked back and forth between the two of us. He cleared his throat. "Bryan, can I see you in the kitchen for a minute?"

Bryan lifted his chin and followed my brother through the living room and into the kitchen. The swinging door closed behind them.

Shifting my weight from foot to foot, I smoothed my dress and stared at that closed door. I wanted to know what they were saying, but it was a private conversation. It would be wrong to listen, except that I knew it was a conversation about me.

Hesitating only a moment longer, curiosity won out, and I followed them. As soon as I got close, I could hear their harsh whispers behind the swinging door. I was just moving closer when Bryan suddenly came back out.

"Where's Dizzy," I asked, glancing over his shoulder.

"He went on." Bryan placed a hand on the center of my back and guided me toward the front door. "We'd better get going. We're already too late for your dinner reservation. We'll miss the dance if we don't leave soon."

As soon as I stepped out onto the front porch and saw the limo waiting at the curb, I glanced shyly at Bryan. "You didn't have to do this for Warren."

"I'm not doing it for him."

Bryan stared at me, the overhead porch light illuminating the intense gleam in his eyes. He reached out and ran a hand through my hair, sifting the individual strands through his fingers. Somewhere in the distance, a car door slammed.

"I'm doing it for you," he said with a small smile. "You deserve a night like this. Come on." He took my hand and led me to the limo.

Everything about the night from that moment on was pure magic. For the first time in my life, I felt like the fairytale princess I'd always dreamed of being. I didn't even try to pretend it was the dress. I knew it was being with Bryan.

Arm in arm and dressed in my finery, I let go of all my concerns, lived for the moment, and danced with my prince. As we moved together, I unashamedly allowed myself the pleasure of touching and looking at him, without even attempting to hide how I felt. He held my hand cradled to his chest, and by the time the last slow song of the evening began, I'd convinced myself he felt the same way about me that I did about him.

Back in the limo, I snuggled close to him, laying my head on his strong shoulder while he stroked my hair. I sighed contentedly. But before long, I glanced out the tinted window and saw we were pulling up to my house.

Was it midnight already? I didn't want the magical night to end. Couldn't bear to go back to a reality where he was so close and yet so distant.

"Bry," I said, tilting my head to look at him.

Staring at me, he stroked my cheek. "Yeah?"

"Come inside with me," I said, and felt the sudden tension in his body.

"No, Lace," he whispered after a long moment. "I can't."

Rejected.

Again.

A sharp pain sliced across my breastbone. I squeezed my eyes shut and blindly reached for the door handle.

His hand closed over mine. "Lace, listen."

"No," I choked out, my throat on fire. "Just tell me this. Why Missy Rivera?"

He cursed under his breath. Taking my chin in his hand, he gently tilted my face back. "Because I can never have the one who really matters to me," he whispered, then brushed a soft apologetic kiss across the side of my mouth.

So this was about War.

Seeing the determined set to Bryan's jaw, the steeliness of his stare, and knowing that once again he would do the right thing, my heart sank.

"Let me walk you inside," he said.

Bleakly, I nodded.

Outside on the sidewalk, I wrapped my arms around myself, trying to ward off the chilly air that made my teeth chatter. He took off his tuxedo jacket and draped it around my shoulders. His warmth and the crisp pine and smoky scent of him lingered in the material.

I fumbled with the key at the front door, and he took it from me. Once we were inside, he dropped the key into the glass bowl next to the phone. It rang with a tone of finality.

"Good night, Lace, I . . ." He trailed off as he caught a glimpse of the disappointment I hadn't been quick enough to hide. He reached out and drew me to him, his gray-green eyes intently searching mine. "You're not going to cry, are you?"

"I never cry."

"What's this," he asked softly, running a fingertip under my eye.

"I'm just tired. The cold wind . . ."

"You're lying."

"So are you, Bryan Jackson." My hands fisted. I'd had enough. "Denying what's between us."

Handing him the tuxedo jacket, I kicked off my shoes. I tossed my hair back and took a deep breath for courage, deciding I could be determined too. As my heart pounded, I slipped off the thin straps of my dress, first one shoulder and then the other. Holding my breath, I looked him straight in the eye, daring him to resist me.

Bryan didn't move. But the dark flash of his eyes and the flare of his nostrils emboldened me.

I reached back and released the hook of my dress, then lowered the zipper. The fabric puddled at my feet, a black and pink pool of chiffon and lace.

With my shoulders back and chin lifted, I stood before him, completely vulnerable and nearly naked in a strapless corset, matching panties, and gartered stockings.

Bryan stood still a moment longer, and then he reached for me. His eyes full of fiery intent, he claimed me, crushing his lips and his body to mine.

• • •

Present day

"Lace."

"Huh?" Dazed by the past, I turned toward the sound of Bryan's voice in the present. In only a pair of boxers, he stood right beside me.

How could that be? How long had he been there? Had I been so lost in the memory that I hadn't heard the door to the sleeping section open?

"I called your name twice," he said, his voice a delicious rumble.

"I didn't hear you. If I had, I would have responded." Mesmerized, I stared up at him from my seat at the banquette.

His lids lowering, Bryan came closer, looking sexy as sin with his brown hair all tousled from his bed.

"What were you thinking about that had you so absorbed?" His expression soft, he took a strand of my hair and rubbed it between his fingers. The subtle yet coveted touch made my scalp and everything else tingle.

"You," I whispered, and his eyes flared. "And prom night."

"Lace. Babe." He swept his appreciative gaze over me, swallowed, and glanced behind us. The door to the sleeping section remained closed.

"It seems to keep coming back to that for us," I said softly.

For me, prom was never far from my mind. How could I forget the most magical night of my life? And to know now that it had been incredible for him as well changed everything.

Those same thoughts seemed to be in his eyes as he looked back at me.

My heart racing, I reached out. "Are you real?" I needed to touch him. I had to. "Is this real? What we shared . . ."

"Was the best night of my life," he said, filling in where I'd left off.

"Oh, Bry." Tears in my eyes, I laid my palm against the smooth skin at the center of his bare chest.

He covered my hand with his. The air crackled with heat like my blood did.

Bryan tugged me out of the banquette, and I stumbled into him. My breasts to his chest, I could feel the rock-hard strength of him through the thin material of the button-down shirt of War's that I'd worn to bed. My nipples tightened.

When Bryan lowered his head, I lifted mine. His breath bathed my lips with smoke and heat, and then his mouth was on mine. I parted my lips at his urging.

A flood of fire swept through me as his tongue touched mine. One firm stroke, then another, and my legs went out from under me. Bryan held me tighter, crushing me to him with his hands now on my back. I needed him to remain upright. The intensity of my longing after all this time was almost too much to bear.

I whimpered as he pressed me back into the partition, the wall a hard surface behind me. His chest, his hips, his thighs, and his erection were even more unyielding. Insistent, he devoured me everywhere his mouth could reach. His lips, his tongue, and his teeth did wicked, wonderful things to me that made me moan.

"Yes, Bry. Yes," I whispered, begging for more.

He yanked my arms up by the wrists, raising them over my head. My hands pinned to the wall in his tight grip, I felt the cool air caress my skin as the oversized sleeves of my shirt slid down to expose my arms all the way to my elbows. He pressed impassioned wet kisses across my cheek and then down my arched neck.

"Dammit, Lace, stop me," he whispered in a raw voice, yet he drew my earlobe between his teeth. "We shouldn't be doing this. We can't."

"Don't stop." I trembled as he traced the shell of my ear with his talented tongue.

Breathing heavily, he eased back and stared down at me with lust-filled eyes. "How am I supposed to get over you when you respond to me like this?"

He's not over me?

That was news to me. It seemed all our previous conversations had been past tense.

"I don't want you to get over me," I whispered, angling my hips forward and rocking over him. My needy body took over, ignoring the faint protesting voice in my mind.

He groaned, then went completely still.

Certain we'd been discovered; I glanced back over my shoulder. But no one was there. The door was still closed.

Confused, my gaze returned to his. Only he wasn't looking at me—he was staring at my arms.

"Fuck." He yanked them down and flipped them over, his grip tight on my wrists.

My fevered blood ran cold. When his head came back up, his hair was in his eyes, and his gaze was bright. The fury on his face almost made me wish War had discovered us instead.

Dropping my gaze, I tugged my wrists free and pulled down the sleeves of War's shirt. But it was too late. The damage had been done. Cold shame doused the raging desire that had consumed me only a moment ago.

"Whatcha shooting up, Lace?" Bryan's hot breath rained condemnation on me. "By the looks of those track marks, I'd say you've got an expensive daily habit."

"Bry, please, don't be angry. I can explain." I lifted my chin to discover that the evenness of his tone was at complete odds with the fire blazing in his eyes.

"Don't want an excuse," he gritted out. "I want to know if War is doing that with you. Is he giving you that shit?"

Not answering, I tried to twist away, but Bryan caged me in with his arms.

"I can't believe you'd do something like this. Not after all you went through with your mom." Exhaling heavily, he dropped his forehead to mine. "Oh, Lace." His eyes were so close, I could make out the pixilated variegation of gray and green, as well as read the concern that filled them.

His gentleness crumbled my resistance. I couldn't shut him out.

"What is it, Lace?" he said again, gentling his voice. "What are you shooting up?"

"Heroin," I said softly.

Bryan

The air brakes on the bus hissed, jostling Lace and me as the tour bus lurched to a stop. I was tense as fuck, struggling to process what she'd just revealed.

Heroin. Could it be any worse?

"What the hell?" War exclaimed from behind us.

Yes. Apparently, it can.

I released Lace and took a step back. I'd been so out of it that I hadn't heard the door to the sleeping section open, and it seemed that Lace hadn't either. Her eyes wide, she pulled the gaping neckline of her shirt back together. Looking guilty as shit, we both stared at War.

War obviously had no trouble putting two and two together. Not hesitating, he came right at me, his eyes narrowed and his hands tightly fisted.

Lace slid in front of him. "War," she purred seductively, her pretty eyes lowered to a placating half-mast. "It's not what you think. Bryan saw my arms and was just getting up in my face about my using."

"That true?" War's gaze returned to me for confirmation.

"Yeah." I nodded, though I was sick to my stomach. My mind and guts swirled with the toxic mess of it. The drugs were a game changer with Lace. I didn't know what I was going to do, but I knew I had to do something. I couldn't—*wouldn't*—just stand on the sidelines any longer.

War leaned down and gave me a pointed look before laying a wet one on her, ravishing the mouth I'd just thoroughly explored.

"Go on to the back," he told her after breaking the kiss. He snapped his fingers like an authoritative ass, and she hustled to obey. "Bullet and I need to talk."

His focus on me, he didn't see the furtive glance she shot me.

"But I want to go into the hotel," she said. "Get a shower in a real bathroom."

"You will, babe. I promise. Just give me a minute with Bullet, all right?"

She nodded and headed to the back without glancing at me again.

Good plan. Though I appreciated that her shower request was likely an attempt to throw him off in some way. But there was no throwing off this confrontation. I wanted it as much as he did.

More, maybe.

War pressed the button to close the door as soon as she passed through. The atmosphere between us instantly supercharged with toxicity as he turned to face me.

"We've been through a lot together, brother." His eyes narrowed. "So I'm having a difficult time understanding why I should find you alone with my woman again, only this time her mouth tastes like fucking cigarettes."

Shit. I scrubbed a hand over my face.

"I get that she's beautiful. And I'm not blind. I know you've had a thing for her since high school." War's voice was low, his expression menacing as he took a step toward me. "But you know the code. She's"—he gave me a hard shove—"off"—and another hard shove—"limits!"

I took what he dished out, standing my ground while my body vibrated with restrained anger. The only reason I didn't retaliate was because I felt that I probably deserved that much.

But not more.

My nostrils flaring, I pulled in air and leaned in, my hands balled into fists. I was revved up too, just as furious about the drugs as he was at finding out that I'd kissed her.

We stared each other down. The physical contact between us seemed to have taken his anger down a notch, but a wall of distrust had risen in its place.

"War." I wanted to explain, believing I owed him an explanation after all we'd been through, so I forced my hands to relax. Violence would make me feel better, but it wouldn't help her. "Listen, I—"

"No. You listen to me, Bullet. Next time you're feeling horny . . ." War's face twisted into something ugly. "Go and get your own pussy."

He turned and stalked toward the back but stopped in the doorway.

"Tell me this, though." His head dipped, turning slightly in my direction, but not all the way. It was like he didn't want to look me in the eye, see the validity of my answer. "You come on to her, or did she come on to you?"

"It was all on me, brother."

"Okay." Some of the tension drained from his rigid stance, and he turned to fully face me. "Then know this. I'm serious about not wanting to find you alone with her again. You feel me?" He let those words hang in the air between us for a minute before hitting me with a hard look.

"I feel you," I said with a curt nod. But I didn't make any promises. I was done making any of those to him.

Breathing hard, War said, "Don't hassle her about the drugs anymore. You gotta know she beats herself up enough about it. I've got the situation under control."

I had major doubts about War's control of the situation. In fact, I had some major concerns about a lot of things now, but I decided for the moment to keep those to myself. To do so, I had to clench my jaw so tight that my teeth ached. I just needed some time to think things through, and then I needed to talk to Lace.

War stepped into the sleeping compartment, but before he slid the door closed behind him, he paused. His voice dangerously low, he said, "Don't fuck with me or her, brother. Or I promise you, friendship aside, I will mess you up."

• • •

Lace

Inside the back bedroom on the tour bus, I watched War throw some things into an overnight bag, his movements abrupt. His muscles were taut beneath his white T-shirt. He'd yet to look at me.

I wondered what had happened between him and Bryan. The door to the front lounge had been closed, so I hadn't been able to hear. My nerves frayed, I pulled on some jeans, but left War's button-down shirt on. A little uneasy, I figured things would go better if I was wearing the team colors, so to speak.

"Come on, babe." War's voice sounded jarringly loud after the protracted period of silence.

He grabbed my hand and led me off the bus. I didn't see Bryan or any of the others. Their curtains were open and the bunks vacant. Apparently, everyone was as eager as I was to be off the bus for some downtime and a bit of space.

War didn't say anything as we picked up our hotel key and headed to our room. He slid it in the reader, and I entered ahead of him, walking straight through to the sliding glass door on the other side of the room. The surrounding Virginia forest was almost completely shrouded in fog. In the early dawn, the Appalachian foothills were a fuzzy purple shadow in the distance.

The door clicked shut behind me, and then I heard a thump as his overnight bag hit the dresser. I wrapped my arms protectively around my waist. I didn't know what to expect, but I knew I'd had enough of this tension and imagining the worst.

Turning to face him, I asked, "What's going on, War?"

"I know what happened," he said with narrowed eyes. "Bryan told me."

My stomach did a major flip at the sight of the hurt on War's face. That wasn't what I wanted. I was a screwup. When it came to Bryan, I just couldn't control myself.

"I can't believe he would pull something like this with you while I was sleeping just a couple of feet away," War said, moving across the room until he was standing in front of me. Reaching for me, he threaded his fingers in my hair.

Wait, back up the conversation. What exactly was he talking about? I'd been afraid Bryan had told him about prom night. Was this only about the kiss today?

War held my head in place, his brown eyes probing mine. "I warned him to back off, but I don't trust him anymore, babe. Not with you." His chest expanded as he took in a deep breath. "I love you, Lacey."

I reeled at that. It had been a long time since War had said those words to me. Not since high school, when he'd been keeping the RCA deal secret from me. Looking back, I'd seriously doubted he'd ever really meant it. Could I trust that he meant it now?

"Maybe I should have said something as soon as we started up again." He gave me a long, searching look. My disbelief must have been visible. "I do love you. You must know I do. And after all that's happened, I need for you to tell me that you feel the same, because I have a feeling that this is gonna come down to choosing sides. And if it does, I want you to know, right here, right now, that I'd pick you over anyone else."

My eyes closed, and I leaned my cheek more firmly into his hand.

This was why I'd fallen for War. The surprisingly demonstrative things he could do, like apologizing in front of everyone before we'd started dating. Like revealing his plans and including me in them after showing me his mom. Like taking me back after our first breakup, and again after Martin.

And now this.

I'd be an idiot to screw this up. War had said exactly what I needed to hear. He didn't seem to have any problem putting me first, before his friendship with Bryan.

It was time I did the same.

I covered the hand War had in my hair with mine. Pulling it down toward my lips, I turned it over and kissed his palm. Then I told him that I loved him too, and stood on my toes to press my lips against his.

War took my hand and walked me to the bed, moving my hands out of the way when I started to unbutton my shirt. "Let me."

Intent on his task, he slowly worked his way down to the last button. His warm hands brushed softly against my bare shoulders, and the shirt, his shirt, fluttered to the floor. He bent down and took one of my breasts into his mouth.

Staring at the landscape painting on the wall across from me, I held his head to my breast, both my hands entangled in his silky hair. I loved him, sure, but wished I felt more than I did.

I would need a magic wand to banish thoughts of Bryan Jackson from my mind forever.

chapter

15

Bryan

An insistent rapping that matched the pounding inside my skull woke me. Bleary-eyed, I squinted at the hotel clock.

Shit. I'd slept the whole fucking day. No surprise, given the amount of liquor I'd consumed.

Someone banged on the door again.

"Hold on!" I shouted, swaying unsteadily as I shoved my legs into my jeans and managed a couple of buttons before I made it to the door and swung it open.

"You look like crap," Dizzy said after looking me over.

I shrugged. *Incidentally, not a good move when you've got a hangover as bad as mine.*

"War told me to get you." Dizzy came into the room, glanced at all the empty mini bottles, and raised a brow. "You drink all that liquor by yourself?"

I nodded, which was another bad idea. The motion made the room rock and my stomach roll. I ran to the bathroom, ejecting what was left inside my tortured guts.

Dizzy walked in just as I was flushing the toilet. He leaned his rear against the counter. "What's going on? The guys and I heard you and War arguing on the bus. Sounded like he threatened you."

I stood up slowly, holding on to the door frame for support before pushing Dizzy aside to unwrap one of the plastic drinking cups so I could rinse the vile taste out of my mouth.

"Can you give me a break here?" My gaze met his in the mirror as I pulled out a toothbrush from my bag.

Dizzy unsympathetically shook his head. "This is because of my sister, isn't it?"

With the toothbrush sticking out of the corner of my mouth, I closed my eyes and nodded.

"He finally find out about prom?"

I shook my head.

No. Not yet. Thank God. When War found out about that, there would be more than just a shove and a warning involved.

Staring at the sink, I went back to brushing my teeth.

"What then?" Dizzy's eyes narrowed. "Don't tell me you slept with her again?"

I spit, drank a sip of water, rinsed, and spit again. "Dizzy, c'mon."

"No, Bry. You come on. You know how War is about her. Remember what happened when he found out about her and Martin?"

"Yeah, I remember. Not easy to forget."

Dizzy knew the basic facts, but he didn't know the whole of it. War had scared the hell out of me, though. I'd found out how deep his feelings for Lace ran, as well as how closely they mirrored mine. This situation between the three of us was such a tangled-up mess.

I gave Dizzy a hard look. "You know Lace is using now too?"

"Yeah, Bryan, I fucking know. She said she's quitting. That she's got it under control."

I snorted. That's what War had said too. "And you believe her?"

"I gotta believe her." Dizzy shrugged but appeared troubled. "What can I do? It's her life. You can't control what other people do. Right?"

Yeah, that was pretty much the same basic conclusion I'd come to . . . after nearly drowning myself in a sea of booze, thus the godawful hangover.

I was really worried how this was all going to play out in the end. War's warning hadn't been an idle threat. He would do anything to keep her, just as I would give up anything for a chance to make her mine.

Knowing that they were both shooting up had ratcheted up my sense of urgency about everything. I didn't want a replay of what had happened with War before.

• • •

Two years ago

"War! Asshole!" I yelled. "Open the damn door!"

When he didn't respond or come to the door, I looked over my shoulder and gave his mom a worried glance. She seemed just as concerned as I was, with her hands clasped tightly in front of her.

"How long's he been in there?" I asked.

"Since last night."

Fuck. It wasn't like him to stay in his room. Not in this house.

"He was really upset when he came in." She bit her lip. "I haven't seen him that upset since the time he tried to see his dad."

Yeah, well, I definitely remembered how that went down, and that wasn't a good sign.

I banged on War's bedroom door again. *Nothing.*

"I'm gonna break it down. Okay, Ms. Jinkins?"

She nodded.

I kicked the door with my booted foot, giving it two solid tries. On the third, the wood splintered and the door swung open.

"Shit!" I exclaimed when I saw him.

War was facedown on the carpet, deathly still. The room reeked of vomit, and spoons and a syringe lay on the floor beside him.

"I'm calling an ambulance," Ms. Jinkins told me and hurried out of the room.

I fell to my knees next to my friend and turned him over.

War groaned.

Thank God. I pulled him up to a seated position and slapped his face a couple of times. "Wake up, dammit. C'mon, man."

"Why, Lacey," he mumbled without opening his eyes.

"Shit. War, listen to me. Your mom's gone to call an ambulance. That's gonna bring in the cops. Me, personally, I don't give a shit, but I know you do. You've got priors. This will land you in jail, and that'll kill the RCA deal for sure. You okay with that?"

War opened his eyes, his legs shooting out straight as he tried and failed to stand. He clumsily wiped the side of his mouth. "Mom!" he slurred. "Mom, c'mere!"

"War." Out of breath, she ran back into the room, a phone in her hand.

"Put the phone down, Mom. I'll be okay. Don't need that kind of trouble. Not with my record."

Ms. Jinkins frowned. Looking uncertain, she glanced at me.

I grabbed War by the shoulders. "Shooting up drugs is serious shit. The next time could be your last." Leaving the choice up to him, even though it was against my better judgment, I said sternly, "If you don't want us to call the ambulance, you gotta promise not to do this kind of shit ever again."

"I screwed up." War hung his head. "I lost her. Lost Lace. I should've listened to you. I should've talked to her first about the RCA deal and explained, but it's too late now."

When he spoke again, his voice was so low, I had to lean closer to hear him.

"I saw her again with him last night, Bry. With Martin Skellin."

I knew. I'd seen her too. It had been like having a hot knife rammed into my abdomen. Long legs, short-ass skirt. She'd been practically having sex with him out on the dance floor. That guy was bad news. There was no way he loved her.

That's what made the whole deal such a brutal wakeup call. Until then, I'd been sure that if she ever broke it off with War, she would end up with me.

chapter

16

Lace

Present day

Bryan in a faded black Gibson T-shirt, and my brother in his leather jacket, were sprawled out shoulder to shoulder on the bus couch, playing a video game. The surround sound system filled the air around us with the sound of simulated gunshots. Since we'd boarded the bus again, I'd felt Bryan glancing at me, but we hadn't spoken since his discovery last night.

On the bench at the banquette, War's arm tightened around my shoulders. I turned to look out the window and saw the mall where War and I had gone shopping earlier today. After I'd agreed to do the song in Atlanta, he'd insisted I have a new outfit. I hadn't found exactly what I wanted, but with a few minor adjustments, it would probably be all right.

Conversation buzzed on around me as we continued heading south on I-95. Sleepy, I leaned my head on War's shoulder as he, Sager, and King continued their game of poker.

War had made love to me twice back at the hotel. He'd never been so tender. I'd been a little surprised by his enthusiasm, given the amount of dope he'd used the night before. But I understood that it had been his way to show me that he cared and to affirm that I was his.

I suspected that my kiss with Bryan was weighing on War's mind. My mind, however, was on much more than just that one kiss . . .

• • •

Two years ago

Bryan's hot skin slid against my naked back as I strummed my guitar. Warm kisses rained down, first along the base of my neck, and then across my shoulders. I sighed from the sheer pleasure of it.

"Are you okay?" he asked from behind me.

"Mm-hmm." I was better than okay. Bryan had just made love to me in my bed after prom, and I was still basking in the afterglow.

The darkness that had fallen over me like a shadow since our kiss on the beach, and seeing him with Missy afterward, had lifted. Being with him with the wall between us gone had inspired me. A melody and words rushed around in my head that I had to get down on paper. I'd loved him so much and had for so long, but now everything finally made sense.

"I mean, are you sore?" he asked, trailing a finger softly up and down my spine while I tried to jot down the last of the notes and words on the music paper I kept beside my bed.

"A little." I set down the guitar and turned my head, smiling shyly at him over my shoulder. "But not too much."

His fingertips traced a featherlight trail along the line of the silk ribbon I still wore around my neck. "I love you, Lace Lowell."

My breath caught as my heart stopped and then restarted. Its previous stumbling, syncopated pace changed to a more harmonious, steady rhythm, reflecting the joy his words gave me.

I shifted, twisting so I could look at him. "I love you too." My lips parted as my shy smile blossomed into a radiant one that couldn't be contained.

My words seemed to have a similar effect on him. Using the roughened pad of his thumb, he reverently traced my wide smile, his lips curving up at the edges as if he'd absorbed my happiness through that simple touch.

"Lace," he said softly, his expression even more intense as his gaze moved over my face.

The gray-green depths of his eyes fascinated me, especially the range of emotions I saw there. Love. Adoration. Desire.

"I'd like to have you again."

My body flooded with warmth at his words. It was a heady feeling to be wanted and desired by the man you loved.

He kissed me between my neck and shoulder. "Slower this time," he mumbled against my skin.

The first time had been wonderful, but over too quickly, a rush to a culmination and closeness with him that I'd never allowed anyone else. And though I'd messed around with War enough to know my way around the male anatomy, I'd still been a little unsure if Bryan had been pleased.

It was intimidating to know that he'd been with other women. A lot of other women. Knowing now that he loved me gave me an additional boost of confidence that had been missing the first time around.

I started to move, but he stopped me, his hands heavy and firm on my shoulders.

"Hold on. Be still. I wanna try something." His fingers tickled a bit as he untied and slid the silk ribbon from my neck. "This is sexy as hell. I'm never going to be able to look at a black ribbon again without remembering this night with you."

He leaned over me and pressed closer, the stubble from his chin rough where it rested on my shoulder. I watched the ribbon slide down to unfurl over my breast. A shiver rolled through me as he moved it, light as a feather, over the tightened bud of my nipple.

"You're so beautiful." His words were warm in my ear before his tongue replaced them.

As his tongue plunged in and out, I became hot and restless, and when he traced around the shell of my ear with the tip, I moaned his name. I reached for his face, wanting to bring his mouth to mine.

"No, Lace." He took my hands and kissed them. "It'll be your turn in a minute. But for right now, I just want you to lie down."

I gave him a speculative look, and his lips curved up into a seductive smile.

"Trust me."

"Okay, Bry," I said. There was no one I trusted more to have a care with me.

"I think you'll like what I have in mind," he said, his voice a persuasive low rumble.

"I'd better," I teased, stretching out on my bed as he shifted to kneel beside me.

He slanted a brow. "Oh, I'm sure you will."

That sounded like a sultry promise.

Still giving me that foreplay smile, he slid another pillow beneath my head. "I want to play a little, prolong things this time around. The rule is you look but don't touch. Not until it's your turn."

Sounds like fun.

An anticipatory thrill pulsed through me as his heated gaze traveled the length of my body. With my heart pounding, I watched his hand open above me.

The ribbon unfurled, and he glided the soft end up and over the slope of my breast. The silk barely made contact with my skin, but I was already so focused on what he was doing that I felt it with an intensity that surprised me. Then he withdrew the ribbon and leaned down.

I felt the heat of his breath, right before I felt the warmth of his lips and the wetness of his tongue as he slowly and thoroughly retraced the ribbon's path. My fingers fisted in the sheets. That felt fantastic. I moaned deep in my throat, and my back arched completely off the bed.

"Told you you'd like it." His lips formed a self-satisfied smile.

I made a face and stuck my tongue out at him.

Bryan's eyes darkened a moment before his face swept down and he captured my tongue in his mouth. By the time he finished with it, I was panting for air and wanting more, so much more than he'd yet given me.

He gave me a wicked grin, and then began teasing and tantalizing with the ribbon and his mouth on my other breast, using just the right amount of heat and pressure to make me go crazy, writhing on the sheets.

"It's not enough," I said breathlessly. My nipples ached and my clit throbbed.

"Not for me either." He moved the ribbon lower, trailing it over my sensitized skin from the middle of my breasts down to my navel, and soft kisses followed. "I don't think I'll ever get enough of you."

My eyes slowly opened. Refocusing on his handsome face, I saw that his lips were parted and his breathing was just as ragged as mine. Knowing that bringing me pleasure was turning him on that much made me feel powerful and sexy.

Without pausing, he moved his attention to the lower half of my body, running the ribbon down one leg and up the other, kissing, licking, and getting so very close, but never quite touching where I wanted him the most.

Going crazy, I shuddered with need. "Enough."

I grabbed his hand and stopped him, and he turned his head, his smoldering eyes connecting with mine. I wasn't going to last much longer, and I wanted to have my chance to touch him too.

I peered at him from beneath my lashes. "My turn to play."

He pressed one more light kiss on my hip bone and then switched places with me, straightening the pillows and stacking his hands behind his head. His eyes gleaming, he grinned at me as if he were the one in charge.

"Comfortable?" I asked, and he nodded. "Not for long."

Pulling in a breath, I took a surreptitious peek at the impressive length of him.

Copying his technique wherever the ribbon had landed on me, I sucked, licked, and tasted every single glorious male inch of him without shyness, because this was Bryan, and I loved him. He was so incredibly sexy; the salty flavor of his skin gave me a stronger buzz than alcohol ever could. I discovered that I loved teasing and working him into a frenzy, just as much as he'd seemed to enjoy doing it with me.

Making love with Bryan was so much more than I'd ever imagined it would be. He was passionate and playful, and yet so very tender. His body and its contrasts fascinated me. He was hard where I was soft. His chest was wide and smooth, his pecs defined, and his abdomen was a row of concrete ridges.

When I paused to lick the flat coins of his nipples, he moaned my name and grabbed the back of my head. Leaning back, it was me this time who breathlessly ordered him to open his eyes.

With those gray-green eyes glittering with heat, he gazed back at me through his thick lashes. I gave him a naughty grin before strategically opening my hand and letting the ribbon drop, the length coiling around the steely tip of him.

"Enough, imp." Bryan growled, grabbing me and flipping me over onto my back. "Playtime's over."

He knelt between my legs and brought our bodies together in a single masterful motion that felt so good, I hummed low in my throat.

Finally, I was getting the more that I'd wanted. Once we were connected and he began to move, the buildup was so quick that it was only moments before we spiraled out of control and climaxed together.

• • •

Present day

"Wake up, Lacey." War's voice washed the memory away like being doused with ice water.

I opened my eyes, lifting my head from his shoulder and feeling disoriented.

"You were moaning in your sleep, babe." War's brown eyes danced as he smiled. "Remembering the two times earlier, huh?"

My cheeks flushed.

"Bryan, dude," Dizzy said. "Pay attention, man. Quit looking at them. You're getting us killed."

Feeling Bryan's attention on me, I pushed against War's solid chest, the pressure of my fingers creasing the soft material of his white T-shirt. "You're embarrassing me. Let me out."

"Come on, babe." He tried to kiss my cheek, but I ducked away.

"War, please."

"Oh, all right. Sorry, babe." He scooted out so I could exit the banquette. "It's just I'm so glad you're back in my life, and I had a good time with you today. What's wrong with that?"

"Nothing," I mumbled with my gaze on the floor.

I shouldn't have been this upset. I wouldn't have been if I hadn't been dreaming in vivid detail about what it had been like with Bryan. It made what I'd done with War seem almost tawdry by comparison.

"I'm sorry too," I said. "I guess I'm just stressed out about Atlanta. I'll feel better after I work on my wardrobe."

Once I was alone in the back of the bus, I was able to catch my breath and regain my equilibrium. I placed the outfit I planned to wear for Atlanta on the bed. Low hip-hugger jeans with a little flare at the knee, a cool silver peace-symbol belt, and then the lacy long-sleeved midriff-baring top that was really lingerie. That was the part I needed to fix. In its present condition, it was completely transparent.

I took out a needle and thread and went to work.

After a while, I heard a lot of banging around outside the door, followed by the sound of the guys warming up with their instruments. I picked up my stuff and wandered back to the front to join them. Bryan's eyes searched mine for a moment before he looked away.

I immediately recognized the melody he was strumming. It was the one I'd been working on after the first time we made love. Luckily for me, he didn't have the lyrics that went along with it. If he sang those right now, it would probably kill me.

Why is he doing this to me?

Bryan

Two years ago

I smoothed a finger over Lace's brow. She looked so peaceful while she slept.

What have I done?

I'd convinced myself last night that because I loved her so intensely, that this must be right. But as daylight seeped in through the blinds in her bedroom, I knew that I couldn't hide from the glaring consequences of my actions.

A couple of soft knocks might as well have been the shots of a firing squad to my guilty conscience. My gaze snapped to the door.

"Bryan, if you're in there," Dizzy whispered from the other side of the door, "you need to wake up, man."

Shit.

Carefully, I moved to the edge of the bed and pulled on the tuxedo pants I'd worn the night before. I glanced back at Lace. She held the black ribbon in one of her hands and was lying on her side as she slept, her beautiful blond hair spilled across the pillow. The sheet had fallen away from her chest.

The beautiful Cinderella without her ball gown.

Dizzy knocked again.

Time for the prince to leave.

I slid the ribbon from her grasp and tucked it in my pocket before gently pulling the sheet up over her. Moving for the door, I grabbed my shirt, jacket, and tie on the way.

Dizzy's amber eyes widened when he saw me. "I hoped I was wrong."

I shrugged. I wasn't going to get into this with him right now.

"War's on his way over." Dizzy ran a hand across his face, and I felt my stomach drop. "If he sees you here with her, it's gonna be over for all of us. Ruin everything for everyone. Right when we've got two labels fighting over us, and a chance for all of us to get out of Southside." He frowned. "Never figured you were such a self-centered prick."

Panicking, I blurted the first thing that came to mind. "War doesn't need to know." My stomach churned. "It was just prom. Getting laid is a rite of passage. It didn't mean anything."

• • •

Present day

"What's that mellow shit you're playing?"

Dizzy's question brought my wandering thoughts back to the present.

Of course he didn't recognize it. Only Lace and I knew that melody. It was the song she'd strummed in her room the night after prom. I played it now, meaning it as a message for Lace, wanting to remind her of what we'd once shared. To remind her of that night when she'd been mine, and mine alone.

"Yeah, man, no mellow stuff." Sager pushed his jet-black hair out of his dark eyes before he put his pick between his lips and plugged in his bass. "What we need is some good road music."

"How about 'Endless Highway'?" King banged his sticks against a practice snare pad.

"No way." Sager made a face. "RHCP's 'Road Trippin'.'"

I sneaked a peek back at Lace while King and Sager continued to argue about the merits of their choices. Her head was down, her blond hair spilling over the embroidered ivory blouse she wore while her fingers deftly weaved a needle in and out of a scrappy piece of white material she held.

"I've got the perfect song," King said. "'Born to Be Wild.' That's us right there." He laid down the intro beat, and Dizzy joined in on rhythm guitar.

"Steppenwolf. Hell yeah. Good one, King." Sager picked up his cell. "Hold up. We need to get this on our YouTube channel."

I slanted a brow. "You guys have a YouTube channel?"

Sager nodded. "TMT. Tempting Men of Tempest." He and King moved back to back, their arms crossed over their chests. "We're dynamite and sin all wrapped up together."

When I laughed, Sager scowled at me.

"Don't be a hater, man. We've got over thirty thousand subscribers."

"Lined up lots of good tail because of it," King said proudly, his lips curving. "Primo poon. Remember Dana?" He wiggled his brows.

"Oh yeah." Sager nodded. "Redheads are sweet. Remember her, Bullet?"

I frowned and glanced at Lace. Her lips flattened as our eyes met.

"Hey, Bryan," Sager said and held out his cell. "Here. We need a cameraman."

I took his phone and began filming as soon as the guys started up again. War wandered over during the second play-through and provided the vocals. Lace put down her sewing and twirled around in the aisle on her bare feet, looking like a young Stevie Nicks in that gypsy top as she sang along with him.

My lips lifted into a nostalgic smile as I watched them. This was how it had all been when we'd first started out, jamming in that old musty garage, covering our favorite tunes. It had been fun and easy when it was just about the music.

The bus lurched to a stop, and I glanced out the window. "Looks like we're stopping for fuel."

"Thanks, man." Sager grabbed his phone from my hand. "Let's go get some snacks, King."

"Wait up," Dizzy called. "I'm coming too. I need some new reading material. How 'bout it, Bryan?" he asked over his shoulder.

"Sure." I glanced at Lace. "I'm betting they have popcorn in there."

"Then I'm in." She turned back. "You want anything, War?"

He shook his head, pointing to the cell he held to his ear. "I need to finish this call."

While the others filed into the truck stop, I lingered, checking on the driver and trying not to look suspicious. But I was determined to find a moment alone inside the convenience store with Lace.

I found her at the back, near the coolers. Placing my hands on her arms, I leaned over her shoulder and wasn't surprised when I felt her muscles tense beneath the gauzy sleeves.

"We need to talk," I said, turning her to face me.

"No, Bry." She shook her head. "What's left to discuss?"

"Lots." I shoved my fingers through my hair. "The messed-up shit you're doing with War, for one."

Over on the adjacent aisle, King raised his voice as he popped off to someone. Usually loud and boisterous with a notoriously quick fuse, the only time our drummer was shy and quiet was around the ladies. At the moment, though, I only had interest in one person.

Focusing back on Lace, I shifted closer, trapping her between my arms so she couldn't move. "I can't get you out of my head, and that was before the kiss we shared on the bus. If you're being honest, I don't think you can either. Emptying the minibar was the only thing that kept me from coming and taking you away from him last night."

I saw the truth reflected in her eyes.

"I've *never* forgotten prom, and how it was between us," I said emphatically, and probably a little too loudly.

I yanked her closer, watching her tongue dart out to moisten her lips. I wanted to pull it into my own mouth, and that was just for starters.

"Don't tell me there's nothing left to say." I slid my hands up to cradle her face and lowered my voice. "Meet me tomorrow morning in the hotel workout room in Atlanta. Eight o'clock."

"I can't." She shook her head.

"Bullshit," I said tersely. "Find a way, Lace. If you don't show, I'll come find you."

Chapter 18

Lace

In the front lounge, I waved my hand in front of my nose as the guys stuffed their faces with fast food. "Jeez, it smells like a grease factory in here."

"C'mon, Lacey. Have one." War offered me a French fry. "You used to love McDonald's."

"No, I didn't." I shook my head at him and raised my brows. "You must be getting me confused with the other love of your life," I teased. "Yourself."

"Dick's Drive-In was her favorite," Bryan muttered under his breath.

When his gaze met mine, my cheeks flamed. I'd been a sucker for those gray-green eyes since I was five.

War frowned. I think he noted my response and didn't like Bryan pointing out things he knew about me that War didn't.

Bryan stood and crossed the aisle, and I turned my head to follow him. As he reached up to rummage around in the top cabinet at the kitchenette, his black T-shirt rode up, providing a glimpse of his bared midsection. The view of his flat abs and contoured hip bones mesmerized me nearly as much as his eyes did a moment before. The black color of his shirt was a perfect backdrop for his tats. I'd told him once that I thought the tattoo sleeves were a waste of money.

Looking at him through my lashes right now, I decided I'd changed my mind. The intricate black Japanese characters that spelled out his mom's and his sisters' names were sexy as hell, and worth every single penny. I imagined tracing the marks with my fingers, or maybe even my tongue.

"Lacey, pay attention." War's frown deepened. "The guys wanna know if you're in for a game of truth or dare."

"Oh, okay. Sure."

"What's going on with you?" War shifted to study me, his brow dipping. "You seem really distracted today."

"I'm fine." I shrugged. "Does this game work like the one we played when we were kids?"

"Basically," King said. "We still find out embarrassing shit about each other. But now we get really drunk too."

I chuckled. "Fun times."

"Rules are twenty dollars and a shot of tequila to whoever passes the truth-or-dare challenge," Dizzy said. "Oh, and the last person left standing usually gets a bonus prize."

"A kiss from Lace!" King shouted as Bryan moved toward us with a stack of shot glasses in one hand and a bottle of Cuervo in the other.

I smiled at King's enthusiasm. "Like that's anything special."

"How 'bout a night to sleep in the back bedroom?" Sager rolled up the sleeves of his Black Flag concert tee. "No offense, Lace, but you and War have been hogging it."

"Not happening," War muttered. "I'm sleeping with Lace, and I'm not sleeping with her in a bunk."

"Uh-oh, is that the only bottle of tequila?" Dizzy asked Bryan.

"Yeah." Bryan nodded. "Just this one."

"Oh yeah," Dizzy said. "I remember who drank the other one."

A look I didn't understand passed between my brother and Bryan. Dizzy removed his jacket and took a seat on the couch beside War and me. Sager, King, and Bryan sat on the opposite one.

"Who's going first?" Bryan asked.

"We'll just do it reverse alphabetically," War said.

"Confusing as hell," Bryan said. "And just to put that out there, that'll put me last."

"Great. What he means is that the game's already his." Dizzy rolled his eyes as he arranged the shot glasses. "No one can hold their liquor the way Bryan can."

"War, you're up," King said, tapping the side of his full shot glass. "Truth or dare?"

"Dare," he said.

King's dark brows rose. "I dare you to share what you said about Avery Jones when she was here on the tour bus."

A heated nonverbal exchange passed between War and Bryan.

"You're such an asshole, King," War growled. "I'm out." He shot to his feet. "I've got better things to do than play this idiotic game with you pissants. I'm going to the back."

He leaned in and gave me a tight-lipped kiss, and I started to rise.

"I'll come with you."

"That's all right, babe. Stay. Come when you've had enough. Knowing these motherfuckers, that won't be long."

I stuck my chin out. "I can hold my own."

"Sure you can." Sager's head bobbed in agreement. "You did with those cops when they hassled you and King." He glanced at his best friend. "You remember that? Don't you, King?"

"Oh yeah." King nodded. "She stood up to them for me. Said we don't get to pick our family."

"Just our *amigos*." I held out my knuckles to King for a fist bump.

"Okay." Dizzy smiled indulgently. "You're next, Sager, *mi amigo.*"

"All right." Sager leaned back and stretched out his arms over the back of the couch. "Give me a truth."

Dizzy ran a finger over his eyebrow piercing. "Did you really do the nasty with Mrs. Neboski on that science field trip to Lake City?"

His lips curving, Sager gave him a quick nod.

"Hot damn!" Dizzy's brows rose almost to his hairline. "I thought that was just urban legend."

Expressions ranging from disgust to admiration went around the table as Sager pocketed his cash and knocked back a shot of tequila.

Bryan refilled the shot glass. "You're next, Lace."

"Okay." I pulled the shot glass with a twenty underneath it toward me.

"Truth or dare?" Bryan asked.

Shit. This could be tricky. Bryan had a devilish glint in his eye that concerned me.

"Truth. No, dare," I said quickly, changing my mind, nervous about how far he might take things.

"Hmm." He ran a finger slowly across his mouth.

My stomach did a little flip. I licked my dry lips as he continued to stare at me, obviously enjoying making me squirm.

Finally, Bryan grinned. "Kiss your brother . . . on the lips."

I snorted. "No way!"

Dizzy shook his head as he glared at Bryan. "That's just sick, man. I'm giving her my turn, and she earns a modify since you went so far over the line."

"Agree." Sager rubbed his chin as he stared at Bryan. "Now she has to kiss *you* for forty bucks. You're almost like a brother to her, anyway. She's already so pissed, I'd watch out. She might bite."

"Promise?" Bryan grinned as he gave me a slow once-over.

My cheeks warmed. "I just might, you ass." I crossed over to him, ignoring Dizzy, who was violently shaking his head at me.

I was surprised my brother didn't have more faith in me. That forty dollars was already mine.

I bent down to give Bryan a peck. As soon as our lips touched, he took over. I forgot all about our audience, which was a huge mistake.

"Lace." War's voice snapped my head up like a whip. "Come to bed." His expression was furious.

Blood roaring in my ears, I swiped my winnings off the table before hurrying after him.

chapter

19

Bryan

Shifting in my bunk as I wore my earbuds, I turned up the volume again, trying to drown out the sound of Lace and War yelling at each other in the back.

I shouldn't have taken things so far with that kiss, but I wasn't sure I gave a damn. I'd wanted to taste her again.

A terrible thought hit me. What if War got physical with Lace? Not that I'd ever seen War hit a woman, but drugs could make you do irrational things.

I pulled out my earbuds, listening intently. Just more shouting.

But now that my imagination had gone there, I couldn't rest until I saw for myself she was okay. I threw my legs over the side of my bunk and started to climb down from my top roost.

"Stay put." Dizzy grabbed hold of my leg before my foot even hit the floor. "Get the fuck back in bed. Haven't you caused enough trouble for one night?"

"I'm going to make sure he doesn't hurt her," I told him flatly.

"He wouldn't dare. Not with you standing by, ready to take her off his hands. Besides, you know Lace can take care of herself."

I wasn't so sure about that. After Martin and now the drugs, I wasn't sure about a lot of things anymore.

"Why can't you let it go?" Dizzy asked in a low voice.

I didn't answer. Dizzy would never understand. I'd never seen the dude have an emotional connection with any woman. He went through them at a faster clip than I ever had. Dizzy had the whole *grab 'em and bag 'em* thing down to an art form. It seemed like an obsession with him more than a game.

Eventually, things quieted down in the back, and my tensed muscles began to relax. But then I smelled something acrid burning.

Fuck.

They were shooting up again. I put my earbuds back in and blasted up the volume. I could certainly relate to Axl's sarcastic introduction to "Estranged" from the live version. As Slash's guitar solo wailed in my ears, I squeezed my eyes tightly shut.

• • •

Lace

I tapped the soles of my stilettoes on the floorboards. On edge, I peeked out around the stage column. The arena in Atlanta was a complete sellout. An ocean of fans bounced in the pit as Bryan stood in front of the band, playing the catchy guitar riff in "We're Through."

Shirtless, War was a sexy sight as well, his upper torso gleaming with a fine sheen of perspiration under the intense heat of the spotlights. A pair of panties arced through the air and landed at his feet. With practiced ease, he bent down, picked up the scrap of pink material, and held it in the air before stuffing it in his jeans pocket.

The crowd roared their approval.

Why couldn't I get all breathless and fluttery inside for War anymore? With his studded belt, low-slung dark jeans, and crooked smile, what wasn't there to like?

Nothing. Only he wasn't Bryan.

My attention swung to his counterpart at center stage.

Bryan's guitar hung crotch-level low. With his light eyes half-shielded by heavy lids, his expression was sublime as he played, entirely in his element. It was a look I'd seen before in a much more intimate setting.

My cheeks warmed at the memory.

The sound of voices backstage drew my attention away. An intense Marcus Anthony was talking to someone I didn't recognize, a suited executive type. The mid-thirties brunette had a curvy figure and wore a stylish Marc Jacobs charcoal-gray pinstripe suit with a really cool pair of T-strap pointy-toed pumps with four-inch spike heels.

Her brows drew together as she asked, "Is she all right?"

"She'll be okay. Sam and Trevor are back with her." Marcus gathered the ends of his shoulder-length hair into his fist. "Avery's a professional."

The suit put her hand on Marcus's arm, and his entire expression softened. A moment later, I saw why as Avery Jones appeared, went straight to him, and melted into his arms. Her eyes were red-rimmed.

I wondered what all the drama was about, but when she looked over in my direction, I threw my hair over my shoulder dismissively. I didn't really care what her problem was. I had more important things to worry about than that haughty bitch. She'd probably just broken a fingernail.

Tugging at the jagged material at the end of my sleeves, I checked the rest of my outfit one more time. Strategic flesh-colored inserts covered everything important up top. My belt hung just right, low around the hips of my skintight jeans. It was all good.

I blinked as a camera flashed next to me. Kimberly had just taken another picture of the guys. I'd wanted to strangle War when he introduced me to the *Rolling Stone* photographer. Like I needed any more pressure, knowing that the magazine was covering the very event where I was to make my debut.

"Kimberly, how are you?" A handsome middle-aged man with steely blue eyes, deep dimple grooves, and close-cropped gray hair approached her and held out his hand.

"Charles Morris," Kimberly said. "I'm surprised to see you here. I thought this was a Black Cat affair."

"It's a concert, Kim." He raised a brow. "As far as I know, those are open to the public."

"All right, Atlanta." War's voice boomed over the venue's speaker system. "Help me welcome former Tempest songstress, Lace Lowell, to the stage."

I spun back around.

Shit.

Shit.

Shit.

My heart raced from nerves and from the line of coke War and I had done earlier.

Holding my shoulders back, I made my way out to him, willing my hands not to tremble. War took them in his and kissed my cheek before leading me to the piano. The weight of an arena's worth of stares draped heavily on me. For a scary moment, I thought I might puke, but luckily, it passed.

Taking a careful sip of air, I settled onto the piano bench. As I lifted my head, my eyes met Bryan's. His gaze was warm, and he gave me an encouraging smile.

I can do this.

I placed my fingers on the keys and began to play the song that I'd written for him. My voice rang out steady and sure. I sounded really good.

Seconds later, I relaxed into the song, and by the time I reached the chorus, I could feel the electrified hush that had fallen over the arena.

Wow. Cool.

War was at my side as soon as I finished. "You nailed it, Lacey," he said in my ear, right before thundering applause rained down on us.

My face broke out into a wide smile.

War took my hand and led me to center stage. "Miss Lace Lowell," he repeated into the mic after the applause died down. "And Tempest." The guys all gathered around, and the six of us took a bow together.

"It's a fucking rush, ain't it, babe?" War asked as he guided me off the stage with his arm around my shoulders.

"It's amazing," I said, buzzing from the adrenaline still rippling through my body. Right this moment, I felt like nothing was out of my reach.

"Warren Jinkins," an authoritative voice said, jarring me from my reverie.

It was the same brunette executive I'd seen earlier with Marcus, only this time she looked pissed as she beckoned War. "Come with me." She turned, her heels clacking on the hardwoods as she said sternly, "You too, Miss Lowell."

I looked at War, but he'd already moved to follow. Surprised, I scurried to his side, never having seen him so intimidated by anyone.

We followed the exec back through the busy corridor. Her shoulders stiff, she led us to an empty dressing room and then turned to face us.

Her light gray eyes flashed at me. "Who gave you permission to be out on that stage tonight?"

"I did. She's one of us," War said. "She used to be in the band."

"Warren." Mary shushed him with an abrupt hand motion and frowned. "This is not a high school talent show. Are you the one paying the nightly rent on this facility? Do you sign the paychecks for this tour?"

His lips flat and brows drawn together, War shook his head.

Mary stepped closer. Even though she had to peer up at him, there was no doubt in my mind that she was totally in charge. "You may *think* you're some wild stallion, but the fact is that you're not. You're just another horse in my stable. You *ever* pull a stunt like that again without my prior approval, and I'll turn you into a gelding. You get where I'm going with this?"

War nodded again. I was surprised he didn't say *yes, ma'am.*

Then those gray eyes brimming with confidence turned back on me.

Uh-oh. I gulped, fighting the urge to squirm under her scrutiny.

"That said, I want to talk to Lace for a minute."

War moved toward me protectively.

"Alone," Mary said, giving him a sharp look, and he hurried out of the room like his ass was on fire.

When War was gone, Mary took in a breath and pinched the bridge of her nose. "You were actually quite good out there."

"Thank you," I said.

"Why haven't I heard of you?" Mary muttered more to herself than me.

I shrugged.

She frowned and typed into her phone. I heard the *bloop* of an outgoing text message. "You could benefit from some voice lessons, though. You're raw, but clearly talented." She fixed me with a level stare. "Have you ever thought about a career in the music industry?"

The way the CEO studied me, I had a strong feeling that how I answered was really important. "I have. In fact, it's something I've always dreamed of doing."

"Solo?" Mary's eyes narrowed. "No band or boyfriend to back you up. Just you at center stage, win or lose. Think you could handle that?"

I raised my chin. "Absolutely."

Mary's brows rose, and she studied me for a moment more. "All right then. Beth Tate, one of my execs, is flying down tomorrow. I want to sit down and talk with you formally in Orlando."

Bryan

I checked the apartment number against the text from War, wondering what was up with all the cloak-and-dagger shit. I knocked, and the door immediately swung open. An attractive woman with a low-cut blouse and a Bluetooth device clipped above her ear swiped her finger over an iPad.

"Welcome, Mr. Jackson. Zenith Productions and Mr. Morris are pleased you could come. Bar's in the corner. And if there's *anything* else you feel that you need or require, don't hesitate to ask. I'll make it happen."

I nodded as I scanned the swanky setup. It eclipsed the meet-and-greet affairs we'd had so far on the tour.

The apartment was spacious and modern with dark hardwood floors, multiple seating areas, and chrome and glass fixtures. The DJ's mix featured a heavy bass line that permeated the entire space. Guests packed the place, most dressed a hell of a lot fancier than I was in my navy button-down and jeans. I wandered in, my gaze drifting to the balcony and the intriguing view of downtown Atlanta.

The more intriguing scenery was inside, though.

Wearing the same sexy outfit that she'd worn onstage, Lace was perched on the edge of a wide white chaise next to War. His long legs were sprawled out in front of him. He noticed me and waved me over.

The man they were talking to turned and offered his hand confidently. "Charles Morris. Zenith Productions."

I gave War a puzzled look. What was he doing here at a party thrown by another label?

"You're a hell of a guitar player," Morris told me with a respectful chin dip. "I'll tell you up front what I told War. I want you both, and Zenith will make it worth your while to break from Black Cat."

His gaze went back to War.

"I'll let you fill Mr. Jackson in on the finer details. I'll give you another call in a couple of days." He shook War's hand, then mine, and kissed Lace's cheek. "I've got other business to attend to, but we'll talk soon."

Once Morris had faded back into the crowd, I turned to War. "What the hell kind of game are you playing? You know we have an exclusive contract with Black Cat."

War's eyebrows went up. "No deal's ironclad. I'm just exploring all my options. There are always buyout clauses, and Morris says he's willing to pay them to get us out. Tempest is a *major* deal now, Bullet. *Rolling Stone* may do a feature on us. We have a top-ten hit, but Black Cat's still treating us like we're second tier. We should be headlining our own tour, man. Fuck, we don't even have a music video yet."

I considered that for a moment. "What do the other guys think?"

War polished off his drink and handed the tumbler casually to Lace. "Could you get me a refill, babe?"

Lace's eyes narrowed, but she did as he asked.

"The other guys aren't included in this deal," War said in a low, confidential tone when she'd gone. "This offer is just for you and me."

"What the fuck?" My heart thumped hard against my ribs.

War looked so nonchalant sitting there planning a deal that would leave the rest of the guys in the group behind. This wasn't taking care of your friends. It made me wonder how well I'd ever really known him.

"Bullet, wake up." War stood, and the toes of his boots touched mine. He swayed, his pupils mere pinpoints. He was wasted again. "This is just business. Zenith's offering ten times what Black Cat's paying. You and I write most of the songs anyway. Face it, the other guys are replaceable."

"Bullshit." I leaned in, my hands balling into fists. "This is bullshit, War. You're forgetting that Dizzy was the one who came up with the riff on 'We're Through.' That riff makes the song what it is. Not to mention that he's a solid rhythm guitarist. Sager and King pull their weight too. They lay the foundation that gives you the freedom to do the improvising you like to do. Tempest works the way it is. The five of us work . . . you said so yourself just the other day. What the hell's going on with you?"

War finally had the decency to look uncomfortable. My gaze slid to Lace, who was watching us from the bar, her pretty mouth pinched into a worried frown.

"What about her, War? What's Lace gonna say when she finds out you're going to stab her brother in the back?" Glaring at him, I dug my hands deep into my pockets and cursed my bad luck that I found no cigarettes. I needed a smoke in a bad way right now.

"She's getting her own contract with Zenith out of this." War shrugged. "She'll come around about the rest eventually."

"You're fucking deluding yourself if you think that's gonna happen."

War straightened to his full height. He was leaner but a half inch taller than me, something we used to joke about, but

I didn't feel like joking now. "She'll understand I did what I had to do."

"What's going on?" Lace returned with War's drink and glanced between the two of us.

"Nothing, Lacey. Just guy talk. Right, Bullet?"

I didn't answer. I stared at War for a long time, feeling completely sucker punched by his actions. My best friend seemed to have suddenly morphed into someone completely different.

Or maybe the problem was me. Maybe I'd turned a blind eye to the subtle changes in him over the past two years. Fame was a rabid bitch that had bitten War. I wondered how long it would be before he decided I was expendable too.

My gaze tipped to Lace. "I didn't get a chance to tell you earlier, but you were really great tonight. You were *meant* to be up on that stage."

"Thank you," she said, looking embarrassed.

"I'd better get going." I glanced at my watch. "It's late. I wanna hit the gym early in the morning." I hit her with a meaningful look.

She dipped her head. *Message received.*

"I'm heading back to the hotel." My gaze slid back to War. "I've got a lot of thinking to do."

Lace

Stunned, I stared down at War as he knelt on one knee on the carpet in our hotel room, an open velvet ring box in his hand. I couldn't believe he'd just proposed to me.

"Lace," he said. His brown eyes were warm, but he cocked his head to the side, seeming surprised that I hadn't tackled him in enthusiastic acceptance.

"Yes." I nodded instead, giving him a tremulous smile as I held out my hand.

War slid the pear-shaped diamond ring on my finger, pulled me into his arms, and kissed me long and hard.

Being engaged to War would give me the security and respectability I craved. I knew he loved me, and I knew him. He wasn't Martin. There wouldn't be any surprises. War wasn't cruel, not completely. Those were the things I told myself quickly and in rapid succession.

Why then did I feel so unsettled and unsure?

He'd completely caught me off guard. I hadn't been expecting anything like this. That was part of it, for sure. There hadn't been any hints leading up to this.

And he'd been acting a little weird, distracted and checking his cell a lot since Bryan left the Morris party. I didn't know what was up with War. I couldn't read him like I'd once been able to.

Why did I have this niggling suspicion that the Morris deal had something to do with the timing of his proposal?

War pulled back from me and favored me with a wide smile. "We should celebrate."

He moved to the safe and pulled out a leather pouch. He dumped the contents on the desk, placing a brown blob on a small piece of tinfoil. Holding a lighter underneath the foil, he heated it up.

Glancing at me, he asked, "You sure you don't want at least a little hit tonight?"

I shook my head, though my mouth went dry with longing as the heroin liquefied and I inhaled the familiar fumes. My hands shook as I turned away. "No. I'm okay."

I stood with my back to him and looked out the window. The lights of downtown Atlanta were softened by the coming dawn, but there wasn't anything soft about my heart. It was pounding its way out of my chest with desire for that *little hit* that I'd refused.

Behind me, I heard each of War's practiced movements. I knew without looking when he reached the point of drawing up the seductive liquid to a syringe. My resolve rapidly dissolving, I turned around.

"Change your mind?" War's eyes met mine.

I nodded. What did it matter, anyway? I closed my eyes as if that would keep me from knowing what I'd become. Feeling worthless, I crossed to him and held out my arm.

He lifted my chin, his gaze moving across my face. "It's just a tiny dose. I've been lowering the amount each time, just like you wanted."

War tied off the tourniquet, his eyes already heavy lidded as he bent over my arm. He'd already had his dose.

Anticipation swirled in my belly as I watched the needle enter my skin. The effect was almost immediate. My brain detached from the world around me as the warm euphoric haze descended. I didn't even notice when War removed the needle.

• • •

When I woke up later, I was curled up on my side. War was sprawled out on his stomach in a pair of black boxers on the bed beside me.

I glanced at the bedside clock. Seven a.m. The dose must have been really small. I'd only been out a few hours, but War was snoring, indifferent to the world around him. He didn't even stir when I slipped out of bed.

In the bathroom, I stripped out of my clothes and looked at myself in the mirror. I'd lost twenty pounds over the past year. Food, fashion, passion, music . . . all were losing their appeal. Everything in my life now took second place to my desire to get high.

Disgusted with myself, I turned from the harsh truth that stared back at me from the mirror.

A junkie. As bad as my mother had ever been.

My life that once had so much potential was circling the drain.

If only I'd refused that first hit when Martin offered, maybe things would have turned out differently. But I'd been too weak. It had been so much easier to give in to the belief that I was as worthless as my mother had always made me feel, than to fight the battle for my self-respect.

I showered and dressed, pausing for a moment to glance down at the sparkling gem on my left hand. I'd made my decision, hadn't I? Yet after only a cursory glance at War, I found myself tiptoeing quietly out of the hotel room and heading downstairs for my rendezvous with Bryan.

On the elevator ride down to the workout room, I used a rubber band to secure my hair into a sloppy bun, but avoided looking at my guilty reflection in the mirrored wall. When the door finally opened, I let out a heavy sigh.

Avery.

Great. She was the last person I wanted to see right now. And besides, what the hell was she doing down here on the workout level with Bryan, anyway?

"Good morning." The redhead took a step back to let me out of the elevator. She allowed the door to close without getting on, her hands twisting on the handles of a jump rope. "I heard you sing last night. You were really good."

"Thanks," I muttered, my eyes narrowing. "Did you have a good *workout* this morning?"

"Yeah," she said, completely oblivious to the double entendre. "I like to jump rope while Marcus does the treadmill."

"Oh, really?" I glanced over her shoulder. "Where *is* your fiancé?"

"He's finishing up. Why?"

"No reason." I shrugged.

Avery stared at me for a moment, her head tilted to the side. "Where's War?"

When I didn't answer, she said, "I'm surprised to see you down here. You both seemed pretty messed up last night."

"We had a couple of drinks. It was a *party*," I said sarcastically. "Anyway, who are you to talk?" Her lips pursed in response to my biting sarcasm, but I wasn't done. I had better than that. "I seem to remember some internet video of you being pretty smashed yourself at some hotel bar in Phoenix."

"I wasn't referring to alcohol." Avery's emerald eyes flashed. "I'd keep those sleeves of yours pulled down if I were you."

Sanctimonious bitch.

"Listen, you don't like me for some reason," she said. "And that's fine. You're not exactly my favorite person either. There's been a lot more tension on the tour since you arrived. But your drug use really concerns me. My brother went down a similar path. It will destroy you, and hurt those who care about you." She sighed. "I really don't want something bad to happen to you. Especially if there's something I can do to prevent it."

"Oh, please," I said. "Save the Mother Teresa act for the fans. I don't need your help or anyone else's."

"Hey." Marcus walked up and kissed Avery's cheek. "I'm done. You ready to go up?"

"Yeah, I guess." Avery stood back while he pushed the elevator call button, and then leaned into him. "Think about it, Lace."

I walked past them without responding. I'd had enough of her highhandedness.

But though I tried not to let them, Avery's words got under my skin. I nervously twisted my engagement ring on my finger as I continued down the hall. I inserted my keycard and took in a calming breath before I entered the small exercise room.

With his sleeveless exercise tank wet with sweat, Bryan was lying on a bench, his tatted muscles flexing under an impressive load of free weights. "You okay, Lace?" He racked the bar as soon as he saw me. "You look a little pale."

I put my shaking hands in my hoodie pockets. Avery Jones had rattled me more than I cared to admit.

"I'm glad you came," he said, holding my gaze. Reaching for one of the folded towels, he wiped his forehead. "I did a lot of thinking after the Morris party." He stopped talking as a woman entered the room. "Let's go somewhere where we won't be interrupted."

His hand warm and insistent against the small of my back, he guided me out of the gym and down the hall. He opened the door to an empty massage room. Flipping on the light after I was inside, he closed the door and I heard the lock click.

My gaze fluttered nervously to his when he turned around. My blood pressure shot up in response to the intensity of his gray-green gaze.

"Bry?" I took a step back, even though he only stared at me. "What are you doing? I thought you said you wanted to talk."

"I do, and we will."

He took a step toward me, and when I took another step back, my ass came into contact with the counter behind me. I was trapped.

Bryan closed the remaining distance between us, pressing his hard body, all of it, against mine.

I placed my hands on his chest, intending to push him away, but my traitorous fingers didn't comply. Instead, they fisted into the damp material of his shirt and pulled him closer. The smell of his crisp cologne surrounded me.

"I'm done, Lace. Done hiding what's between us."

My face probably registered my shock as his head lowered, and he kissed me.

How many times have I wanted him to say something just like that? A million and one at the very least.

Thoughts gave way to sensation as his talented lips moved expertly against mine while his hands slid down to my ass. He grabbed me, pulled my hips into alignment with his, and pressed his erection against me.

He felt delicious, better than anything in the world, and I wanted him so badly. Drenched in desire, I shivered, allowing him to coax my lips apart. His tongue entered my mouth and slowly slid across mine. My pulse fluttered, beating wildly as his fingers opened and closed, massaging the soft flesh of my ass.

Breaking the seal between our lips, he lifted his head, breathing out my name before he trailed hot, open-mouthed, body-melting kisses down my neck. I was just going to slide my hands underneath his shirt when he caught them and brought them to his lips.

Suddenly, he froze. "What the hell is on your finger?"

My passion-hazed brain took a moment to process his question.

"You're fucking engaged, aren't you?" Bryan's voice was deadly quiet, but his expression was so wild and wounded, I would have stepped back if there had been any room.

"Why, Lace?" He took a step back and scrubbed his face with both hands. When he refocused on me, his eyes had a tormented glint to them. "How could you do this to me? To us?"

"What *us* is there, Bryan?" Anger slithered through me. "Prom was a long-ass time ago. You left me behind the same as War did, but he wants me. He makes our relationship a priority. When have you ever done that?"

"When *could* I possibly do that?" Bryan bit out, his expression anguished. "First War, then Martin, there was always someone else for you. But I can tell you this, and I want you to listen well. If you *were* mine, I'd love you better. I'd love you enough to tell you when you're wrong."

He pulled in a ragged breath, his eyes blazing with emotion as they met mine.

"The drugs, Lace, they'll bury you alive. Like they did your mother. They're keeping you from seeing the truth that's right in front of you. How incredibly strong you are. How much you have to give. How much you mean to the people who *really* care about what happens to you. Like your brother. Like me."

"War cares about me," I said, protesting weakly, my eyes burning at his harsh words while I recognized the truth in them. I dug my fingernails into my clenched palms.

Bryan's declaration was beautiful, but I told myself it was too little, too late. War was the safer choice, the wiser choice. I'd taken a risk on Bryan before, and look at the downward plunge my life had taken afterward.

"It's admirable how loyal you are to him, and you've been a good friend to me too." I peered up at him through my lashes. "That is, when I remember to keep my distance. But that's difficult for me to do when there will always be a little part of me in love with you." I sighed. "I don't think anyone ever gets over their first."

"Lace, don't," he said low.

My eyes burned beneath the strain it took to refuse him. "You know how I always wanted a Prince Charming to come and sweep me off my feet?"

"I remember." His gorgeous face was intense as he focused on me.

"What I've been looking for is a man to take me away from my shitty life, a man who would do everything in his power to keep me safe, a man who would put my happiness above his own. War is that man. I was too young and had too much going on to see that before, and I . . . I made a lot of mistakes. I don't deserve him. I'm certainly no prize, but most of the time he treats me like I am. So, we've got to stop doing this, Bryan. It has to be over between us. I've made a commitment to him."

We stared at each other a moment, the room completely silent except for our quiet, tortured breathing.

When Bryan reached for me, I didn't avoid him. I reveled in his touch, the warmth as his fingers curled into my upper arms.

"All right, Lace. You've had your say. Now it's my turn." His eyes glistened, a green forest shimmering with rain. "You say you've decided War's the fucking one." Bryan's voice was quiet but harsh. "How the hell can that be when he's giving you heroin? Some knight in shining armor, he is. That's bullshit. He's facilitating your destruction. That's not putting your happiness above his own."

I shook my head in denial, but Bryan was hard to resist. His words, the pull of his personality, and the sincerity in his gray-green eyes weakened my resolve, and that was before he gently skimmed his knuckles down my cheek.

"You need to ask him about the Morris deal, Lace. You need to remember the past and think about the future. Then you need to open your eyes and see who really loves you. I always have, and I always will."

"What about Avery?" I said desperately, too afraid to believe that he'd really said what I'd always wished for him to say.

"Avery was never more than a friend. What little there was between us was destined to fail. The truth is I didn't want it to succeed. You're the only woman I've ever cared for. The only one I've ever *made love* to. The only woman I've ever loved."

"Stop," I cried out. "Why are you telling me this now?" Tears gathered in my eyes, but I blinked them away. "It's too late now. You make me want to believe in a happily-ever-after for us, but that's not reality. That's a fairy tale. That's something the woman I once was believed in, but I'm not that woman anymore."

"That's not true." Bryan firmed his jaw and weakened my resolve. "That woman is still here. I'm looking right at her.

You have more than enough faith for both of us. You've just lost your way. We both have, being separate from each other."

He reached for me, but this time I drew away.

"Talk to War," he said grimly. "And then you'll see. He's the one who isn't who you think he is. He's changed. He's the one who's not who he used to be."

chapter

22

Bryan

The bus ride from Atlanta to Orlando turned into six and a half hours of living hell. I didn't see Lace at all, but thoughts of her in the back bedroom with War—with that ring on her finger—made me want to tear the hair out of my head.

I let out a loud sigh of frustration. Now that I'd decided to risk everything, give up everything for her, she wouldn't let me. If only I could just grab her and whisk her away, away from War, away from the haze of deception and drugs, maybe then I could convince her.

As one hour bled into the next, I remained alone in the front lounge, settling for killing digital zombies on the bus game console, instead of going back and doing real harm to Lace's drug-enabling fiancé.

When the bus eventually pulled up to the drop-off area at the Contemporary hotel, I disembarked, got my key, and headed straight for my room without stopping to make small talk with anyone.

The happiest place in the world, my ass. Orlando was jammed with parents, children, teenagers, and tons and tons of strollers. Fortunately, my boots kept my feet from being maimed by errant wheels as I wove my way around all the flotsam and jetsam to the elevators.

When the doors opened, I had to squeeze sideways to fit inside. Though there was barely any room to breathe, it wasn't half as crowded as my brain was right now. Crammed with thoughts of her. Of us.

But what more could I do? I'd said my piece. Lace knew where I stood. Now I had to wait, but I was *not* a patient man.

She'd better talk to War soon.

As I exited the elevator, I cursed my bad luck that there wasn't even a real concert to keep my mind occupied tonight, just a short set inside the Magic Kingdom that Tempest and Brutal Strength were obligated to do for one of the tour sponsors who had rented out the entire park for an after-hours affair for their employees.

Once I finally reached my room, I entered and dropped my guitar case on the floor. I threw my sunglasses and small overnight bag on the white duvet that covered a king-size bed. A quick scan revealed an earth-toned interior with modern decor like the lobby. Nothing to provide any real distraction.

I crossed to the sliding glass doors and looked out at the view of the lagoon. As I watched a parasail drift back down to the water, I wished I could drift out of this nightmare to a safe landing.

Needing some grounding, I slid my cell out of my pocket and dialed home. The call was picked up on the first ring.

"Hello," my mother said, sounding out of breath.

"Hey, Mom. Did I catch you at a bad time?"

"No, sweetheart. I just came in from work and was cleaning the kitchen."

I heard the sound of running water being shut off. "Are Miriam and Ann okay?"

"They are. Both made the honor roll again, but we're all looking forward to the winter break. What's up with you?

I haven't heard from you in a couple of days. The tour's in Orlando now, right?"

"Yeah." I turned from the window and flopped onto the bed.

"How's Disney World?"

"I just got here. It's a little surreal, I guess. Not exactly a rocker kind of place with all these rug rats running around."

"I can imagine." She laughed. "How's Lace?"

Shit. My mom always had an alarming ability to home right in on whatever it was that was bothering me.

"She and War got engaged last night," I said softly.

"Really?" The line was silent for a moment. "I would've thought that relationship would have run its course by now."

I barked out a humorless laugh and rubbed a hand over the ache in my chest. "Apparently not." In a quick rush, I said, "I love her, you know."

"I know."

"How could you? I never said anything." Worried, I asked, "Was it that obvious?"

"It was always obvious to me, but I'm your mom." She sighed. "Seems like this has been building for some time. What are you going to do about it, Bry? Have you told her how you feel?"

"Oh yeah, but it didn't go over quite the way I'd hoped."

"Well then, she's not as smart as I thought she was." After a short pause, Mom said softly, "I'm sorry, Bry. Maybe you should consider just letting her go."

I'd been trying for the past two years. Longer, if I was being truthful.

"There are other girls out there," she added. "Any one of them would be lucky to have you. You're a real catch."

"Thanks, Mom. I'm glad you think so." I glanced at my watch. "Hey, I'm sure you're tired after your shift. I'd better let you go."

"I'm okay. It's great to hear from you, Bry. I'm so proud of you and all that you've accomplished, but I'll be glad when you actually get to come home."

"Me too. Love you, Mom."

After ending the call, I threw my cell onto the comforter and stalked to the minibar. After a quick examination, I slammed the door. Figured that all this place would have was granola bars and healthy shit. I needed a drink.

. . .

An hour later, my left elbow was propped up on the bar at the Outer Rim. I looked out over the lagoon from inside the large open-air atrium as a monorail whooshed through the building on the track above me.

The bar was small and concave. It only sat four, but all the seats were filled, as were the couple of low loungers by the windows. Apparently, being happy was easier with a little liquid lubrication. For me, it was going to take a hell of a lot.

I tried yet again to generate some interest in the blonde beside me. It had been wishful thinking that she'd be able to distract me. Even with my mind blurry from four drinks, it wasn't happening. She was too small on top, too curvy on the bottom, and her eyes and smile were all wrong. In other words, she wasn't Lace.

I was so screwed.

The blonde took the cherry from her drink, pulled off the stem, and leaned in close with a flirty smile. "Wanna see what I can do?"

"Not really." I was serious.

Not getting it, she laughed and proceeded to try to wow me with her tongue-tying prowess.

Suddenly, the hairs on the back of my neck prickled, and I glanced over my shoulder.

Lace. She stood by the gift shop, forgotten souvenirs in her hand. As her wide eyes met mine, she brought the pile of T-shirts she held to her chest like a protective shield and then spun away.

I squeezed the blonde's hand. "Nice trick, baby. Sorry, but I gotta go."

"Wait," she said, but I ignored her.

I threw a couple of twenties on the bar and hurried to the shop. As soon as I entered, I spotted Lace in the checkout line and called out to her.

She tensed before turning to face me. "Hey." Her smile didn't reach her eyes. "Pretty girl."

"I didn't notice." I took a step closer.

"The only one you'll ever love, huh?" Lace's cheeks reddened. She twisted the shirts, as if embarrassed that she'd said that out loud.

"Yes, dammit." I grabbed her arm and pulled her around the counter and over to a secluded corner, next to a bargain bin of Mickey Mouse swimsuits and flip-flops. "Have you talked to War yet?"

"No, not yet. He—"

I moved her back. "You didn't like seeing me with someone else, did you?" I grabbed her hands and pinned them behind her back, tugging them down and forcing her to look up at me as I growled out, "Well, join the fucking club. I don't like watching you with him either."

Her eyes darkened with understanding.

"You need to talk to War. Today, Lace."

She licked her lips and nodded.

I stared at her mouth. "I've laid it out to you how I feel, and I believe you feel the same."

She was fighting it, though. She needed a push, and I was going to give her a big one.

I came closer, crudely rocking my erection against her. "That's for you, babe. I've been sitting next to that blonde, but the whole fucking time, I've been thinking about you. It's always you. For years, it's been you."

Her breath caught. "Stop it, Bry," she begged in a rough whisper.

"Give me a reason to stop, Lace. Or so help me, I'm going to take that blonde upstairs and pretend that she's you. That's what I do. That's all I can do if you won't meet me halfway."

Lace closed her eyes, her pulse beating furiously in her neck. I held my breath, waiting for her to answer.

"Excuse me," an unfamiliar voice said.

"Huh?" I let go of Lace's hands and turned to look over my shoulder.

"I need to reorganize the suits," a shop lady said. "You two on your honeymoon?" She raised a brow as she started to sift through the bin.

"No," Lace said before slipping past me and practically sprinting for the exit.

"Lace, wait." I caught her by the elbow.

"Let me go." Her voice was low, and she looked flustered as hell. "I can't do this right now. I've got a meeting with Mary Timmons, and I'm already late."

"You didn't answer my question."

"It sounded more like a threat," she choked out.

Fuck me, but I liked the defiant glint in her eyes. This was my Lace, the one without the drug haze. The one who didn't back down from a challenge. The one who could believe, who could stand at my side and fight for us.

"You know what I want," I said.

She shook her head, so I spelled it out for her.

"I want you to tell War it's over. I want to be able to stop hiding how we feel about each other. I want to hold your hand so everyone will know you're mine. I want to laugh and flirt with you again. I want to walk and talk with you, take you out on dates. I want to be the one in the back bedroom with you on the bus instead of him. I want to make love to you and then hold you all night long. I want to wake up next to you in the morning. I want you, babe. Just you."

Lace closed her eyes. "I can't give you what you want," she whispered, but I saw the surrender written in her eyes when she reopened them. It told me everything I needed to know.

What I wanted, she wanted too.

chapter 23

Lace

I yanked my arm free from Bryan's grasp and ran from the shop as if an animatronic Disney villain had sprung to life to pursue me.

When I reached the bank of elevators in the center of the building, I stopped to catch my breath and glanced back. Bryan was leaning against one of the columns of the shop, one ankle crossed over the other, his hands in the front pockets of his dark jeans.

To the casual observer, he might look relaxed, but I knew better. His gray-green eyes were watchful. His sculpted chest muscles and bulging biceps were coiled springs, ready to come unwound. I knew because I was just as tense. I felt exactly the same way.

I watched a mother and her teenage daughter both do a double-take when they passed him. Bryan Jackson was every woman's bad-boy fantasy—tall with long legs, a tight body, tatted arms, and handsome as sin. And what they saw on the outside was just a small part of all the amazingness that was him.

The elevator door opened, but I paused before getting in. I was so tempted to run back to him. Who the hell wouldn't be after what he'd just said? But I had to stop doing this. I'd made my decision, hadn't I? However, I couldn't help but wonder if it had been the right one.

A man and his son hurried onto the elevator, and the man beckoned me. "Better hurry on," he said, and I did, though numbly. "What floor do you need?"

"Twelve," I mumbled, giving him Mary Timmons's floor number before moving to the back. I shook my head as if that was all it would take to clear away my confusion, fretting as the elevator zipped upward.

What if Bryan went back to the blonde at the bar? The thought made me tremble with nausea. I didn't feel good, kind of woozy like I had a fever. Forcing my thoughts back to the upcoming meeting with Black Cat's CEO, I rubbed my chilled arms.

When Mickey Mouse's recorded voice announced my floor, I stepped out of the elevator and trudged down the monochromatic hallway to Timmons's room. Outside the door, a woman with gray-green eyes almost as beautiful as Bryan's smiled pleasantly at me. She had a cell pressed to her ear.

"Just a second," she told whoever she had on the line. Balancing the phone between her cheek and shoulder, she held out her hand to me. "Hi, Lace. I'm Beth Tate, head of PR for Black Cat."

"Nice to meet you." I nodded and shook her hand.

"Mary shouldn't be long," Beth told me, then ended her call. Sure enough, the door popped open a moment later.

Surprisingly, Charles Morris came hurrying out. He straightened his tie and buttoned his suit jacket. As Beth slipped past the Zenith Productions exec on her way into the room, I noticed Charles had pink lipstick smeared on the side of his mouth. When he looked at me, I pointed it out, trying to be discreet while hiding my surprise.

Was that Mary Timmons's lipstick? This was an interesting development.

Rubbing the color off with his thumb, Charles cleared his throat and ran a hand through his close-cropped hair. "Whatever Mary offers you, I'll double it," he said, his voice gruff.

I didn't know what to say, but I got the distinct impression that I was caught in the middle of something between him and her that was more than just a competition for my representation.

"You still have my card from Atlanta?" he asked as the door cracked open again.

"Charles," Beth asked with a frown. "Are you still here?"

"Tell Mary this isn't over." He glanced over Beth's head. "I'll see her in Miami."

"I don't think . . ." Beth trailed off as he walked away with a dismissive wave over his shoulder. Her lips flattened, but her expression was neutral when she turned back to me. She opened the door more widely. "Come inside. Mary will see you now."

"Okay," I said, entering and taking in the huge suite that dwarfed the standard hotel room War and I shared. It contained a large sitting area that took advantage of floor-to-ceiling windows that showcased a gorgeous view of Bay Lake.

Mary sat on the middle of a beige sofa with her spine straight and her shoulders back. "Have a seat." She gestured to the orange chair beside her.

As she shuffled through a stack of papers on the coffee table in front of her, I was surprised to see her hands shaking. An aftereffect of her encounter with Charles Morris? No doubt, the man was a force to be reckoned with. But I got the distinct impression that Mary Timmons was too, and was accustomed to getting what she wanted.

She smoothed her short brown hair into place, and I heard the door click closed behind Beth. All business now, the exec leveled me with a serious stare.

"I want to let you know up front that Black Cat is interested in signing you." She tapped a finger against the manila file. "But there are a couple of things that came up in your background check that concerned me."

"Oh?" I raised a brow, affecting calm, but inwardly I tensed.

"After graduation, you moved in with a man named Martin Skellin. Is that correct?"

My throat too tight to speak, I nodded.

"He's a convicted drug dealer." Mary tossed the file on the table. "I don't know if you were aware, but he was murdered last week. Shot in the back of the head, execution style."

My eyes wide, I inhaled sharply. I hadn't known, but I wasn't surprised. Martin had been skating on thin ice with the higher-ups long before I'd left him.

I gave the news of his death about ten seconds of my time, only a few of those seconds feeling bad about it. After all, he hadn't felt the least remorse about beating me and turning me over to Strader, who I likely wouldn't have escaped alive.

"That's awful." I swallowed to moisten my dry throat. "But I don't know how that's relevant to me."

"People are often measured by the company they keep."

"Guilt by association. Great." My hands balled into fists. "Look, Martin Skellin was an asshole. He knocked me around. I left him when he tried to pimp me out to a competitor to pay off a debt. My time with him isn't something I'm proud of, but who he was or what he did has nothing to do with me."

"Hmm." Mary seemed to give that some consideration. "I understand you're engaged to Warren now?" She glanced at my hands, I nervously twisted the engagement ring. "Isn't that a little sudden?"

Uncomfortable under this interrogation, I shifted. A fine sheen of perspiration broke out on my upper lip. "Not really. War and I have known each other for years. Why all this interest in my love life?"

I wasn't sure what I was expecting from this meeting, but I was beginning to feel uneasy. I wished now I'd taken War up on his offer to come with me. He'd warned me Mary was a hard-ass. Now I realized he'd been way understating it.

"It takes a strong personality to go solo," Mary said, studying me. "I need to be sure you have what it takes to handle it. There will be no boyfriends or fiancés to hold your hand on the road."

"I realize that." I straightened. "I can take care of myself. I've been doing that for a long time now."

"Yes, I know about your childhood. I can't even imagine what it must have been like for you." Mary's expression softened. She stood and tugged at the hem of her suit jacket. "I can certainly sympathize, and I admire your resilience, Lace, really, I do. But I have my concerns."

She moved to the windows and continued. "You're untrained. You're young, and you're inexperienced. But more than that," she turned back around, her brow furrowed, "I'm concerned about your judgment. I've heard about all the partying you've been doing on this tour."

I gulped and looked down at my ankle boots. I was sunk. The woman didn't miss a thing.

"All that said, I'm still willing to offer you a signing bonus of thirty thousand. I just need your word that drugs won't be an issue."

"They won't be." I nodded, telling myself it wasn't a lie, not really. I was quitting. Drugs wouldn't be an issue for me anymore.

"Good. I can assure you that Mr. Morris wouldn't match that much up front."

My head snapped up.

"Don't look so surprised. I know all about what Morris has been up to." Mary tapped her fingers against her folded arm. "I think it's very shortsighted of him to try to lure Warren and Bryan out of Tempest."

"What do you mean?" My eyes narrowed in confusion. "I was under the impression that Morris's offer included all the guys."

"No." She shook her head. "Zenith's deal is very personnel-specific. Morris is an unrepentant disassembler. He likes to take things apart and put them back together in a way he thinks is best."

I put my hands over my churning stomach as the reality of what Mary told me just sank in.

War had been planning to sell out the rest of the group, just like he'd done to me with the RCA deal. This was what Bryan wanted me to know. I wished he'd just told me himself.

It was obvious why War had kept this bit of damning information from me. Proposing to me on the same night he'd just brokered that sleazy backroom deal with Morris was a real manipulative move on his part, an obvious attempt to tie me to him.

Did War honestly think I would overlook the betrayal of my brother or King and Sager, just because he put a ring on my finger?

Bryan was right. War *had* changed. And if he thought I would turn a blind eye to all this . . . well, he didn't know me any better than I knew him.

"I put an end to it," Mary said, oblivious to the fact that my world had just been turned upside down. "Morris has assured me that he's withdrawing his offer." She sat on the couch again and leaned forward. "But back to you. I know Charles has offered to increase whatever I offer you, but you're smart enough to see through all those dollar signs. His offers are always back-end loaded and full of stipulations. Basically, if you don't meet his demands, you get nothing. The most likely scenario is that you'd end up owing Zenith money."

She handed me a piece of paper.

"Read this over. My offer is very simple." She slid a check across the table toward me. "A thirty-thousand-dollar advance on a three-year exclusive contract with Black Cat. Do things my way, Lace, and I think there's a good chance that you'll be a star."

I picked up the check and stared at it. Mary's signature was a wide scrawl, matching the one on the contract.

My vision tunneled in on this moment. There really wasn't a choice. Although I was still reeling from what I'd just found out about War, I was sure of this decision. I needed to do this. It was a chance for me to finally turn my life around.

I picked up the pen and signed.

The rest of our meeting passed in a blur. Mary shook my clammy hand, and Beth came back in to congratulate me.

Soon I was on my way back down the hall, then inside the elevator to my floor, completely numb. In front of the door to my room, I inserted the keycard and went inside, grateful the room was empty. I didn't feel up to a confrontation with War at the moment.

Shivering, I leaned back against the door. The air-conditioned air felt too cold on my feverish skin.

Suddenly, I realized what was going on. It wasn't stress making me feel this way, nor was it the flu. I was having withdrawal symptoms from the heroin. I'd had bouts like this before when I'd tried to quit, but I'd never made it this long without a dose. And I'd never had symptoms this bad.

I just needed one more teeny-tiny dose to get me over this hump. Just enough to get me through today.

After that, I was done for real.

I opened the safe and pulled out the small satchel. My hands were shaking so violently, I almost dropped the bag. I stumbled to the bed and sat down, then flicked on the lamp and unzipped the bag.

Bryan

In the lobby, beneath the concourse level where the bar and gift shop were, I stuck out like a bad ink stain in my all-black outfit of jeans, shirt, and boots, sitting on the corner edge of a beige suede sectional. A modern sphere mobile spun lazily overhead while I tapped my fingers impatiently against my leg.

Where is Lace? She should have been down here twenty minutes ago.

I ran my hands across my face and up through my hair. The light sweet scent of her vanilla fragrance still lingered. I wanted her soft curves back in my hands. I wanted my mouth on hers. I wanted to hear that low sound of arousal she made whenever our tongues touched.

I wanted her. Now.

I shifted, glancing at War at the other end of the sectional, where he sat talking to Dizzy.

Everything was so fucked up. War was the wrong guy for her—I could finally see that. Sure, I'd once made a promise to him, but this wasn't high school anymore. And I never promised I would stand idly by while he let her spin out of control. I had to get Lace to acknowledge what was between us. I was her first, and dammit to hell, I would see to it that I was her last.

"Where is she, man?" Making eye contact with War, I threw up a hand. "Did she text you? It's not like her to be late."

"I dunno." War shrugged, glanced down at his phone, and then looked over as King and Sager burst out laughing. "What's so funny?"

"King," Sager said with a smirk. "And his response to this cop who was hassling him at that truck stop in Richmond. I recorded it and put it on our YouTube channel. Come over. You guys need to see this."

War, Dizzy, and I moved over to the chairs where Sager and King were sprawled. We leaned in over the laptop, and King turned up the volume.

"You been smoking some marijuana?" the cop on the screen asked in a condescending tone.

"Not yet," King said with his usual sassy grin.

The cop's brows rose. "I'm just checking. I don't know if you knew, but a lot of drug deals go down in the area around here."

"Really?" King bowed up. "I get my drugs somewhere else." He folded his arms over his barrel chest and stared down at the much shorter uniformed man. "Are you telling me this because I'm Hispanic? If you don't mind, Officer, could I have your badge number?"

I watched the cop and King, but zoned out on their conversation as my ears picked up the unmistakable sound of my raised voice in the background.

"I'll *never* forget prom and how it was between us."

Fucking shit.

I glanced nervously at War. *Oh yeah, he heard me.*

He frowned as his gaze slid to me, and then back to Sager. "Play that part again. And turn up the volume."

My heart damn near stopping, I said, "War . . ."

"Just shut the fuck up!" War growled.

My muscles locked tight as the tape replayed. With the volume up, you could hear pretty much the whole incriminating conversation between Lace and me.

There was a long moment of stunned silence when the clip finished. No one moved, and no one spoke. Even the lobby noise seemed to fade away as War and I stared each other down. I felt the dynamic between us shift forever.

"You lying asshole!" War shouted, his face a furious mask. "How long have you been fucking my woman behind my back?"

"It's not like that—"

But I never got the chance to complete that thought. Without warning, War's fist flashed out and connected with my jaw.

I staggered back, gingerly touching a thumb to the blood on my lip. My gaze narrowed. "I'll give you that one, but let's take this somewhere else. I don't want to *talk* about this out here."

"I don't care what you want!" he shouted, and my guts seized up at the anger and betrayal in his gaze. "I trusted you, Bryan. Like a brother." He shook his head. "Can't believe you'd do this to me."

"I love her, man."

"Don't we all." War's lips twisted and he turned to Dizzy. "Did you know about this?"

Dizzy nodded, shifting in his seat and not meeting War's eyes.

"Listen." I pulled in a calming breath through my nose, but it was time to get this out in the open. Meeting War's furious gaze, I said, "It was only that one time in high school. But I've wanted there to be more between us, and you need to know I've asked Lace to choose."

I didn't tell War that if she chose him, I would keep trying to win her over anyway. And that's really what it all came down to. War and me, our friendship, having each other's backs . . . that shit always came first for me, but not for him.

The band was War's idol. Everything and everyone else was a distant second. The Morris deal was proof of that.

War didn't see the conflict for me, because there wasn't one for him. If he were in my place, I knew in my gut that if it were the band or her, he wouldn't have a problem with walking away from her. In fact, he'd done it before with the RCA deal.

My best friend's jaw tightened. "You guys covering for Bullet too?" War's furious gaze sliced through me before swinging to Sager and King.

"Leave us out of it," King fired back.

"That's his plan," I bit out. "As long as we're clearing the air, War, let's get everything out in the open." Speaking to all the guys, I said, "War's taking an exclusive solo deal from Zenith. He's breaking up the band."

"What the fuck, asshole?" Our very large, very angry friend King glared at War as he puffed out his chest, looking even bigger than usual.

"You're so full of shit." I held War's gaze and gave it to him, the destructive truth pouring out of me like pus from an infected wound. "Acting all self-righteous. Giving us that tired, worn-out old speech about the band and all of us being a priority. None of us are a priority to you, Warren. Not Lace, not me, not the guys. To you, we're all replaceable."

Suddenly, the hair on the back of my neck stood on end. It wasn't the same feeling I'd had earlier with Lace watching me. This one was more like an icy chill, like cold fingertips running down my spine. I glanced over my shoulder as a couple of paramedics jogged toward the elevators, rolling a stretcher between them.

I turned back to the scene unfolding with the guys.

"You're a sorry bastard." Dizzy's amber eyes were narrowed with accusation and focused on War.

"You're the one who's replaceable," King said, standing up and looming over War. "*Pinche güero culero.*" *Fucking white asshole.*

The chill I'd just had morphed into a horrible premonition the moment I heard Dizzy's cell phone ring. When he answered it, his look transformed from puzzlement to shock. Without a word, he broke for the bank of elevators at a flat-out run.

My entire body flooded with ice water, and I bolted after him. I caught him at the elevator, jumping inside it with him just before the doors closed.

His face pale, Dizzy hit me with a frightened look. "Those guys that just went by were for Lace. Beth Tate found her in her room." His eyes teared up. "Bry, she said Lace isn't breathing."

chapter 25

Lace

A low humming sound hovered around the edges of my consciousness while a diffuse bright light up ahead propelled me forward. As I followed it, the light coalesced into rays of sunlight streaming through the trees . . .

• • •

Two years ago

"Lace," a deep familiar voice called.

I blinked, dragging my gaze away from the fresh-tilled dirt and craned my neck to look at him. His hands in the front pockets of his dark jeans, the wind blowing layers of his silky hair into his gray-green eyes, Bryan stepped forward.

"War's looking for you."

Disinterested, I shrugged, returning my attention to the grave in front of me. My hands balled into fists.

How dare that bitch die on me.

Without saying anything, Bryan dropped to the grass beside me. He didn't ask if he could join me, and I wasn't about to tell him he couldn't. I needed him, more than anyone else. War didn't know what to say to me because he didn't really understand. He didn't understand about a lot of things.

My mother's death had totally shaken me. Not because she'd overdosed, but because she was gone. My anger toward her had always fueled my fervor to succeed. Now that she wasn't here, how was I going to prove her wrong, show her that I was worth something?

Bryan and I sat silently together, the only noise the steady hum of the traffic from a nearby freeway. As I continued to stare blankly at my mother's name on the marker, his warm hand covered mine. Nothing in my entire life felt more right than him beside me, holding my hand.

Bryan's soft voice broke the silence. "Did you ever go back to University House to see her?"

"Once," I said with a sigh.

"Oh, that's right. I remember."

"She didn't. She didn't even know who I was."

"I'm sorry, Lace." He squeezed my hand.

"Don't be. I knew how she was. I was stupid to think she would ever change. You ever try to see your father?"

"No. The last time I saw him was in middle school. Good riddance, if you ask me."

I nodded. Having a shitty parent was a bond, a common hurt and vulnerability we shared. "She can rot in hell for all I care."

"You're not her, Lace Lowell," he surprised me by saying.

"No, I'm not. I'll get out of here. I'm going to make something out of my life."

"I know you will." Bryan's voice resonated with sincerity. His faith in me never wavered. "You ever hear back from the counselor about your scholarship application?"

I shook my head. "That's a long shot. They have over two thousand applicants for that one spot." I pulled my hand free, smoothing both palms over my jeans as he continued to closely watch me. "Anyway, it only covers books and tuition, not living expenses."

"Your uncle hasn't changed his mind about you staying on after you graduate?"

"No. He's getting married, and his fiancée has kids of her own. They're gonna have a full house as it is."

"You could stay with us."

My eyebrows lifted and I gave Bryan a measured look. "I don't think your mother would allow that, do you?"

"I guess not."

We both got quiet. Something way beyond friendship had been building between us lately that neither of us was quite ready to address.

I pulled up my knees and dropped my chin on them, whispering, "I'm not going to cry for her."

"I don't expect you to."

"I lost track of how many times she told me I was a burden to her. Mostly, she ignored me. But there were a few times, usually when she was really wasted, that she would let me crawl into her lap." I pressed my lips together to keep them from trembling. "She would stroke my back and sing to me."

I risked a glance at him.

Bryan returned my look, the light of empathy so compelling in those beautiful eyes of his. "It's those few times like that with my old man that made me really hate him. It's so unexpected, the kindness after the neglect, that it almost feels like a betrayal."

I looked away, nodding. That's exactly how I'd felt with my mom. "Why didn't she love me, Bry?"

That was it, really, the part that bothered me the most about her passing. She might have been the world's worst mother, but there was a part of me, a part that I despised, that still longed for her approval.

Bryan's arms went around me, and his chin rested on the top of my head. I leaned back into him, my throat so tight, it burned like fire.

"If only we could choose our parents, huh?" He kissed the top of my head, and my knotted muscles loosened. "She was your mom, Lace," he said softly. "But she was a wretched human being. She didn't deserve someone as wonderful as you."

...

Present day

The incessant buzzing sound in my ears grew louder.

Stop.

I wanted it to stop. I wanted to stay back there in that memory. With him where everything made sense.

Safe.

Cherished.

Comforted.

In Bryan's arms.

The noise in my ears wouldn't go away, though. It solidified into voices—strong, assertive male voices.

"She's breathing. She's coming around," one of them said.

chapter

26

Bryan

Hunched over and sitting in the uncomfortable plastic chair in the ICU waiting room, I slowly lifted my head from my hands as War returned with a cup of coffee.

"Any news?" he asked, taking the chair opposite me.

I shook my head, keeping up the uneasy truce we'd formed as we waited.

I glanced at the door to the ICU for the umpteenth time. This had been our basic routine for the past twenty-four hours—monosyllabic communication punctuated by visits from King and Sager and periodic updates from Dizzy. As a family member, he was the only one actually allowed back there with Lace.

My stomach was a massive, churning, burning ball, despite the most recent reassurance from Dizzy that she remained stable. Sure, she was for now, maybe . . . but what about the next time? Heroin sucked people into its vortex, and more often than not, spit them back out into a pine box.

I should have done something, no matter whose girl she was. The moment I'd discovered that she was using, I should have dragged Lace off that bus and straight to the nearest rehab facility.

Should've.

Shouldn't.

Shit.

I squeezed my eyes shut, but the terrifying memory of that chaotic scene at the hotel was something I couldn't force out of my mind.

Beautiful, vibrant Lace. Her body completely still, like a corpse . . .

• • •

One day ago

"Shane, I can't find a vein. She's used 'em all up," the older paramedic said in a clipped voice.

"Go for the intraosseous, then," the other paramedic said, continuing to breathe for her through a tube they'd put down her throat.

I felt as helpless as I'd been as a thirteen-year-old boy when that drug dealer had hurt Lace. Like back then, I stood in the doorway.

Beside me, Dizzy made desperate bargains with God as we both watched the paramedics work on her.

There was a pop and a crackly sound as they punched a large needle into Lace's shin bone. My muscles tensed and my hands fisted, I offered my own silent prayer.

C'mon, Lace.

Suddenly, her body jolted. Her eyes blinked open, and her chest rose as she took in a loud shuddering breath that sounded more like a gurgle.

"Narcan's working." Shane turned Lace's head to the side, and she spewed vomit all over the hotel carpet. "Glad we had the ET tube in already."

The EMTs wiped her face clean and reattached an oxygen bag. Together, the two men lifted her onto the stretcher and tightened the straps.

Shane looked at his partner. "Let's get her to the hospital."

The other EMT nodded and spoke into a radio hooked to his shoulder. "We have a code three. Heading to the truck. ETA twelve minutes."

"Stand back," Shane barked when they reached the door.

I blinked rapidly, my eyes burning as I stared down at Lace's, which were totally unfocused. She was incoherent and thrashing violently but ineffectively against the restraints.

"Tighten the straps, man," Shane said. "Narcan's making her agitated."

I stepped out of the way, and once they'd wheeled her past, Dizzy and I hurried after them. We had to take a different elevator and rejoined them in the lobby, where a ton of eyes tracked our progress. By then, it registered that War had joined us. He looked as freaked out as we were.

Out on the circular driveway in front of the hotel, someone flashed a cell phone camera.

Beth Tate appeared out of nowhere and stepped in front of us, holding up her hands. "No pictures, please. Show a little respect."

I stood with Dizzy and War as the paramedics loaded Lace into the back of the ambulance.

Dizzy jumped in the moment Shane's partner clipped the stretcher into place. "I'm her brother."

At the same time, War and I both reached for the handle to climb inside.

"Sorry, guys." Shane's partner shook his head. "Only one's allowed in the back. We're taking her over to Celebration Health. You can meet us there."

Shane slammed the ambulance doors shut, and I felt like my heart had stopped as I watched the ambulance drive away . . .

• • •

Present day

The automatic doors of the ICU whooshed open in front of War and me, and the memory cleared as Dizzy stepped through them.

"The breathing tube is out." Dizzy gave us both a strained smile. "The doctors say she's gonna be okay. She's awake. They've just moved her to a private room on the sixth floor."

I let out a pent-up sigh. Finally, I could see her. Talk to her. Touch her.

"She's asking for you," Dizzy said.

Yes. Thinking he meant me, I took a step forward.

"But, War," he said, and I froze. "I gotta warn you, she's totally coherent. She knows all about the Morris deal, and she's pissed."

Dizzy shot me an apologetic look before he moved off with War.

Frustrated, I shoved my hands into my pockets, my fingers clenched around the pack of cigarettes that I couldn't smoke in the hospital. But I wasn't about to go outside, not until I saw Lace.

I pressed my lips tightly together. *Deal with it, Bry. You just have to wait a little longer.*

I stood alone in the empty ICU waiting area that was cold and quiet except for the television droning in the background. I eliminated any other options. I didn't want to upset her, but we had to talk. I was past done with letting War run the show. His method of "taking care of her" had almost gotten her killed. No way was I going to let them pick right back up where they'd left off.

That decided, I strode purposefully to the elevator bank, pushing the call button and raking my hand impatiently through my hair as I waited for the elevator. Fortunately, it was fast.

When I reached the sixth floor, the nurses looked up and threw speculative glances my way. I was probably quite a sight as I clomped past the nursing station like Sabbath's vengeful iron man in my heavy boots and leather pants. I found Dizzy waiting out in the hall outside her room.

"Hold up, Bry. She's still talking to War."

The door was open, and I peered over Dizzy's shoulder. Looking extremely pale and fragile, Lace lay in the hospital bed with an IV pole beside her and her blond hair spread over her pillow like a puddle of melted gold.

Totally focused on War, she didn't see me. One of her hands was in his. My eyes narrowed to jealous slits as I watched War sift a strand of her hair through his fingers. Lace's eyes drifted closed, and every single muscle in my body tensed.

That was my cue. I should have left before it got worse. *But I didn't.*

Was there a scenario where I could make myself leave her?

"No." Lace's voice was as raspy as a two-pack-a-day smoker. "But I will." A tear slid down her cheek and rolled into her hair. "Dizzy said you know everything . . . about Bryan and me."

Whatever War said in response was too low for me to hear.

"I'm sorry, War." She nodded. "I've made a mess of it all. But I'm alive, and for some reason, God's giving me a second chance. I'm going to take that chance, and I'm going to do better. I'm tired of the roller coaster I've been on. I'm tired of all the lies, especially the ones I've been telling myself. I really thought I could quit whenever I decided to. But I realize now that's not true."

She closed her eyes for a moment. "I had a really long conversation with the hospital social worker before I left the ICU. She asked if the overdose was a suicide attempt."

"Was it, Lacey?" War asked softly.

"No, of course not." She shook her head. "Though she helped me see that in a way, that's what I've been doing all along with the drugs. The end result is still the same. I know that self-medication isn't the answer. I've got to face my problems to overcome them."

"It's all my fault," War said, and his raspy voice deepened. "You being here. I should never have given you the drugs in the first place. I never imagined something like this would happen."

"Neither of us did." She reached up a hand and touched War's face.

"I love you, Lacey."

"I love you too, War," she said, and he leaned his face into her hand.

Her declaration sliced through the stitches of hope that had been holding my heart together these past twenty-four hours.

Rubbing my hand against my chest, I turned away. A dark shroud descended on my thoughts. I forced my feet to move down the hall as my heart turned to stone.

Lace

"A part of me will always love you," I said, yet I slid my hand away from War's face. Our gazes locked for one long last moment. "You've been a huge part of my life for so long, Warren Jinkins. But I don't feel like I really know you. Not anymore."

My fingers twisted in the hospital sheet, and I forced myself to go on, though the regret that was so evident in his familiar features had me wavering. I stared down at the IV in my hand for a couple of monitor beeps before I continued. A clean break was best for all of us.

"You've changed, Warren, and not for the better. You're not the guy I fell in love with." If I hadn't been so desperate, so drugged out, I probably would have realized that sooner. "You promised you wouldn't keep secrets from me."

He frowned. "Lace." My name sounded like a plea on his lips.

"When were you planning to tell me about the Morris deal?"

"Nothing has been finalized," he said defensively. "I was just putting out feelers. We've all talked about how totally undervalued we are by Black Cat."

"That's not what I heard." My eyes burned with unshed tears, and I forced my heart to harden. "It's really scary to me how quickly you abandon those who are loyal to you."

"It's not like that, Lacey." A tiny flicker of something I hoped was shame flashed in his eyes.

"Bullshit. It's exactly like that," I said, letting my anger loose. "I don't know how you can stand there and look me in the eye and say that."

"Because you don't know everything." A muscle twitched in his jaw. "You need to give me a chance to explain before you push me away. Don't make the same mistake you did after you found out about RCA. Now, just like back then, it was *never* part of the plan to abandon you. If you'd stuck around instead of leaving me and hooking up with Martin, you would've found that out, and things would've turned out differently."

"That's ancient history," I said, sad about all the many mistakes by both of us that couldn't be undone. "Tell me how this time is any different. Now's your chance. I'm listening."

He didn't speak, so I continued.

"I'll tell you then. This time it's worse. This time there are three people you're screwing over. There's only one person you're ever really looking out for, War, and that's yourself."

"That's not true. I was looking out for you, and Bryan too."

I shook my head. He didn't get it. "War, you go off and do these things, like with RCA and Morris. You make these monumental decisions that will have a drastic effect on people's lives, and yet you don't stop to ask for or even to consider their opinions or feelings. That's not normal behavior. That's manipulative and self-serving."

"Oh, so now after your near-death experience, you're an expert on psychology." His face twisted with cruelty I hadn't allowed myself to see before, or maybe I had and thought my love would make a difference. "You accusing me of being manipulative—that's a little hypocritical, don't you think, considering you were screwing around on me with my best friend?"

I sucked in a sharp breath. The monitor beeped faster with my increased heart rate. "War." This time my voice was plaintive.

"I knew he always had a thing for you, Lacey, but fuck. I trusted him, and I trusted you."

"I know." Tears stung my eyes. "I'm sorry."

He turned his back to me. The line of his shoulders was stiff below the ends of his hair. "How long has it been going on?"

I sighed, but he deserved the truth. "Only the one time, and it was me that's to blame for it."

His shoulders dropped, but when he turned around, I powered on.

"But it doesn't really matter, does it?" My gaze slid from his, and I looked out the window, watching slivers of orange peek through the gaps in the metal window blinds. The sun was finally setting on this disastrous day. And it was time to end this relationship that had gone on for far too long.

I slid off the ring that I never should have accepted and held it out to him. "Here. You and I both know this isn't going to work anymore."

War's expression darkened and he looked away again. "Keep it," he said, his voice gruff.

"No." I shook my head. "Maybe you can get your money back."

"Yeah." His gaze came back to me like a slingshot. "What about my heart that you're ripping to shreds?" He took a step closer, his eyes unmistakably glassy. "How am I gonna get that back? Lacey, you almost died. I realized a lot of things while you were there in the ICU. Mostly, how much you mean to me. I'm sorry about the Morris deal, and the way I handled the RCA thing. But I believe we can get past that if you'll try. Let's start again. There's still time to work things out."

My bottom lip trembled. This was the sweet side of War, the part of him that had stolen my heart at the beginning. "We're not kids anymore, Warren. It's too late for do-overs."

Warm tears of regret spilled onto my cheeks. What remained of this battered and bruised heart of mine would always belong to another, and that wasn't fair to War.

I held out the ring, but he reached out and closed my fingers around it.

"Keep it. To remember the good times." War held my eyes for a long moment, shared sadness flowing wordlessly between us.

I would keep the ring to remember the things that had gone right, to remind me that love was possible, even though War's love was flawed, and mine for him was too. With our hearts both belonging elsewhere—to someone else in my case, and to the band in his case—we were never the right people for each other.

War gave me a tight nod of acceptance before leaning down to kiss my forehead, a strand of his hair trailing through the wetness on my cheek as he straightened.

He paused in the doorway to whisper, "Good-bye, Lacey," and then he was gone.

• • •

When my eyes opened again, I discovered that the room had fallen into shadow. It was silent except for the slow, quiet beeping of the heart monitor. Scanning the room, I found a familiar figure slumped in the chair.

"Dizzy," I croaked, my throat dry.

He shifted, the leather of the lounger groaning beneath his weight, but he continued to snore. When I swallowed and tried again, my brother opened his eyes and blinked the sleep away.

"You okay?" he asked, rising and crossing to my side. The concern in his amber eyes made me determined to reassure him.

"Not yet, but I will be," I said with forced confidence.

He didn't speak, but his expression softened and he covered my hand with his.

"I really screwed up everything, Diz. You were right the other day about my life being out of control. I've been living on the edge for a while. It was only a matter of time before I fell off."

"What are you going to do?"

I took in a fortifying breath. "It's too deep a hole and too steep a climb to get out of as quickly as I'd like. I'm going to take it one step at a time . . . and the first step is rehab."

"Good. I'm glad to hear that. I couldn't stand to ever see you like that again. I love you." He smoothed a hand over my hair. "I wish I'd done things differently. When we moved in with Uncle Bruce, I thought that you didn't need protecting anymore. At least, that's what I told myself, so I wouldn't feel guilty. I never should have—"

"Stop." I put my hand on his arm. "You protected me when it mattered. Really. The mess I'm in right now is my own."

Dizzy frowned, regret swimming in his eyes. "I want to help any way I can."

"I appreciate that." I gave him a tentative smile. "But this is something I have to do for myself. And if we're being honest here, I think you'll admit that you've got issues of your own that need sorting through."

He dropped his head, refusing to meet my eyes.

"Mom really screwed us both up good," I whispered.

Bryan

With one arm slung over my eyes, I lay in my bunk on the bus with the curtain pulled closed. I had my earbuds in, but no music, just static. Endless, purposeless, white noise filled my ears, like the life that stretched out before me without Lace in it.

I hadn't heard War come onboard yet. He was probably still at the hospital with her. That's where I would be if I were him.

"I love you."

Her saying those words to him instead of me cut deep. It was wrong, yet it replayed in my brain on an endless loop.

Baring my soul to her, exposing the ugly truth about the Morris deal, none of that changed her mind. I'd always believed deep down that someday we would be together. I'd purposefully kept my relationships distant or chosen ones destined to fail, anticipating, hoping that one day she would be mine.

But now I was going to have to figure out how to move forward and start to live a real life without her. Maybe with a new band. Could I stand it? Seeing her with War again? I turned over on my side and punched the pillow.

The curtain on my bunk slid back, startling me, and Dizzy poked his spiky head into the gap. "You awake, man?"

"Yeah." I pulled my earbuds out. "How is she?" I asked because I had to know, even though I had no right to, even though I knew I should cut the fucking cord that bound us together.

Might as well rip out my own heart. It belonged to her.

"She's in a good place, all things considered," Dizzy whispered. After a glance behind him, he said, "Listen, why aren't you answering your cell? She's been trying to call you. She wants to talk to you before they transfer her to the rehab facility."

"Yeah, so?" I shrugged noncommittally.

"Are you okay?" Dizzy scratched his head as he studied me.

"Just too many hours awake, I guess."

"All right. If you say so." Dizzy didn't look entirely convinced. "Here's the number at the hospital."

I glanced at the piece of paper he handed me. The number on it was in her handwriting. I wanted to trace it with my finger, but resisted somehow.

"Call her, okay? She really wants to talk to you, and she can't talk to anyone once she gets there because she'll be in lockdown." Giving me one last pointed look, Dizzy slid the curtain back into place.

Once more, I was alone with only my thoughts to torture me. I flipped onto my back and stared without blinking at the metal ceiling of the bus, staring so long my vision blurred. I wanted to hear that beautiful voice of hers, but what would that accomplish? What was left for her to say? Nothing I wanted to hear, I was sure.

I crumpled the note in my fist and tossed it at my feet.

. . .

Lace

I stared out the window, watching the night give way to the morning as the sun rose above the clipped hedges that lined the perimeter of the Second Chances rehab facility.

Outside, I could hear the fountain softly gurgling, but inside, a torrent of conflicting emotions drowned out all but the futile rage within me. I'd been able to keep my mind occupied while I filled out reams of admission paperwork, then met the staff and been shown to my quarters.

But now I was alone.

Overwhelmed and adrift, I longed for a shot of something to numb the pain. It would be so much easier to escape into the drugs than to face what lay before me.

Why hadn't Bryan called? I'd delayed the transfer for over an hour, hoping to hear from him. I loved him so desperately that I'd take *anything* from him, but I hadn't gotten anything.

A dark wave of emptiness crashed over me, leaving me hollow in its wake. This was even worse than the morning after prom. Worse than the first betrayal by War. Worse than Martin.

Because now, I didn't have a backup plan.

This time, there was no one waiting in the wings to help. The one I'd always counted on to catch me when I fell was ominously absent and silent. And the truth was, I had no one to blame but myself. I'd fallen too far and pushed him away one too many times.

I fell back onto the mattress and turned onto my side, the cheap polyester comforter scratchy against my wet cheek.

This time I was truly on my own.

chapter 29

Bryan

I glared poisoned daggers at War's back as he walked offstage after our lackluster performance at the arena in Miami.

My former best friend and I were no longer on speaking terms. If it weren't so pathetically sad, it would almost be comical the way we communicated now, using other people as intermediaries. Though it hadn't been too much of a problem during the Miami sound check, it had been a big problem during the concert. It was really fucking hard to hit your cues when your lead singer wouldn't make eye contact with you.

After the encore, Dizzy had cursed up a storm and stomped offstage with the latest groupie in tow. From their position against the far wall, King and Sager continued to cast dubious glances my way as they conversed with a couple of roadies.

Watching War with his arms thrown around two women did nothing to improve my foul mood. How could he do that to Lace when she'd given him her love, and he'd supposedly given her his?

Apparently, he could manage just fine, and two weren't enough for him. He crooked his finger to get the attention of a brunette whose blouse was so low cut, I could see her nipples.

My eyes burning with anger, I took another drag on my cigarette as War made out with all three of them.

Asshole.

So intent was my focus that I practically jumped out of my skin when someone laid a hand on my arm. My gaze swept over the curvy form of an ebony-haired beauty as her black-painted fingernails traced a line to the center of my bare chest.

"Bullet," she purred. "Don't you wanna get laid?"

I froze. Sure I did, but not tonight and not by her. I was so sick of this fake shit. I might not have Lace, but I wanted something better than this, something real.

Then I looked at the woman again, *really* looked at her. Behind the outward overtly sexual display, I knew that there was a living, breathing person inside, one with feelings. That's something I couldn't ignore anymore, and wouldn't settle for anymore.

Her hand trembled, and she definitely had stars in her eyes. She couldn't be much older than my sister Miriam. In fact, I'd very carefully avoided thoughts like these for a long time. But all these women who threw themselves at us had one thing in common.

Hope.

Hope to hook up with someone famous. Hope that they'd be the one to tame one of us. Hope that when we hooked up with them, it would be the start of something beautiful, and not just a sex act.

One time, never twice. Leave 'em satisfied, but always leave 'em.

I couldn't do it anymore.

The loud sound of a slap had me turning my head just in time to see War disappear inside the temporary dressing room with his trifecta.

Hell, fucking no.

"I'm sorry, babe." I gently removed the woman's hand from my arm. "It's not you. It's me. Maybe . . ." But she'd already turned away and moved to Dizzy before I'd even finished speaking. Appeared she was about to make him a similar proposition.

So much for my attempt to save the world, one groupie at a time.

At the sound of Brutal Strength's set starting in the background, I skirted around a group of tour personnel and didn't stop to knock at the door I'd seen War enter. I threw it open so hard, it clanged against the cinderblock wall. In spite of that, it took several moments before anyone inside even noticed me.

His leather pants unlaced and his legs splayed wide, War sat lazily on a folding chair, guzzling whiskey straight from the bottle. The woman kneeling between his legs was going down on him while he watched the other two women going at each other.

One of the girl-on-girl duo glanced over at me. "Hmm, Bullet's here. Come on over, baby."

War's head snapped up, and he glared at me. "You're not invited to this party, Jackson." He took a long swig from the bottle. "Now get the fuck out!" he shouted at me before pushing the woman's head back down.

I saw red, total fire-engine red. Sirens blaring in my ears, the works.

I stepped into the room. "Give us a minute, *ladies*." My voice was cool, but inside, I was on fire, shaking mad.

The woman in front of War sat back on her heels and gave me a confused look. When I glared at her, she wiped her mouth and motioned for the other two to follow her out of the room. As soon as the door closed, I spun around to face War.

Our illustrious lead singer laced up his pants and met me in the center of the room, his own eyes ablaze. "This better be a fucking emergency."

Furious, I took a step forward and shoved him with both hands.

"What the fuck, man?" War knocked my hands aside and gave me an equally hard shove back. "You busting in here just to pick a fight with me?" He mockingly crooked the fingers of both hands. "Well, come on, Bullet. Bring it. Though I don't get you at all, man. It's me that should want to beat in your fucking face in for what you did to me."

All the anger and hurt I felt about Lace choosing him instead of me coalesced into my clenched fist. I reared back and let War have it.

There was a satisfying smack as my fist connected with his jaw, sending a shock wave all the way back to my shoulder. The force of it knocked War clear off his feet. His body slammed into the liquor cabinet, and bottles of booze fell like rain off the shelf, crashing onto the concrete floor.

He scrambled to his feet and rubbed his jaw. "You bastard! You're the one who fucking screwed my woman!" Then he came at me like a blitzing middle linebacker.

I managed to dodge him just as the door flew open and Dizzy, Sager, and King burst into the room.

As I was rounding on War, Dizzy stepped between us. King grabbed my arms from behind, and Sager did the same to War. I saw the PR chick from Black Cat had followed them into the room. Beth closed the door behind her.

"Let me go!" I struggled to break free from King's grasp. The guy was the same height as me but built like a fucking tank. I couldn't budge him.

My gaze flashed back to War. "You don't fucking deserve her, asshole. She loves you, man. She almost died barely twenty-four hours ago, and you're getting yourself a blow job the minute she's not around."

"*Used* to love me," War muttered. "She served me walking papers at the hospital." He shrugged out of Sager's grasp. "I didn't start this shit."

Holy shit. Lace broke it off with War!

I staggered back, remembering her message. She'd tried to call me before she went into rehab. My mind reeling from the implications of this earthshattering news, I didn't even notice that King had released me.

"I warned you, brother." War pushed his face near mine, practically nose to nose with me, close enough that I could smell the fumes on his breath. His skin was red and twisted with anger. "Bitches are trouble. Told you, but you didn't listen. And now she's come between us. Messed us up. Messed up the band."

"Wasn't her that did all that. It was you, asshole," I growled. "You'd sell your own mother if the price was right."

"Whoa," Dizzy said. "Easy, guys. Let's leave the mothers out of it."

"I can't believe you." War shook his head. "You've got that bitch up so high on a pedestal, you can't even see her faults."

The shrill ringing of a cell phone cut through the charged silence that followed the last comment.

"Yes." Beth eyed us all warily as she answered the call. "I'm here now." She paused, nodding as she listened. "No, you were right, Mary. I'll call you back as soon as I'm done."

Beth pocketed the cell. Her heels clacked on the concrete as she took a couple of steps forward. Her demeanor was entirely professional. Apparently, she was totally unfazed by what she'd just seen.

"You guys obviously need a keeper. Mary's calling in Ian Vandergriff to handle things."

I cringed. Vandergriff had a reputation in the industry. He was the manager who'd been brought in to straighten out the Dirt Dogs after their lead singer had passed out onstage for the third time in two weeks. I'd heard it had taken less time than that for him to bring the entire group to their knees. The guy was a total hard-ass.

Shit.

Beth glanced back and forth between War and me. "Vandergriff's salary is going to come out of your tour bonuses, by the way."

Great. Just fucking great.

chapter

30

Lace

Twisting my hands in my lap, I sat on my bed and stared out the window at the courtyard. I was still lonely, but the view was now a familiar tableau. The soft gurgling of the fountain was the only sedative I had left. No more methadone to keep me company. It had been tapered off days ago.

Now it was just me and my sober self.

Well, me and Dr. George, who the other rehabbers harshly referred to as Sawbones. I wasn't really sure why. The wrinkled old psychiatrist seemed benign with his gray hair and beard, his kind eyes and soft tone, like some benevolent grandfather figure. Not that I'd ever had one.

It wasn't the upcoming session with Sawbones that had my stomach turning somersaults. It was my first mandatory group session. I wasn't relishing the thought of unpacking all my baggage in front of a bunch of strangers.

A quick glance at the clock had my stomach flipping faster. Time was up.

I took in a careful breath and straightened my shoulders. *You can do this, Lace Lowell.*

I pushed off the bed and stepped into my slippers, then flipped off the light switch and opened the door.

"Hey," a musical female voice called out before I'd taken two steps down the hall. "Hold up."

I turned and saw a young woman with long platinum hair locking the door to the room next to mine. She beamed a double-dimpled smile my way as she walked over, one so infectious, it even put my brother's to shame. Despite my nerves, I found myself grinning back at her.

"I'm Bridget Dubois. I've seen you in the cafeteria. You got in last week, didn't you?"

She didn't pause to let me answer, speaking each sentence in rapid-fire succession.

"You're coming to the group session, aren't you? You look a little pale. Don't be nervous." After a micro-pause, she added, "Really, don't be."

Tilting her head at me, she arched her white-blond eyebrows expectantly. She reminded me of a pixie with her petite frame, sparkly blue eyes, and exuberant manner.

"I'm Lace Lowell." I held out my hand, which she took and squeezed once before letting go.

"Nice to meet you, Lace." She studied my face for a minute before waving for me to follow her down the hall. "Don't worry. You don't have to talk the first time in group if you don't want to. Believe it or not, I didn't."

She gave me another dimpled smile. "I think you'll be surprised. It's really helped me to know other people have gone through the same stuff that I have. No one's perfect. We're all just trying to make it through the best we can."

As we entered the cafeteria together, she continued to jabber while I looked around. The tables had been moved to the side, and there was now a circle of plastic chairs near the windows.

Bridget gestured discreetly at a middle-aged man and an older woman loading up on snacks from the small buffet.

"That's Miles. He's an accountant who's a cokehead like me. The woman is Maribelle Lewis." She gave me an expectant look. "You know, the punk rock singer?"

I shook my head.

"Well, she's a pretty big deal here in Orlando. She's got really bad teeth from the meth. Don't stare. It pisses her off. She can be kinda mean."

I took a seat in the circle beside Bridget and tried to focus on her rather than Maribelle or the upcoming session. "Why are you here?" I asked quietly.

Bridget's gaze slid away. She stared out the window for a moment before looking back at me. "Usual story," she said with a shrug. "I fell in love with the wrong guy. Got pregnant. Family disowned me."

Her tone was light and breezy, but her expression told a different story. This girl had been hurt deeply. There was more to Bridget Dubois than I'd initially thought.

"Lace." Dr. George took a seat on the other side of me and squeezed my shoulder. "Welcome to the group. We don't have many rules, except that what's said here remains confidential, and that we only speak in generalities about any physical abuse, mental issues, or drug problems. No graphic details here, please. Today's topic is responsibility. I thought perhaps we'd start with you today."

My gaze flew to Bridget. "But . . ."

Bridget patted my knee. "Doc, I told her she could just listen the first time."

"Yes, of course she can." He nodded. "Lace, you've been doing so well, I thought you'd be eager to jump right in." His gaze moved to the brunette across from him. "Brenda, why don't you start us off?"

Listening to the others share, one after another, I started to relax. A lot of the stuff they shared was frighteningly familiar. Bridget was right. Minute by minute, I was feeling less like a freak, less like a loser, and less like a loner to be here.

I *could* do this.

I made eye contact with Dr. George, and he nodded his approval.

"My name's Lace Lowell. I'm addicted to heroin, mostly, although I've done some cocaine and other stuff too. I'm an addict like my mother was. I've been using for about two years now. I tried to get my boyfriend to help me taper off, but I realize now that wasn't going to work out. I need professional help like I'm getting here, and I have to take responsibility for my own choices. I'm the one who made the decision to take that first dose, and in the end, it has to be me who decides not to do it anymore."

• • •

I cursed under my breath, ripped out the page, crumpled it, and tossed another disappointing sketch aside. The wadded-up ball of paper joined the growing discard pile that looked like white snowballs against the green grass.

I was irritated and jumpy. Though my fingers were busy, my mind shifted into reverse. I'd figured out today why Dr. George's nickname suited him. He had this nasty ability to cut through all his patients' bullshit like some old-time surgeon dispensing with a gangrenous limb.

He'd certainly cut uncomfortably deep in the private session with me today.

"You need to be self-reliant, Lace. Stop looking for a man to come rescue you every time you get into a bind."

He was right.

I pushed my hair back behind my ears and let out a heavy sigh. That was exactly what I'd been doing. First with War, then after that fell apart, with Martin, then War again. And I always had Bryan in reserve.

I sucked.

I blinked back the burn of frustrated tears as I stared down at the sketchpad on my knees. That pathetic dependence on the men in my life needed to stop. It was a trap, letting someone else's approval define me. I was the only person who could redefine things.

Sawbones had also made me confront my unresolved feelings toward a father I'd never known. There was a dotted line that connected my lack of a father figure to the lack of judgment I'd used in choosing the men in my life.

But worst of all, Dr. George had forced me to go back to a place today that I'd never wanted to return to . . . my childhood. He'd pushed and prodded until I told him everything.

How worthless my mother made me feel. That I meant less to her than her next high. How still to this day, it galled me to have been denied the love of someone I hated so much.

The level of vitriol I'd spewed had been shocking. I hadn't realized until that moment just how much anger and resentment I still carried around. The drugs had obviously been my way to cover that all up. Dr. George showed me that I needed to stop repressing and find a healthy way to deal with those emotions.

No more bullshit. I needed to let go of the past and wipe the slate clean. And I needed to have a plan for my future.

It was up to me and me alone to be the woman I'd once believed myself to be, a woman who, despite her shitty mother and lack of a father, was strong and capable of doing whatever she set her mind to. Sure, I'd made mistakes, a shitload of them. I had a lot of owning up to do. But I was ready to make amends. Whether or not the people I'd hurt forgave me was up to them.

Though I knew the hole I'd dug for myself was a deep one, I no longer felt overwhelmed by hopelessness. Getting off the drugs gave me clarity, and it was the first step on the ladder to getting out of that hell.

I could see light up there at the top, and that's where I wanted to go.

• • •

I took in a deep calming breath. Seven more days done. I'd made it two weeks now without drugs, which was a huge accomplishment. It had seemed like forever since I'd been this clearheaded.

The first couple of days in rehab had been easy, though, compared to these last few. The more honest I was with myself, the more we examined my motivations and emotions in therapy, the edgier I became. Dr. George had suggested I continue with my sketching to deal with it, but so far today, the task had just been an exercise in frustration.

A shadow fell over me, blocking out the sun.

"Hey, Bridget," I said, knowing who it was without turning around. She'd become my constant companion since that first group session. No matter what I tried to do to dissuade her, there was no shaking the irrepressible girl.

And the fact was, I liked her.

"Whatcha doing?" Bridget picked up a ball of paper from the discard pile and uncrumpled it. "Wow! This is really good."

I glanced over at the drawing of an evening gown. My favorite type to draw, they reminded me of the dress I'd worn to prom.

"It's okay." I shrugged. "But the hemline's not right."

"What's wrong with it?" Bridget asked, sitting down beside me on the concrete bench.

I reminded myself to be patient. The jitters made me want to pop off when Bridget was hyperactive or dense, but I didn't want to do that. She had a good heart. Plus, she'd been extremely supportive of me, even holding a cool washcloth to my head last night when the withdrawal shakes had woken me up.

"The hem should probably have a decorative border," I said, "maybe eyelet lace. I don't know."

Bridget studied the drawing, smoothing it out across her thin tanned legs. "I think you're right. Like that stuff they wore under their dresses in the late fifties. A really cool lime-sherbet color might work."

Actually, that would look really great. I reached under the bench and pulled out my colored pencils, then shaded in the color while Bridget watched.

"Told you," Bridget said with a satisfied nod when I was finished.

I gazed at the golden-tanned platinum-blonde. I'd been ready to dismiss her idea out of hand. In fact, I'd been trying to keep her at arm's length, which had been my pattern with practically everyone else in my life except for my brother, Chad, and Bryan. War, I really hadn't had to keep at arm's length emotionally, because he'd stayed at that distance during the entirety of our relationship.

Yeah, I'd learned a lot about myself in rehab.

"You're into fashion?" I asked.

"Duh, isn't everyone?" A mischievous grin spread across her face. "I've got a stash of *InStyle* magazines in my room. Wanna see?"

"Sure." I raised my brows, surprised to uncover a rebellious streak in Bridget.

I grabbed my stuff and followed her back inside. The Second Chances facility was completely closed off from the outside world. No phone. No television. No internet. No contraband magazines.

I sat on the bed beside her while thumbing through her stack. "These are brand new. How'd you manage that?"

Bridget smiled, dimples flashing on either side of a mouthful of pearly-white teeth. "I have all the latest gossip magazines too."

She quickly explained how she'd gotten them. Apparently, one of the security guards had a crush on her.

When she pushed a *Rolling Stone* issue toward me, I went completely still, my hand resting on *his* face. TEMPEST, BIGGER AND BADDER THAN BS was the headline.

Kimberly must have taken the photo of the group in Atlanta. War finally got his wish to be on the cover of *Rolling Stone*.

Vaguely, I realized that Bridget had stopped talking.

She glanced back and forth between the magazine cover and my pale face. "You look like you've seen a ghost."

I swallowed. *No. Not quite, though one still haunted my dreams.*

"You know those guys?" she asked.

"Yeah." I nodded. "We went to high school together."

"Holy shit!"

"Don't get all starry-eyed. It's no big deal. The lead singer used to be my boyfriend. The rhythm guitarist is my brother." I left out the other details. Did they matter anymore to anyone but me?

Bridget looked at me with skepticism, taking the magazine and flipping it open to the article. "There's a picture of you in here."

I glanced over. Sure enough, they'd included one from my performance in Atlanta. That dream was done. I'd ruined it like all the other ones.

When I tried to close the magazine, Bridget stopped me, her finger on the page and her blue eyes wide. "War says a lot of nice things about you in here."

"He did back then," I said. "I don't think he would say anything flattering anymore."

"Men are bastards, huh?" Bridget closed the magazine and leaned closer. "Lace, come on. You can tell me. If it'll help to talk, I'm happy to listen. After all, I'm your best friend."

I stared into the sparkly but sincere eyes of the woman beside me. *Is she my best friend?* She was definitely the only one.

Bridget held my gaze, nodding as if she could read my thoughts. "You're prickly sometimes, but then so am I. We're doing hard work in here, and that can make anyone irritable. Most people like to ignore their problems, but you and me, we're facing them head-on."

I gave her a small smile. "I guess we are."

"No guessing about it. I was there when you told your story, remember? You had a crappy childhood, but you don't use it as an excuse. That's unusual. There's an inner strength in you, a resolve. You're gonna make it, Lace Lowell. You're a winner, and I like to be on a winning team."

My eyes stung from the unexpected praise. I was getting way too sappy in here.

"Thanks," I said, hearing the thick emotion in my voice. "I don't really see myself that way. But going back to drugs isn't an option for me. They cost me everything that I cared about."

Vividly remembering the disappointment in Bryan's eyes when he'd seen my tracked-up arms, I let out a long sigh.

Bridget patted my hand. "It gets easier." Her expression sobering and worry darkening her eyes. she suddenly looked much older than her age. "At least, it does in here. Five more days till I'm done. How much longer for you?"

"Fourteen."

Bridget mock cringed. "If you ever need anything when you get out, call me and I'll come running. I promise."

"I promise too." I gave her a genuine smile. "Teammate."

chapter 31

Bryan

I nodded to Vandergriff, a.k.a. the Buzz Buster, as King had dubbed him. Our band's new enforcer was built like the Incredible Hulk, his muscles bulging beneath the cheap polyester suit he always wore. We had to check in with the guy twice a day, morning and night.

He'd traveled with us on the twenty-eight-hour bus ride from Miami to Minneapolis, and on the four-hour flight up to Vancouver for tonight, the last stop on the tour. His methods weren't pleasant, but he'd been successful. The only one of us he hadn't gotten into line yet was War.

I searched the backstage area, but there was no sign of him. I hoped our lead singer wouldn't screw up this final concert, but I had an awful feeling that he would.

War and I hadn't spoken a word to each other since Miami. Actually, he pretty much wasn't on speaking terms with anyone in the group. The Morris betrayal had opened a rift between him and the other guys too. It wasn't something that would be easily forgotten or forgiven.

Not that War was much interested in bridging the gap. If anything, he'd gotten more temperamental, more demanding, and more unpredictable.

Tempest had barely taken the stage on time in Minneapolis because of him. He'd locked himself in a room backstage with a couple of fan girls the roadies had pulled from the audience. Apparently, the usual groupies wouldn't do for His Highness anymore.

"When was the last time you saw him?" Dizzy asked me as he tightened the strings on his Gibson.

"Not since we landed, and he made that big scene about the lukewarm beer in first class."

"King's right." Dizzy cringed. "The dude's got it bad."

"What?" I rolled my shoulders.

"LSD."

"Shit. You're kiddin' me."

Dizzy barked out a laugh. "LSD. Lead singer's disease, man. War's got a real bad case."

Speaking of the diseased monster, War had finally arrived, and he was obviously wasted. His head was slumped to his chest, his arms draped around two women, and his legs wobbled under him like limp noodles.

I glanced over to see if Vandergriff had noticed. Sure enough, Buzz Buster was already heading straight toward War with a dark look on his face. He dismissed the two girls and grabbed War just as he fell forward.

War lifted his head, his lips twitching, right before he blew chunks all over Buzz Buster's shiny black dress shoes.

"Bullet. Dizzy," Buzz Buster called, then cursed. "Come help me with this asshole."

"We're screwed," Dizzy mumbled as we hurried over. "We've only got thirty minutes before we're on."

"I'm fine," War slurred, rocking back on his heels. He put his hand on his hip, but his attempt to appear belligerent was sabotaged by the fact that he almost fell over again. "Get me my shades!" he yelled at one of the roadies as he pulled his black bandana lower over his red-rimmed eyes.

"I don't believe you, man." I shook my head.

"Yeah, well." War's gaze cut to me, his stare surprisingly steady considering the intensity of the alcohol reek emanating from him. "I can't believe you either, asshole."

We glared at each other. The undercurrent of restrained violence between us saddened me more than I was willing to admit. Numbly, I nodded when Buzz Buster ordered me to keep an eye on War while he and Dizzy went to round up some Red Bull.

Frustrated, I raked a hand through my hair. The tour, the group, my friendships, my life . . . everything was going to hell. Maybe I should try to salvage some of it.

"Listen," I said to War, taking a step closer. "I'm sorry. Sorry about busting you in the jaw. Sorry about you and Lace. I know how you must feel."

"You don't know anything," War growled.

"I know what a low tolerance you have for rejection. I was there when your father—"

"Shut up!" War shouted, his eyes narrowed. "I don't care about that bastard, and I don't give a fuck about that bitch Lace either."

A cruel grin twisted his lips. "The only reason I was ever with her was because I enjoyed watching what it did to you. It used to be nice having you trail around after me like a puppy, always ready to do my bidding. But it got old after a while. In fact, all this shit's gotten old."

Buzz Buster returned and thrust a Red Bull into War's hand. "Drink up. And keep it down."

War took a long swig and wiped his mouth. "Listen, all," he said, projecting loudly enough that everyone backstage turned in our direction. "I have a special announcement to make."

He pointed at me.

"I'm not working with this motherfucker anymore. I'm quitting after tonight's show." War stumbled to the edge of the stage, brushing past Dizzy. "Now let's get this shit over with."

I didn't move. Shock had frozen my feet in place.

chapter

32

Lace

I stood in the foyer, staring out the glass doors at the circular driveway.

Waiting for Dizzy to arrive, I was filled with equal parts trepidation and excitement. I was ready as hell to get out of this place, to see my brother, to watch television, to surf the web, and to wear something besides a Second Chances track suit. On the other hand, I was really worried how I'd handle things out there in the real world . . . on my own.

After paying the rehab bill, I still had ten thousand dollars left from the signing bonus that Mary Timmons had given me. But I knew I wasn't going to keep it. I was planning to give that back and work out some kind of repayment plan for what I'd already spent.

I'd taken that money under false pretenses, and being a cheat and a liar didn't sit well with me anymore. Not with the person I'd set my mind on becoming.

A dark blue sedan with tinted windows and a rental car sticker pulled up in front of the building. Dizzy jumped out of the driver's side and jogged around to the front of it. I pushed through the front doors and rushed outside, dropping my bag just as my brother lifted me up and twirled me around in a circle.

"Lace," he said, hugging me so enthusiastically that I could barely breathe.

"Diz," I wheezed. "Too tight."

"Sorry." He loosened his grip, and when he leaned back to look at me, a look of relief passed through those eyes so like mine. "You look fantastic. But how are you feeling?"

"It's not like I had a terminal disease," I grumbled, though I guessed I probably had. Anyway, I knew what he meant.

Looking in the mirror this morning, I'd seen that my skin and hair had regained their previous luster, my cheeks were attractively fuller, my eyes sparkled with awareness, and the jeans and T-shirt that had been loose when I checked in were actually a little snug now.

Getting your life in order and eating three meals a day instead of shooting up will do a lot of good for you.

"Where'd you get the car?" I asked.

"At the airport. We're staying there tonight. I have us an early flight out in the morning. I can't believe they wouldn't discharge you until five."

"Yeah, well, Sawbones is a stickler for doing things by the book." In response to Dizzy's questioning look, I explained. "Dr. George, he's the psychiatrist who runs the facility. I arrived in the evening twenty-eight days ago, so that's when I get released."

I bent down to get my bag when movement near the car caught my eye. As I straightened, I saw *him*. "Bryan."

My heart stopped and then restarted, beating twice as hard as before, just from looking at him leaning back against the hood of the sedan. His black shirtsleeves were rolled up, his arms folded over his chest, and his long legs encased in formfitting jeans.

Bryan was the last person I expected to see, but he was a welcome sight, nonetheless. When he hadn't gotten in touch with me before I'd been admitted, I'd assumed he'd finally written me off as a lost cause, just like everybody else.

His lips formed a seductive grin. "Lace," he said, drawling in that special way of his, and the world tilted a little beneath my feet.

"I wasn't expecting you," I managed to say, even though my voice was noticeably breathy.

For several moments, he held my gaze. Something in my eyes must have given me away, because he sauntered toward me, all swagger and verve.

I held on to the pretense of being unaffected by him until he leaned in and the warmth from his breath tickled my ear.

"You look gorgeous."

My stomach fluttered. "You didn't return any of my phone calls," I said, trying to recover my equilibrium, which was always a struggle around him. "I thought you'd given up on me."

"And I thought you'd given up on me." He leaned back to look at me, his tone filled with regret. "I'm sorry I didn't call. I only overheard part of your conversation with War at the hospital, and bailed when you said you loved him. I understand from Dizzy that I should have stuck around for the rest."

"Hey, are you guys gonna stand out here all day and stare at each other?" Dizzy raised an amused brow. "Or are you ready to go?"

I pursed my lips, and Bryan just laughed.

Mesmerized by the crinkles around his eyes, I blinked up at him. It had been a long time since I'd seen him look so happy, or since my own heart had felt so light. But then again, Bryan could always make me feel that way.

Reluctantly, I released my fingers from his arm and climbed into the passenger seat. There was so much more I wanted to ask him, so much I wanted to believe his presence here meant. The chain connected to his wallet jingled as he slid into the back.

Our eyes met in the mirror, and a heavy, expectant vibe zapped across the space between us.

Is this finally going to be the beginning of an us?

During the thirty-minute drive to the airport, I felt Bryan's heated gaze on me. My body prickled with awareness. To keep my mind off the hungry male lounging in the back seat, I tried to make small talk with Dizzy. My jaw dropped when he told me about War quitting the band.

"You're kidding?" I shook my head, but I refused to feel guilty. That was a burden the old Lace would have taken on. What War did was his own damn business. "What are you guys going to do?"

"I'm glad you asked," Bryan said without a pause as if he and my brother had this rehearsed. "Diz and I were hoping you would consider—"

"No." I thought it best to put the kibosh on that idea right away. "I decided inside rehab to leave that part of my life behind."

"Why?" my brother asked, his brows knitting in confusion. "You're so good at it, Lace."

"And you have a contract with Black Cat," Bryan added.

"I did a lot of thinking about it. The touring, rock-star lifestyle is too much of a temptation for an addictive personality like mine. Besides, I realized that being part of a group was what I really loved most about music, and I can get that in other ways. The singing, going solo, that was War's idea for me. It's not really what I want, so I've decided to go back to school and study fashion design. I've started sketching again." Shrugging, I said, "It makes me happy."

Both guys were silent as they processed that blitz of information. As Dizzy steered the sedan through the tollbooth, Bryan broke the silence. "Whatever you want to do, Lace, I know you'll be good at it."

A surge of emotion clogged my throat. He had always been so supportive of my dreams, and his approval meant so much to me.

I gave him a long look that said *I want to climb into the back seat with you and lick your neck.* I think he got the message because he returned my look and one-upped me with a sexy smile.

We dropped off the rental and took the shuttle back to the airport. After we checked into the Hyatt Regency inside the terminal, Dizzy suggested we grab a bite to eat together at the steakhouse. I eagerly nodded my agreement. The cafeteria in rehab had been okay, but I was ready for some real food. Dizzy went ahead to get us a table.

The instant we were alone, Bryan grabbed my arm. His warm, calloused fingertips traced a path to my palm that made me shiver.

"Eat fast," he said softly, his piercing gray-green eyes glittering with a hungry intensity that I knew didn't have anything to do with food. "You're coming to my room after. There are things to be said that can't wait."

I nodded mutely, a sudden case of nerves unsettling my empty stomach. I wanted him, of course I wanted him, but it had been a long time since prom night.

I ordered a steak, but was iffy about it later. Bryan and I sat opposite each other at the table. I listened disinterestedly while he and Dizzy went through a list of possible replacements for War.

As long as I avoided direct eye contact with Bryan, I was able to continue interacting on a reasonable level. The one time I slipped up, the sensual look he gave me had made my entire body tremble with anticipation.

Lucky for me, by the time the food arrived, my nerves were somewhat under control, and my appetite had returned. I did an admirable job on the steak but resisted dessert. Right now, only one thing, one man, was tempting me.

"Hey, man, I'm going to head on up to my room with Lace," Bryan said to Dizzy when the check finally came. "She and I need to talk."

Dizzy glanced at me. I saw the trepidation in his eyes, and I understood it. I had reservations myself. Not about whether to go with Bryan—that was as inevitable as the coming sunrise. No, it was the uncertainty about what might happen afterward that worried me.

"I've got my own keycard," I told my brother, hoping that would reassure him. "I'll come to our room later."

"Diz." Bryan leaned an elbow on the table. "It's okay. I'll take good care of her. That has always been my intention."

His voice was low and deep, and I totally got that there was more than just a promise to Dizzy in those words. Imagining just what type of immediate things taking care of me might involve made my mouth go dry and my heart rate accelerate.

My brother insisted on paying the bill and gave me a hug before I left the table with Bryan. I looked back at Dizzy, and for a moment, I wavered. Maybe this wasn't such a good idea after all.

"Lace." Bryan took my hand, and my uncertainty dissolved.

I wanted him, and he wanted me. The rest was just details to work out.

Holding hands, we made our way to the elevator. As soon as the doors closed, Bryan's warm hands settled low on my back, right above the curve of my ass. He pulled me close, positioning me in just the right place.

Instant hot desire hummed through my veins, and I knew I was lost. He and I were a foregone conclusion that had been on the back burner for years. It was time to turn the heat up to high.

I placed my hands on his chest, feeling the warmth of his skin and the staccato rhythm of his heartbeat through the thin material of his button-down shirt. Wrapping my arms around his neck, I tilted my face up to his.

Anticipation flooded my body as his mouth lowered to mine.

chapter 33

Bryan

I watched Lace's eyes close, golden lashes fanning over her blushed cheeks. Her surrender made me feel powerful yet humble at the same time. I'd waited so long and wanted her so desperately.

"Bry." She breathed my name like a plea, one to take and possess her, which was what I had every intention of doing.

"Lace," I said, like she was my answer and I was hers, which I most certainly was. This was the start of our beginning, and we were starting it right.

I slanted my mouth across hers, and her fingers tangled in the hair at the back of my neck. That turned me on more than I could stand. Finally, at long last, she was mine.

I plunged my tongue between her sweet parted lips. A fire burned inside me as soon as I got my first taste. Her mouth was salty from the steak, minty from the mints that had been handed out after dinner, and hot as fucking hell.

Her moan made me immediately realize my tactical error. Taking her mouth wasn't going to be enough, not nearly, and I couldn't do all the things I wanted to do to her inside this elevator.

"Babe." I lifted my head, and her dazed eyes fluttered open. Her lips were wet and swollen, and her breaths were shallow. A primal surge of satisfaction swept through me.

Oh yeah. I liked that it was me making her look like this. Me and no one else, the way it was always meant to be.

I put my hands on either side of her head and pinned her sexy body between my arms. "Just so we're clear . . . you and me now. No one else ever again."

"Yes, Bry," she said, her eyes hooded as she peered steadily back at me. The passion that simmered in her beautiful eyes made me want to rip her clothes off right then, elevator cameras be damned.

Good thing the door decided to slide open at that moment. Even so, I went completely cave man, threw her over my shoulder, and stalked to the room.

She giggled, and I fucking loved the sound of it. It had been too long since I'd heard her laugh, since we'd been together like this.

Grinning, I stopped in front of the door.

"Put me down," she said, sounding out of breath.

"Hell fucking no." I slid the keycard out of my front pocket. "I'm the one giving the orders tonight, babe."

Once the door opened, I carried her to the large bed and tossed her into the middle of it, right on top of the fluffy comforter. She pulled herself upright, yanking the comforter out of the way and leaning on her elbows. Her expression anticipatory, she parted her sexy lips as she watched me take off my shirt. No woman, no woman at any time, came close to making me feel the way she did when she looked at me.

While I removed my boots and socks, Lace sat up and lifted her shirt over her head.

"Next time, I get to do that," I told her, giving her a serious look.

"Okay." She tossed her hair over her shoulder, her mouth widening into a playful smile.

My eyes devoured her. The creamy slopes of her perfect breasts spilled out of her purple bra, the dusky rose nipples barely concealed by the lacy edge. She was by far the sexiest woman I'd ever seen, and I went hard as fucking steel when she lowered her head and gave me a flirty *come take me* look through her lashes.

Hell yeah, I'll take her.

I'd never been more ready in my life. I unbuckled my belt and started to unbutton my jeans, but she reached out and covered my hand with hers.

"Let me." Her voice was husky as she stared up at me. She'd been so young our first time, a little hesitant, but not now. Now she was all woman, and she was all mine.

My gaze burned as the magnitude hit me of where we were, and what we'd gone through to get here. Unable to speak, I nodded.

Her hair slid forward as she lowered her head and spread apart the button fly on my jeans. I moved things along by pulling my boxers and jeans off together. My breath caught when her delicate fingers closed around me. My cock jumped in her hand, hers to command, like I was.

Fucking hell.

I pulled her up, only to push her back on the bed. Not willing to wait a second longer, I climbed in and slammed my mouth down on hers with a growl. I wanted to be inside her . . . *now.* That voice inside my head that had been telling me to take it slow? I told it to shut the fuck up. I was done with preliminaries.

I thrust my tongue deep into her mouth, giving it to her a little rough. Apparently, she liked that just fine, because she started to writhe beneath me.

Warm skin, soft curves, she felt fucking fantastic, but her jeans needed to come off. My chest heaving, I was barely able to draw in enough oxygen to fuel my raging desire. I drew back and unfastened her jeans, then yanked them down.

In only her purple bra and panties with all those curves and creamy skin, Lace was amazing. I'd been telling myself for years that my memory had exaggerated her perfection. Not so much. She was my every fantasy made real.

"Fuck, you're gorgeous." I framed her beautiful face in my hands. "I love you. Never stopped loving you. I need you to know that."

"Stop looking so serious." Her fingers ghosted across my lips, settling over my mouth like a soft kiss. "I love you too." She smiled, dazzling me with her happiness and her words. "I've always loved you."

Her declaration settled deep in my soul, the cure to the restlessness that had plagued me since I'd given her up as a teen.

Lace was the cure, my own sweet remedy.

chapter

34

Lace

I stared at this handsome man, watching as his cautious veneer fell away. The guardedness dissolved like a mist, there and then gone forever right before my eyes. The love that remained was a bright beacon, a shining light at the top of a tall tower.

Bryan was the culmination of all my dreams. I was helpless to resist him, not that I ever wanted to.

So many wrongs in my life. Have I finally gotten something right?

I pulled his head back down to me, feeling his grin against my lips right before his tongue dipped inside and slid slowly across mine. One languid stroke, and my body became a hot whirlwind of sensation.

We took turns tasting each other. He was hope, if hope had a taste. Bold, brilliant, and blinding. The heavy weight of him crushed my breasts, and the hard length of him pressed between my thighs. Feminine and masculine, we were two opposing puzzle pieces that fit perfectly together.

I traced across the breadth of his shoulders with my palms and raced down the indentation of his spine with my fingertips, grabbing his ass in my hands and writhing against him.

"Bry," I said on a moan. "I want you." I was on fire, burning everywhere our skin touched.

"I want you more."

He gave me a wicked smile before torturing me by doing wicked, wonderful things to me with his mouth. With long, purposeful licks he teased me, his tongue sliding across my skin—up and over and near, but not quite touching the nipples that ached to receive the same attention.

My heels dug into the mattress, and my head thrashed. Desire roared hot and then hotter still when his mouth finally closed over my nipple. I arched off the bed.

"More," I begged greedily.

When he took me deeper into his mouth, I whimpered. Wetness rushed to my core when I felt the edge of his teeth, and his tongue lash the throbbing tip.

He thoroughly explored every inch of my breasts with restrained nips that jolted through me like lightning, followed by light, soothing strokes that prolonged the pleasure. Worshiped, I was on a sensual high as I watched him through my lashes, praising him by panting his name.

I started to protest when he lifted his head, but stopped when his hands moved lower, on their way to where I most wanted him to go. Delicate shivers racked me as his skilled fingers glided lightly across my fevered skin.

I moaned low and long when he skimmed his palm over my throbbing wet center. His touch was teasing, as soft as a breath, but it made my entire body flush with heat.

"That's it, babe." He stared down at me, his lids heavy and his gorgeous light eyes darkened with passion. "So sexy. So beautiful." He increased the pressure over my swollen clit, rhythmically rocking his palm.

"Bry . . ." Breathlessly, I lifted my hips and rolled with his motion, pulsing beneath him.

"Don't hold back, Lace. I want to see you come for me first, and then I promise I'll give you more."

While he watched, so possessive and so attentive to my needs, I came fast, and I came hard. Tremor after tremor rolled through me. This man owned me, and my body surrendered to him as readily as my heart had done so many years ago.

Before the glow of my climax had dimmed, Bryan grabbed and rolled on a condom. Positioning himself, he slid deep inside me. His cock a hot brand, he reclaimed me as his.

"Lace, oh, Lace." He caged me within his arms, and as he promised, he gave me more, more than I'd bargained for, more than I'd ever dreamed.

My eyes were locked on his. I was his to have, my body and my soul, molten metal and malleable.

"You feel so good," he said low, stroking inside me deep, his passion-roughened voice adding another level to the pleasure.

"Only this good because it's you." Peering up at him, I urgently caressed the smooth skin and flexing muscles of his back. "I'm only like this for you." My hands on his ass, I squeezed the tight flesh and lifted my hips to take him deeper.

"Only you." He groaned, and his muscles bunched beneath my grip. "Only ever you."

My body tingled with heat. My skin shimmered, every nerve ending sheared. His cock was thick, filling me so perfectly. I burned, this time hotter than before, a sun about to supernova as he moved in a practiced rhythm that was insanely deep, impossibly hard, and meant to unravel me.

As his cock provided the perfect friction against my sensitive flesh, his name slipped from my parted lips. His handsome face was all I could see, his amazing body all I could feel. Pulse after electrical pulse surged through me.

Chanting my name, he drove into me deeper, his strokes faster and more erratic. Taking everything he gave, I lifted my hips and strained for the pinnacle—slippery, hot, and wet. His skin damp, his muscles taut, he strained for it too. His heavy breaths lifted the hair from my temples, and mine filled the air. We were out-of-control harmony, the slap of his hips against mine perfectly tuned.

I cried out as it hit me, a bolt of pleasure so deep and sharp that it hurled me over everything I'd known.

Roaring my name, Bryan threw back his head and his cock stiffened as he erupted inside me. His pleasure was my pleasure, taking me higher than I'd ever been, and he was right there with me.

All that he was, I accepted. All that I was, he received. All the bests in my life were him, always him.

chapter 35

Lace

After the haze of sensual bliss cleared, reality reasserted its claim. I didn't want it to. I wanted to bask in Bryan's love and the afterglow of our lovemaking. Savor it.

So I did, reveling in the pleasure of him holding me and holding him right back. Only maybe I held him a little more tightly. But eventually, the condom had to be disposed of, and I had to get cleaned up.

"I love you," I said, giving him a gentle peck. Even just the touch of my lips to his made my knees wobble. A little unsteady, I padded into the bathroom for a quick shower.

When I returned, Bryan was propped up in bed on his elbow, still naked, the sheet draped casually around his waist. He was distracting as hell with his hair tousled and all that exposed skin over tight muscles. I was totally into him, and he knew it. His amused eyes gleamed back at me beneath his lowered lids.

My heart constricted as if he'd squeezed it in his hand.

Bryan Jackson was the perfect man for me in every way, the standard to which no other man could possibly measure up. The second—well, technically the third time—with him only made me more certain of that fact. With Bryan, making love was a two-way exchange, a gift we gave to each other, the physical expression of our love. We'd only just finished, and I already wanted to do it again.

Badly.

The old Lace would have jumped right into taking what she wanted without considering the consequences. My life had made me the person I'd been. Desperate, needy, grasping for happiness where I could get it, not expecting it to last.

This, though, with Bryan, had to last. Starting now, I had to do things differently.

I inhaled deeply and offered him a tentative smile. He studied me a minute, and his forehead creased.

"What's wrong?" he asked warily. "What's going on inside that beautiful head of yours?"

I couldn't fool him. There was no use trying.

I moved to the side of the bed and took a seat with my back to him. Gathering my thoughts, I knotted the bathrobe sash tighter around my waist. I only hoped tighter would give me the courage I needed.

"That was amazing," I said. "You're amazing. I want to do it again. But first, I think we should talk."

"I agree." His voice was deep and certain, and he scooted in behind me, his legs stretched out on either side.

That felt really good. Bryan was warm, strong, everything I needed.

He brushed my hair off my neck and kissed the spot where it met my shoulder. A shiver ran down my spine. Turning me around, he shifted me, arranging me so I sat on his lap. That felt even better.

He gazed into my eyes, and I realized I'd never seen him look as serious. "I want you to move in with me when we get back to Seattle."

I wanted to. There was nothing I wanted more.

My heart leaped, but I closed my eyes and covered my face with my hands, so he couldn't see how much I wanted to say yes. To be with Bryan 24/7, to wake up every morning looking into those gorgeous gray-green eyes, to go to bed with him every night—it would be awesome, the best, a dream come true.

Only it wouldn't be right to accept, not yet.

"That sounds wonderful." I let out a wistful sigh, dropping my hands and opening my eyes to find him staring at me expectantly. "I really want to, but I can't. At least not yet."

"What do you mean, you can't?" His muscles tensed beneath me. "The way I see it, we should have done this years ago. Maybe if we'd—"

"Don't. Please don't. Regret is a dead end," I said sadly. "One of the things they taught us in rehab is to use the lessons from our past to build the future we want. The best isn't behind us, but in front of us."

I ran my hand down his stubbled cheek and trailed a finger under the black leather cord with the silver skull bead that he wore around his neck. I stared into his eyes, willing him to understand. But his guard was up again, and it made me sad to see that.

"Bry, I want a future with you, but to have it we need to establish the right foundation. You went from being my best friend in high school to being my lover. Even if things hadn't gone all wrong for us, I don't think I would have been ready to handle something like that back then. And I'm still not."

"What the hell's that supposed to mean?" He set me aside abruptly and made a sweeping gesture with his arm, indicating the bed. "Were you not just there with me? You know as well as I do what we did was a whole hell of a lot more than just two people getting each other off. It's always been more with you and me." He scrubbed a hand through his hair. "Are you saying that this was a mistake?"

I shook my head. "No, of course not."

"Good." He gave me a curt nod. "Because it's not prom night anymore. But let me lay it all out this time, just so we're clear, and there's no chance for misunderstanding. I love you. I want you with me all the time. Don't make it more complicated than that."

"I'm not trying to." I put my hand on his arm, laying my fingers over the black scrolling of his tattoo, but he shook me off.

My throat tightened as I watched him stand, going for his pants. While he yanked them back on, I pulled the lapels of the robe closer together, suddenly feeling scared and cold.

"Bry, please listen and try to understand."

"I'm listening." He turned back around, his eyes flashing with confusion and pain. "But this doesn't make sense."

"It does. You would have to be blind not to see what a wretched mess my life is right now. I need to get things straight first, get myself straight before I get into a relationship."

"I'm not just some random guy you hooked up with, Lace. We already *have* a relationship."

Shit. I panicked. That wasn't how I meant it at all. Bryan was taking everything I said and turning it inside out.

"I know that . . . God, I know that. I'm so grateful for that, for you. You're my best friend," I said, finding it difficult to breathe. This was going even worse than I'd feared.

Noticing how freaked out I was, he moved back to the bed and knelt in front of me, his expression softening. "I know this is scary, Lace." His voice gentled as his gaze drifted over me. He covered my clutched hands with his. "All the more reason for us to be together, so I can help you."

"No." I shook my head. "That's just it. I can't let you do that for me."

Frustrated, I dug deep for the right words. If only I could explain it so he could understand.

"Look, Bry, I can't keep jumping from relationship to relationship every time I need a rescue. I've got to learn how to take care of myself for a change. It's going to take work to become a better person, and that's work only I can do."

I glanced up at him, hoping that I'd finally gotten through, but my heart stuttered when I saw how completely closed off he was to me now.

His gaze hardened. "So you're telling me you want me to put my life on hold again. To be on standby. To wait."

"Yes." I held my breath as I waited for his reply. "I want to be a woman you can be proud of. Someone *you* need and can rely on, the way I rely on you."

"How long do you estimate this process will take?" he asked, his voice a low rumble.

"I don't know. Just until I prove to myself that I can do it on my own, I guess."

An oppressive silence filled the room. The air-conditioning kicked on, and as cold air blew against the back of my neck, icy trepidation trickled down my spine. I knew even before Bryan spoke what his answer would be.

"No, Lace," he said, his jaw rigid. "I can't. I won't wait. I've already waited through two guys for you, and I've done all the waiting I'm gonna do. I want you now, so you need to decide. I need a yes or no answer right now."

My heart froze, and my chin dropped to my chest. A cold fist tightened around my throat. "Then it has to be no," I whispered. "I can't give you less than the best of me. I won't." Stubbornly, I added, "You deserve better."

Bryan didn't say anything, and that said it all. When I looked up, he was scooping his shirt off the floor.

Stop, my heart cried.

Please don't go, my eyes pleaded.

But his face was an impenetrable fortress. No mere wall between us, no rampart to tread. I was outside the castle, and he was too far away for me to reach now.

"Good-bye, Lace."

chapter

36

Lace

For a long time, I stared at the door Bryan had slammed closed behind him, and I didn't move at all. So long my rigid muscles went from tense, to burning pins and needles, to completely numb.

But sensation eventually returned, and I had to feel the pain. Razor sharp, thousands of cuts, every memory with him brutally ripped away. Bryan had just blown my world to bits. Razed to the foundation, it all crashed down on me.

Obliterated, my heart lay scattered like shrapnel all around me. Big, sobbing shudders shook my body as I looked at the tangled sheets, as I breathed in the lingering scent of his cologne, as I tasted him. Hope rapidly faded, washed away by the salt from my tears.

I jerked up out of the bed and turned my back on it. Sinking to the floor, I pulled my knees to my chest and wrapped my arms around them.

Surely, I'm doing the right thing.

I rocked back and forth, staring straight ahead, tears blurring my vision. My future gone. Bryan gone. All I had left was pieces of me and pain.

And unlike before, there was nothing to ease that pain.

For a fleeting moment, I seriously considered getting up, getting dressed, and going out for some drugs. But if I went down that path again, there would be no coming back from it a second time. I would end up in the ground just like my mother.

My arms tightened. *No fucking way.* I steeled myself and stuck a fork in that chapter of my life. It was done. Over. I was never descending into that pit again.

I'd have my cry. I was entitled to that. It had been a long time since I'd cried, so I made it a good one. I felt sorry for myself and all that shit. Stuff regular people go through, processing without anything to numb the pain.

Not a step forward, maybe, but holding myself steady on the ground I'd gained.

• • •

When the sun came up, my throat was raw and my Kleenex box was empty.

Processing time over, I got up off the floor. I had to use the bed as a crutch because my legs had cramped so badly, but I wasn't going to allow myself to linger in this sad place. It was time to be tough and resilient, a woman who changed her world instead of allowing her world to change her.

My steps steady, I went into the bathroom and cleaned myself up. Taking a long, hot shower, I washed and conditioned my hair. I scrubbed twice with the fragrant hotel soap, scouring the traces of Bryan's scent from my skin.

God, the scent of him. I almost wavered, but I couldn't. I just couldn't.

Pressing my lips into a firm line, I stepped out onto the bathmat and wrapped a towel around myself. With a hand towel, I wiped away the condensation from the mirror. I stared at the pink-faced woman who looked back at me. Her eyes were red-rimmed, but her gaze was determined.

I liked her.

She was hurt. She ached inside, but she would do what needed to be done.

She was worthy. A keeper.

She was sick and tired of life knocking her the fuck down.

Now it was time for her to start fighting the fuck back.

Lace

I pounded on my brother's hotel-room door with my fist.
"Hold up. I'm coming." His muffled reply came through
the door before he opened it. When he saw me, he did a
double-take. "What the hell! What did you do to your hair?"

"Cut it, obviously," I said matter-of-factly as I brushed
past him to enter the room.

"What's going on, Lace?" he asked when I turned around.
"Where's Bryan?"

"I don't know." I blinked back the burn of painful tears
and avoided looking directly at him. Sinking down onto the
mattress, I smoothed out the wrinkles in the comforter. "I
asked him to wait for me, to give me some time to get my head
sorted out. He didn't like that plan."

"Damn. I'm sorry." Dizzy dropped onto the bed and
glanced at me, his eyes filled with questions I didn't really
have the answers for. Not yet, at least. I was working on that.

The haircut was symbolic. The long feminine locks were
gone, lopped off. *Out with the old, in with the new* was my
motto going forward. Well, maybe not all the old—there was
room in the new for a little reboot of the Lace from Southside

249

High, a 2.1 version of me. The me I could have been before my mistakes.

To me, my retro 1960s Twiggy haircut proclaimed all those things with its side part and short smooth layers framing my face. Most importantly, it was edgy, exemplifying the confidence that I could do this on my own.

"I'm not going back to Seattle." I ran my hand over the shortened, ear-length strands that were going to take some time to get used to. "There are just too many memories there."

"Kinda late to be deciding that." Dizzy looked at his watch. "Our plane leaves in a couple of hours."

"I already paid the change fee."

"Where you gonna go then?"

"Vancouver. I have unfinished business at Black Cat. Some things I need to make right. I think it's probably as good a place as any to start over."

"Okay, Lace." The lines between my brother's brows smoothed out. "No reason for me to go back then either. I'll come with you."

I laid my head on his shoulder and let out a breath. "Diz, I have to do this on my own. Anyway, what about the band?"

"What band? No War, remember?"

"Still. The rest of the guys are in Seattle, and they need you there."

"You're probably right." He nodded while his eyes searched mine. "You're sure about this?"

It was my turn to nod. "I love you."

"I love you too. But you're not alone and not that far from Seattle. I'll be just a phone call away." He exhaled and put his hand on mine. "I'm your big brother. I know I have problems of my own, but we're family. You can't get rid of me that easily. I won't let you."

Giving him a small smile, I said, "I don't want to get rid of you, Diz. I just have to do this. For me. For the me I want to be."

"I understand." He held me by the shoulders, and his lips formed an encouraging smile. "I know you can do it, Lace. Between me and you, I've always known it would be you who would figure out a way to overcome our past."

chapter

38

Lace

Ascream pierced the air, waking me, and I rolled over in my bottom bunk. Pressing my spine into the wall, I clutched the small duffel of belongings and my brother's confidence in me to my chest.

You're here, Lace Lowell.

I'd found a place to stay in Vancouver all on my own. I had a job, such as it was, and was making my own way instead of accepting whatever life threw at me.

No one was doing those things for me. No War. No Martin. No drugs. Just me.

Don't give up. You're okay. It will be okay.

That was my mantra, one I had to repeat often to myself when fear crept into my heart, waking me like it had tonight. But the unfamiliar snores and breathing of women around me made me feel more alone and less certain.

Hearing rustling on the bunk above me from a new occupant added to my fear. Would the new person be nice, threatening, or—best-case scenario—apathetic like everyone else? Most shuffled along like me, barely making ends meet, chanting mantras of their own to keep moving forward.

I pulled out my cell, and my finger hovered over the text log. But I couldn't call him. A few weeks wasn't enough time to prove anything.

LACE: You up?
DIZZY: Gunshots again?
LACE: No, just someone screaming
DIZZY: I worry about you there. It's not safe.
LACE: The hostel's all I can afford.
DIZZY: You should let me pay for an apartment.
LACE: No.

I clutched my backpack tighter and continued to type.

LACE: You're already doing too much.
DIZZY: What am I doing? You won't accept anything.
LACE: You listen.

I couldn't owe anyone else anything more. I needed to start my new life with a clean slate.

Problem was, late at night like this, I felt weak. I wanted Bryan. Ached for him.

Warm tears leaked from my eyes. I wanted to hear him tell me like he used to that it would be all right, that I could do anything. His faith in me had kept me steady in high school as I'd pursued my dream, a dream that now felt far beyond my reach.

Don't give up. You're okay. It will be okay.

LACE: I need to do this on my own. I can do this on my own.
DIZZY: I know you can.
LACE: Thank you. You okay?

Dizzy: I'm fine.
Lace: The band?

I avoided direct questions about Bryan.

Dizzy: No band. Sager, King, and I hang out some.
No word from anyone else.

My chest squeezed tight. That meant nothing from War or Bryan. That silence hurt, but I powered through it.

Lace: Good night. I love you.
Dizzy: I love you too, sis. Proud of you. Good night.

• • •

I dropped into the leather chair outside Mary Timmons's office at Black Cat Records again, my designated spot the past three Monday afternoons in a row. I flipped through the magazine selection. I'd read them all by now, but picked up an *Us* magazine that I practically had memorized.

I glanced over at her secretary. "Did you let her know I'm here?"

"I did." She nodded and went back to typing at her computer.

"Okay. Thanks." I looked out the window at the bright blue sky and the lonely cargo ship floating in the bay. My mind zoned out as I prepared for a long wait.

"Ms. Lowell?"

My mind snapped into focus.

"Ms. Timmons will see you now."

Finally.

The secretary held open the door for me, and I entered, getting my first look at the inner sanctum of Black Cat's CEO.

Pretty impressive. The huge corner suite filled with dark, ornate furnishings felt very Old World. Outside the windows, English Bay played the role of moat for Mary Timmons's castle.

The elegant brunette sat on her throne, as intimidating as ever with her hands steepled together in front of her while she stared at me. Hopefully, the queen wasn't about to send me to the gallows.

Taking a seat in one of the chairs across the imposing desk, I stared right back at Mary. The new Lace, the one who had cheated death, didn't take shit from anyone. After all, what could this woman really do to me? I didn't need anything from her.

I pulled the bulky envelope from the inside pocket of my pea coat and placed it on the desk in front of her. "That's the cash from the signing bonus, less the twenty thousand for my rehab. But I intend to pay every penny back."

Gathering my courage, I gripped the wood armrests on my chair to steady myself. *Keep going. You can do this.*

"I took that money under false pretenses," I said, keeping my voice steady despite my pounding heart. "That doesn't gel with who I am now, or at least with the person I intend to become. So I wanted to offer you an apology."

Her perfect eyebrows raised, Mary glanced at the envelope and then back to me.

Okay, at that point, I began to squirm a bit. She hadn't said a word yet. This woman had the intimidation routine down to a scary-ass science. I could learn a few things from her.

Tilting her head slightly to the side, Mary leaned back in her chair, still every inch in control of this meeting. But I sensed a subtle softening in her manner. Or then again, maybe it was just wishful thinking on my part.

"You're done with the drugs, then?" she asked bluntly.

I was a bit surprised by this question. First, that she would even ask it, and second, wondering if she would believe me. After all, I'd lied to her before. But I owed her the truth.

"It was a real struggle at first," I said, "but it's gotten easier."

The drugs had been an escape from an out-of-control life. Now that my life was going where I wanted it to, I didn't crave them anymore. Or not as much, anyway.

"Three weeks sober," I said proudly. "Seven, if you count rehab."

Mary nodded, still studying me. "I would definitely count it."

That was nice, but what was her deal? I'd given her the money back. Why wasn't she saying anything about that?

Underneath the weight of that steely stare of hers, I found myself rambling. "It'll take me a while to pay back the rest. I mean, I didn't realize how much everything costs up here in Canada."

"You're living in Vancouver?"

"Yes. I needed a fresh start, and I didn't want to return to Seattle where I might be tempted to fall back in with my old crowd."

"Lace Lowell." A regal brow rose. "You've impressed me."

Stunned, I tried to school my features so I didn't gape at her. *Really?*

"It's been a long time since anyone's done that," she said softly, reaching for the envelope. She opened a drawer and tossed the envelope inside without checking the contents. "Here's what we're going to do. You'll come into the studio from ten to three, Monday through Friday. I want you doing some studio vocals. You'll work with our voice coach. Then—"

"I can't," I said quickly.

That damn brow of hers rose again. "Pardon me?"

"I can't," I repeated, despite the glare that said *Off with her head.* I'd better make my case before any blood got spilled. "I wait tables in the day. I'm saving up so I can take classes at the Centre."

Her eyes narrowed in surprise. "The Blanche MacDonald Centre?"

I nodded. "I want to get a degree in design."

"What about your contract with me, Lace?"

"If I'm not mistaken, I voided that with the drug use." I sat up a little straighter. "Frankly, I thought you'd be glad to be rid of me. Lost cause and all."

"I thought you told me your dream was to be a singer. Was that another misrepresentation?"

"No. That's what I said. I just think fashion's the better choice for me." I sighed, wondering where she was going with this.

Mary's lips flattened and her fingers steepled together again. "The better choice or the safer choice?" Her eyes held mine in a challenging stare.

Damn. This woman was perceptive as shit. Neither Bryan nor my brother, who knew me extremely well, had asked me that. "I love music. It helps me process."

With notes and melodies, I constructed a world to escape from reality. But fashion was my armor to take on reality, not to run away and hide from it.

"It's my first love," I said without hesitation. "But—"

"No buts." She stopped me with a precise slice of her hand. "The way I see it, there's no reason you can't do both. They might even mesh really well together. Image is such a big part of the music business. I'm sure you realize that quite a few entertainers have their own fashion lines."

My eyes widened while she continued talking. *That would be so cool.*

"You'll have to quit the waitressing, obviously. Unless you're in love with that career path too?"

Frowning, I wondered if she was teasing me. *Mary Timmons?*

Not sure what to say, I shook my head.

"That was a rhetorical question. I'm glad to know you're on board with my plan. Let me just make a call." Mary picked up her cell, sliding her fingers quickly across the screen before holding it to her ear. "Beth . . . No, I wasn't calling about the Tempest thing. I haven't made a decision about that yet."

Wow. At just the mention of the band, my memory hauled ass right back to that last night with them in Orlando. I felt the familiar ache in my chest. The sutures on my heart were holding so far, but the prognosis was still day to day. I missed Bryan constantly.

What good is a new life without him with me to share it?

I let out a weary sigh, refocusing on Mary's phone conversation.

"Yes. I've got her in my office now. I'm sending her right over. Take her to HR. I'm bringing her on as a part-time employee." Mary ended the call and her eyes met mine. "Four hours a day okay with you? Twenty thousand for the first six months."

Heck yeah, I'd take that.

Numbly, I nodded. There was no way in hell I could even come close to earning that amount working for tips. When Mary spun her chair away, I pushed to my feet, thinking I'd been dismissed.

She swiveled back, holding up a finger. "One more thing, Lace."

"Yes?" I gulped, my stomach doing a little nauseating side shimmy.

"Where are you staying?"

"A hostel on Pender Street." Dreaming of Bryan at night, trying to make myself into a woman worthy of him during the day.

Mary frowned. "That's not a very good part of town."

A total understatement. That part of Vancouver made Southside Seattle seem like Disney World.

She opened her desk drawer, pulled out a couple of business cards, and handed them to me.

"One of those is for a driver I keep on call. The other is for the manager at Sutton Place. I don't want you wasting what little free time you're going to have on public transportation, and I want you sleeping in a safe place."

"Okay," I managed to say, trying to process all the surprises she was lobbing my way.

"You'll like the Sutton. It's convenient, and in a nice neighborhood only a couple of blocks from the fashion school you hope to attend."

My *deer in the headlights* look must have registered with Mary, because her face softened.

Why haven't I ever noticed how beautiful she is before?

"I'm not going to sugarcoat it. Working this schedule is going to be a challenge, but I think you can handle it." She huffed out a small laugh and shook her head. "I've seen a lot in this business, but I've never seen anyone quite like you. Showing up at my office three weeks in a row"—*so she'd known!*—"shows you've got courage and mental toughness. Bringing the money back and owning up to your mistakes demonstrates integrity on your part."

Mary stood and held out her hand, and I grasped it.

"You have talent too, Lace. I'm really looking forward to seeing what you do next."

chapter

39

Bryan

Holding the guitar by the neck, I slammed it into the wall, grunting with satisfaction when it splintered apart in my hands. Letting go, I watched my favorite acoustic drop to the carpet, ruined, just like my life without Lace.

I've done all the waiting I'm gonna do.

What an arrogant ass I'd been. My life was at a total standstill without her.

Swiping my beer off the table, I sagged into the chair. I drained the bottle, settled back, and closed my eyes. Alone with my thoughts, and they were all of her.

What's she doing? And who is she with?

I felt completely empty without Lace, nothing more than a brittle, burned-out husk. It was all wrong. Nothing made sense anymore.

"Bry?" my mom asked, and I opened my eyes. "Are you okay? I heard a noise."

"Yeah, Mom." I turned to see her step inside the garage, which had been converted into a studio.

"Is it all right if I come in?"

"Sure." I ran a hand through my hair. "You don't have to ask. This is your house, even though I bought it for you. I just

260

put the studio in, so I had somewhere to practice whenever I'm around."

"I know." She pulled out a chair and sat beside me. Her gaze flicked to the broken guitar before she scanned my face. "I'm worried about you."

"Don't be," I bit out.

"Bryan Hunter Jackson. I'm your mother. That's not an option." Her hands went to her hips. "I want to know when you're planning to stop moping around and take charge of your life again."

I didn't bother to respond. She was absolutely right.

My mother scooted her chair closer, smoothing out the apron she wore over her scrubs. She must have just gotten home from work. Her hand dropped down on top of mine. "What are you going to do about Warren?"

"What can I do, Mom?"

"You've been friends a long time."

"I know."

For all his faults, I couldn't just turn off how I felt. I was worried about War. Not to have him around anymore was like missing a limb. But not to have Lace was like missing my own heart.

"I tried to smooth things over before he quit the band. When War shuts you out, though, you're out. He's very absolute about things. You're either with him, or you're against him."

"Hmm." Mom folded her hands under her chin and looked thoughtful. I had a feeling where she was going to go before she spoke, and I wasn't wrong. "Do you remember what I told you when you first got back from Orlando?"

"I remember," I said, thinking she was going to reiterate all the reasons that ending things with Lace made sense. In my mind, those reasons still had some merit, but in my heart, it felt all fucked up.

"I'm afraid that maybe I gave you some bad advice."

Surprise widened my eyes as I looked at her.

A frown creased her brow. "I think I've let my history with your father color my judgment. So many times, he made promises. And so many times, he broke them. But I kept taking him back, hoping each time that things would be different."

"I know, Mom. I was there, remember?"

She nodded. "I saw that same pattern developing between you and Lace. I'm afraid you love her too much," she said, and her voice cracked. "And that she'll hurt you like your dad hurt me."

"He hurt all of us," I said softly.

"Yes, I see that now. I'm sorry I allowed that to happen."

"It's okay, but Lace isn't like him."

"I don't know that for sure. But I realize now, that's not for me to decide. That's up to you."

I was silent for a moment, letting that sink in.

She lifted her chin and looked me straight in the eyes. "I told you once that sometimes love means letting go, but maybe that was just my old bitterness welling up. I was trying to protect you, Bryan. I was trying to protect you back in high school, when Lace came to visit us and all those record deals were on the line. But maybe I was wrong to interfere, both then and now. In fact, I know I am. I should be encouraging you to make your own decisions. Live your life. Take risks, even."

My mom was right. Damn right. It hit me like a punch to the gut.

Lace was worth the risk. My stupid pride had blinded me from seeing that. It had kept me from agreeing to her stipulations, and acknowledging how brave she was to want to prove herself before we moved forward together.

"Thanks, Mom." I put my arm around her shoulders and kissed the top of her head. "Lace and you are a lot alike. Both so beautiful. Both so resilient."

"I love you, son." Mom laid her palm against my cheek, and I covered her hand with mine. Tears sparkled in her eyes as she smiled at me. "You're a good man. You'll figure it out and do the right thing. And whatever you decide, I'm behind you."

• • •

After my mom left, I did some heavy thinking. I thought about high school, and how I'd stepped aside from pursuing Lace because of my friendship with War. I thought about how difficult that had been watching the two of them—the two people I loved most in the world—grow close.

In the beginning, I told myself it was okay because War had done right by her. Sure, he was overly jealous, but I couldn't fault him for that. Even wanting her for myself, I couldn't fault him for doing everything in his power to keep her for his own.

However, I could fault him for the crap he'd pulled as we neared graduation. As things had started to go well for the band, War had changed. He'd consistently put his dream over Lace's. Though in his typical manipulative fashion, he'd called his dream her dream, and made excuses for modifying it without consulting her or anyone else. That had led to a downward spiral for her, for him, for me, for all three of us.

Loving someone, do you manipulate them, or do you encourage them to be the best they can be?

That's what it comes down to with love, isn't it? Real love, love worth having, requires putting the other person's needs, desires, and dreams above your own.

Lace wanted that. I wanted that. But I screwed it up.

I slid my cell out of my pocket and called Dizzy's number. It only rang once.

"Yo, man," he said. "What's up?"

"I screwed up. With Lace."

"You did. About fucking time you acknowledged that."

"Don't be an ass. Will you help me fix things with her?"

"Depends."

"On what?"

"What you have in mind."

"For starters, I want to set up a scholarship for her to study fashion. But I want it to be anonymous. A grant. A need-based thing."

"I'll help you," he said.

My lips curved.

"What else?" he asked.

"I don't want to interfere with her efforts to prove herself, but I want her safe while she does that."

"Me fucking too."

"Where is she, Diz?" Wherever she was, I was going to be. As soon as I could make it happen.

"Vancouver. Waitressing and living in a hostel. But Mary just offered her a better job, doing part-time vocal work at Black Cat. Just the right time for her to find out about anonymous funding and enroll in fashion school. I'm also thinking it's time for you to appear and lay your cards out. Is that what you're thinking?"

"Oh yeah." I ran a hand through my hair. "You think she'll forgive me?"

"Not for me to say, Bry. But if you give her yourself, all of you, I don't think she's gonna turn that down."

I sure the hell hoped not.

Life fucking sucked without her in it.

chapter

40

Lace

I heard the haunting acoustic melody as soon as I passed Black Cat's reception desk on my way in to work. I walked a little faster, trying to balance the backpack on my shoulder and my coffee without spilling it. The somber sound compelled me forward, directly toward its source.

In studio six, I found a guitarist I'd never seen before. His auburn head lifted, and gorgeous emerald-green eyes that I felt certain I'd seen before focused on me.

Comprehension suddenly dawned. No doubt about it—this was Avery's twin. The physical similarities were striking.

My heart rate kicked into a higher gear as he gazed curiously back at me. He was really good-looking, if you were into beautifully handsome men like Michelangelo's David. Dark and dangerous was more my speed, but I shouldn't go there. I clamped my mind shut to keep Bryan's memory out.

Yeah, as if that will work.

"Don't stop on my account," I said, stepping into the small ten-by-twelve room. I glanced at his guitar with the hummingbird pick guard. "That's a nice instrument. Really sweet tone. And you play it well."

"Thanks." He slid off his stool with a grin, his full lips revealing a flash of white teeth. "Justin Jones." He held out his hand.

Duh, I thought, dropping my backpack and moving my coffee to my left hand so I could take his. "Lace Lowell."

I returned his infectious grin, his calluses rough against my skin as our hands touched. If I hadn't already heard him play, that alone would have clued me in to the fact that Avery's brother wasn't a casual musician.

"We've both got the alliteration thing going on with our names, haven't we?" I said with a laugh.

"Yeah." He leaned his head to the side as if intrigued by me.

Well, I sure as hell was intrigued by him. It was really strange. As quickly as I'd taken a dislike to Justin's sister, I found him to be inexplicably affable.

"Oh, you're both already here. Good."

Beth, the congenial PR woman for Black Cat, entered the room and insinuated herself between us. After only a week working in the studio, I'd come to realize that Beth was also Mary's closest confidante.

"Mary wants you to work together for a while. She feels that your voices and music sensibilities are compatible." She handed me some sheet music. "Today she wants you to focus on some covers. Just basic stuff. Dalton will be here after lunch to record, and we'll go from there. Sound good?"

We both nodded. I turned back to Justin as soon as she was gone. He was standing close, looking over my shoulder at the sheet music. Way too close.

"'Roadside,' huh? Not too bad."

I took a step away from him. Better get this out of the way. Justin seemed like a nice guy, but I wasn't going there. Not with him. Not with anybody else. Not ever again.

Deep inhale.

"Listen, Justin. I'm really looking forward to working with you, but I just need you to know that I'm not interested in anything else, okay?"

He scanned my face, not saying anything for a minute. "Bad breakup?"

I snorted. "Breakup would imply there had been an actual relationship in the first place." I'd tried for a lighthearted tone, but self-pitying tears were stinging my eyes. "There's just a guy that I'm never going to get over, you know?"

"No worries. I promise not to think of you as an entrée if you promise to think of me as a friend."

I grinned. "I can totally do that."

I'd been so lonely up here in Vancouver without the guys, without my brother. I even found myself missing Bridget's nonstop chatter.

• • •

By the end of the second week, Justin and I had already cranked out a half dozen original songs.

Meanwhile, I'd enrolled in fashion classes at the Blanche MacDonald Centre. Miraculously, the exorbitant tuition that had been far beyond my reach, even with my new part-time job, was one hundred percent covered by a very generous anonymous grant.

Avery's twin and I were productive in the studio and enjoyed each other's company. Like me, Justin didn't seem to be interested in serious relationships. Though I couldn't help but notice that he had a lot of one-night stands. Anywhere we went, women would come on to him and slip him their phone numbers.

We fell into an easy pattern of hanging out together whenever we had free time. Justin was staying at the Sutton also, and I discovered that he felt as isolated in Vancouver as I did.

His sister lived in an apartment near the waterfront, just far enough away to be inconvenient for day-to-day visiting. Plus, she had a busy schedule, *thank God*. Their dad was sick and living on Vancouver Island with Marcus's parents, Avery's soon-to-be in-laws.

I shared most of my story with Justin. We had the common background with substance abuse, and appointed ourselves each other's accountability partners.

Since our personalities were a lot alike, I wasn't sure if that was a plus or a minus. We both liked to shop. He was *really* into men's fashion. If it hadn't been for the aforementioned one-night stands, I might seriously have wondered which way Justin swung.

The only thing I kept from him was the nitty-gritty details about my relationship with Bryan. Those I held tightly to myself. Though the way Justin looked at me, when I got myself tangled up again in the past, when I didn't want to do anything but sit in my room and stare at the wall and remember, made me wonder just how much more he knew about me and Bryan than he let on.

Today, we'd finished up another song and were in the break room at Black Cat, negotiating our afternoon plans. Justin leaned against the counter in front of me while I stirred creamer into my coffee.

"Mintage Vintage," I said, my voice a little whiny as I lobbied for us to check out my favorite vintage clothing shop. "We did Armani Exchange yesterday. Speaking of that . . ."

I bit my lip. Maybe I shouldn't mention it. Justin already gave me a lot of grief about jogging alone. But yesterday at the Exchange, I'd gotten a feeling that someone was watching me. Actually, I'd had the feeling a lot over the past two weeks. But this time, I'd smelled cigarette smoke, and the fine hairs had stood up on the nape of my neck.

"What?" Justin asked.

"Nothing," I mumbled.

What could he do? It was just a feeling, after all. I'd never actually seen anyone. It was probably just my imagination.

"You don't look like it's nothing." Justin looked over my shoulder, his face brightening with a huge smile. "Avery."

I spun around just in time to catch his twin's disapproving frown.

"I thought you were visiting Dad," Justin said. "When did you get back in town?"

"Today." Avery looked back and forth between the two of us. Her expression was as tight as that stick up her ass. "Can I talk to you for a minute, Justin. In private?"

He nodded, following her out into the hall.

Even though I couldn't make out what they were saying, I didn't need to be a genius to figure out that it was about me. And knowing Miss High and Mighty, I could imagine that it wasn't complimentary.

When Justin came back in, he was alone, his expression as cloudy as Vancouver during a rain.

"Where'd she go?" I asked.

"To work on some solo material." He scrubbed a hand over his face, something I knew he did when irritated.

I quirked a brow. "She thinks I might be a bad influence on you."

"I told her it was more like the other way around," he said. "She's just being overprotective."

"Oh." I put my hand on his arm. "Don't worry about it. She and I just don't get along." I peered up at him through my lashes. "Don't take this the wrong way, but I think your sister's a stuck-up bitch."

"Hmm," he murmured. "Why do I get the idea that you and Avery are a cat fight just waiting to happen?"

Lace

Later that night, I set aside my feelings of being watched and squinted at my cell. It lay like a cobra on the couch beside me, ready to strike. I needed to make the call, but imagining the reception I was likely to receive made me hesitate.

I'd been putting this off for weeks. Atonement was part of my healing process, one of the steps. He would probably hang up on me. And if he didn't, there was likely to be some yelling. It wasn't going to be easy to atone for past mistakes with him.

I let out a big sigh. It was past time to get this over with.

Selecting his number, I pressed SEND, and he picked up on the first ring.

"Lacey?" War's voice was as smooth as it had ever been, but there was a hard edge to it that he'd never used with me before.

Well, at least he wasn't shouting. *Not yet.*

"How are you?" I swallowed nervously.

"I'm fuckin' great," he snapped, and then let out a loud sigh. "What do you want?"

Okay, not yelling, but close. I'd better get right to it.

"I want to apologize, War. I really messed up with us, with you, and with . . . with Bryan," I said, stumbling on his name.

I never said it out loud anymore. Ever. Whenever I found myself even starting to think about him, I pulled on my running shoes and went jogging.

What's he doing? Who's he doing it with? Does he miss me the way I miss him?

Obviously, I ran a lot.

War didn't respond. I could hear him breathing through the phone.

"I'm sorry," I said, rushing to fill the silence. "That's all I called to say, really. Except for one other thing." I bit my lip. "War, you and Bryan are best friends. You need him, and he needs you. You need each other."

"He put you up to this?" War didn't just ask the question. He snarled it.

"No." My chest burned. "I haven't seen or heard from him in five weeks." A short pause followed, and I couldn't stop myself from asking with a desperate squeak, "Have you?"

"No." There was a pause on War's side of the connection. I could hear music in the background, and a female voice speaking in Spanish.

"Where are you?" I asked.

"None of your business. I gotta go."

Dead air filled my ear.

There was no good-bye. I also didn't miss that War hadn't accepted my apology.

• • •

My cell rang at two in the morning, but quit ringing before I could locate it. I stumbled back to the bedroom and crawled under the covers. I was sound asleep when it started up again.

Shit. Shit.

I found it this time, between the cushions of the couch, and glanced at the display. Hesitating only a moment because the number was unfamiliar, I redialed the missed call.

"Hello?" a woman answered, and I recognized the musical voice right away.

"Bridget. Is everything okay?"

"Everything's fine."

Very few things are fine at two a.m. "What's going on?"

"Listen, Lace." Bridget sniffed. "Could . . . would it be okay if Carter and I came and stayed with you for a little bit?"

"Sure," I said without hesitation, remembering that Carter was her five-year-old son. "But I'm in Canada now. Do you and Carter have passports?"

"Yes." Another sniff from Bridget, and then I heard a boy's voice.

"Mommy, why are you crying?"

"I need to go now," Bridget said quickly. "I'll call you back when I have the flight information. And Lace?"

"Yeah?"

"Thanks," she said softly. "You don't know how much this means to me."

"No problem. That's what best friends are for."

chapter

42

Bryan

Dizzy and I sat in the club chairs in the Sutton Place lobby, waiting for Lace.

Watching so intently, I saw her silhouette as she passed by the gold-framed lobby windows. *Finally*. My heart pounded hard against my ribs. I couldn't wait to be close to her again, maybe very close if things went the way I hoped.

Lace breezed into the marble foyer and stopped in front of the table that always held a large vase of fresh-cut flowers. But she wasn't alone. She was with him. *Again*.

My rapid heart rate screeched to a stop, and my gut twisted into a jealous knot. I'd wanted to give her the time she needed to regain her confidence before making my move. But maybe I'd waited too long.

Dizzy jumped up and flew across the room to greet her.

I'd spilled my guts out to him weeks ago, telling him the way I felt about her and what I was planning to do. He'd been cautiously supportive of my decision, but he hadn't given me any indication how I would be received by her today.

Watching the brother/sister reunion, I held back, my hands in my jeans pockets, almost shaking with the control it took not to grab her, throw her over my shoulder, and just run off with her.

Lace looked good. Fantastic, in fact. Her cheeks glowed, rosy from the cold, and she was wearing the same vintage pea coat she'd worn on the tour. The short hair still gave me pause, but I could see that the style was actually extremely flattering. The waifish cut emphasized her beautiful amber eyes, which had always captivated me.

Hell, all of her captivates me.

Those eyes widened as she spotted me. Her gaze locked with mine, and her face drained of color. The guy at her side that I'd momentarily forgotten seemed to sense her distress and moved closer, glancing in my direction.

Justin Jones. Avery's twin.

Fuck me.

Apparently, I was getting a taste of my own medicine. At least Marcus Anthony wasn't around to gloat. For once in my life, I empathized with the dude. But just as I'd seen him do with Avery, I was going to do whatever it took to get Lace back.

I stared at Justin, giving him the glare that clearly said *you'd better move away from my woman or I'll take you out in the back alley and work you over.*

He raised an auburn brow. I'd seen Avery do that same thing when something amused her.

I sauntered toward Lace, wedging myself between them, shutting Justin out completely.

Amuse yourself with a view of my backside, motherfucker. That's all you'll be getting. You can't have her.

"Bryan," Lace whispered.

The sound of her voice had the usual effect, only worse because it had been so long. Too long. I wanted to wrap my arms around her and fill my lungs with her addictive sweet vanilla scent.

"Lace." I put my hand on her arm instead. I had to touch her, needed to feel the warmth of her skin against mine.

She swallowed. "What are you doing here?" she asked, a trembling uncertainty in her voice.

"Mary flew us all in for a meeting," Dizzy said quickly, glancing at me.

Good save, Dizzy. I shot him a grateful look. The *all* he referred to meant everyone but me. I'd been in Vancouver a while, making sure Lace was safe while giving her the space and time she said she needed.

But that was done. I was done. I couldn't do the sidelines shit anymore.

"Oh, but I thought . . ." Disappointment dimmed the light of expectation in her expression. Her response gave me a boost of hope.

"Aren't you going to introduce me to everyone?" Justin asked from behind me.

This dude was pissing me off. I wanted him g-o-n-e.

"I think you know who I am." I turned to him, my eyes narrowing, but Dizzy defused the situation.

"Justin, hey," he said, pointing to himself. "I'm Lace's brother. The antisocial dude, as you've probably guessed, is Bryan. I'd keep my distance from him for the time being, if I were you."

While Dizzy played nice, launching into a discussion about opening power chords and rock ballads, I zeroed in on Lace.

"Babe." I moved closer, using the low, soft tone on her that always made her eyes darken. "I need to talk to you."

It worked again. Her pupils dilated, and she swayed toward me as she licked her lips.

"All right," she whispered. "Where? When?"

"*Now.*" I wanted to add the stipulation that we do the talking while we were naked, but I figured that might defeat the purpose of actually, you know, talking. "Can we take a walk?"

"Sure," she said to me, then turned to her companion. "JJ." She thumped his arm, and he focused on her while rubbing where she'd thumped him.

What a wuss. Babes hit harder than that in Southside.

"I'm taking off with Bryan."

Justin gave me a narrow-eyed look. "Okay."

I gave him the same shit back, wanting to just lay him out cold. No warning. But I figured that would be as counterproductive as the naked thing. And not nearly as fun.

"I'll see you later," Lace said over her shoulder as I steered her away.

That pissed me off. Justin had hogged enough of her time. I was back officially, and I was making my move. I wasn't going back into the shadows again. It was Lace and me center stage as a couple from now the fuck on.

"Did you have a nice flight?" Lace asked as we stepped outside together through the door the uniformed hotel attendant held open for us.

"Huh?" It wasn't the cool breeze that distracted me. It was how pretty she was with the twinkling lights from the topiaries sparkling in her golden hair.

"The flight. With the guys." She gave me a funny look. "You know, from Seattle to here, Vancouver."

"Oh, well, about that." I rubbed the back of my neck with my left hand. My other was on her lower back where it was going to stay.

"What's going on?" She stopped on the sidewalk and turned to look at me, tilting her head.

"How do you mean?" I took her hand, since her back was out with us being face-to-face now.

"You rub your neck when you're nervous."

Ah, so I did.

"Just spit it out, Bry."

This exchange reminded me of so many conversations we'd had walking home from school, in alleyways before shows, or bars after performances, or on the beach with stolen snatches of time, just the two of us.

"Where do I start?" I asked, not pausing for her answer. "How beautiful you are? How much I missed you?"

"I missed you too," she said softly with a wistful expression.

That was promising. So was the spark of fire within her heart-arresting amber eyes.

"What's the story with your hair?" I blurted.

"You don't like it." She ducked her chin.

Stepping closer, I wedged a finger under her chin and gently lifted her head. "It's flattering. I'm sorry. It's just very different, very short."

"I needed a fresh look to boost my confidence."

"I understand," I said, remembering how she changed her clothes to project her mood. Why not her hair too? "But you needed nothing but yourself. You can do anything you set your mind to."

"Not the SAT."

"Maybe not that. What the hell use is that stupid test, anyway? But fashion, you kick its ass."

I swept my gaze over her. The wrap dress she wore looked like an entire multipack of watercolors spilled onto crushed velvet. It clung to her curves. The thigh-high black suede boots she'd paired with it lengthened her already long legs, and her choker was flirty and sexy.

Distractingly so. It reminded me of the one she'd worn to prom.

"You look like a *Vogue* runway model from the sixties."

"Thank you, Bry."

"Just speaking the truth." My voice went rough as I read a whole bunch into her shortening my name. "Mintage Vintage is your place like Janet's used to be back in Southside. Armani is your second favorite."

"How do you know all that?" she asked, her eyes searching mine.

Shit. I needed a cigarette bad right now, but I didn't have any on me since I'd been trying to quit.

"I visited Armani recently. But I haven't shopped at Mintage in days." She narrowed her gaze. "You didn't come in on the plane today with my brother, did you?"

"Huh-uh." Busted, I shook my head.

"How long have you been here?"

"Let me ask you something first. Do you have it straight in your head that you can do anything you set your mind to, and that you're way too good for me, and not the other way around?"

"How long, Bry?"

"Two weeks."

"Holy shit!"

"I wanted to be sure you were safe." My brows drew together. "I don't like how chummy you are with Avery's brother."

"I got that part. JJ's not into me that way. You have nothing to worry about."

"Why don't I have anything to worry about?" Holding her captive with my gaze, I placed my hands on her slender shoulders and walked her backward, right into the alcove doorway of a French bakery.

"Because . . ." Trailing off, she licked her lips.

My gaze dipped, and as I imagined kissing her, my cock jumped. It had been rock hard from the moment I'd laid eyes on her.

"Because you love me." I met her gaze again, my eyes blazing with that truth. "Like I love you. Like I'll always love you. There's been no one in my bed since you got on the tour bus. There's never been another woman inside my heart but you. There will never be anyone else who owns me heart and soul like you do."

"Oh, Bry." Her eyes widened.

"I can breathe now that I have you. I *want* to breathe now." I framed her face in my hands, plunging my fingers into the silky softness of her shortened hair while sweeping her creamy cheeks with my thumbs. "Apart from you, my life is terrible. I have to remind myself to get up, get dressed, eat, at least try to go through the motions."

"Yes, all of that." Her eyes bright, she nodded. "It's like that for me too."

Encouraged, I continued. "I fucked up, Lace. I know you have self-worth issues. I get it on two levels, first because I know you so well, and also because I have some of that same emotional baggage from growing up the way I did in the same place as you."

"I know. Truly, I know." She covered my hands, pressing my fingers deeper into her skin.

"Getting you, I should have affirmed you, supported your decision."

"Thank you," she said, her voice thick with emotion. "That means a lot to me."

"I'm your prince. I faltered when I should have stayed at your side. But I'm here now, and I'll never leave. Can you forgive me?"

"Yes, I can. Easily."

I swallowed hard. Lace's forgiveness meant the world to me. "You said once that something you always admired about me was that I always try to do the right thing."

"I don't know anyone more honorable than you, Bry."

I gave that a nod as if it weren't a big deal, but my heart was on fucking fire. "From now on, all my efforts to do the right thing are for you. Your dreams are our dreams. My dreams are yours. What the hell does it matter if I stand center stage at Madison Square Garden, Wembley, or anywhere else, if you're not there to watch and share those triumphant moments with me?"

chapter

43

Lace

"**I** love you, Bry." I lifted onto my toes. In my four-inch heels, I didn't have as far to go to reach his beautiful mouth, but it felt far, too far, and too long since I'd kissed him.

"I love you, Lace."

He said my name low and soft, the way I craved. The way I'd dreamed of him doing for weeks, the way I'd imagined when touching myself and thinking of him. Something I'd stopped doing early on, because it made me too sad and lonely.

He angled his head one way, and mine went the other. His eyes were a flash of metal with a hint of alpine green. His breath was humid, a tease before the headlining moment.

I sighed when he pressed his firm lips to my slightly parted ones. That tiny seam was all the welcome he needed. His wet tongue speared between my lips.

I drove my hands into Bryan's hair, grabbing fistfuls. Crushing my breasts to his hard chest, I sucked on his wicked tongue. His hands dove low and he grabbed my ass, lifting me and pressing me harder into the glass door behind us. The kiss was hot. He was hot. He set me on fire.

In Orlando, his taste was hope. Here in Vancouver, it was a homecoming.

He ripped his mouth from mine. "I've gotta have you now." His gaze electric gray with crackling green, he shifted me in his hold while twisting the doorknob to enter the shop.

There was only one person inside, and it smelled like freshly baked bread.

"Can I help you?" the employee asked from behind the counter.

Bryan nodded and gave him a determined look. "Yes, I'll take one of everything in your display."

The young worker's white paper chef hat nearly fell off his head. "That's a lot of money."

Bryan glanced meaningfully at the swing door. "If you look the other way while I take my girlfriend in the back, there'll be a twenty percent tip on top of the bill just for you."

"I, uh, I don't know," the guy stammered. "I just got this job. I should ask my boss, but he's not here. No one is, I—"

"Dude," Bryan bit out. "I love her, and we just got back together. I haven't seen her in weeks."

"Okay. Okay." The guy's eyes went wide. "I get it. My girlfriend's overseas."

"Done," Bryan said, already on the move.

In a couple of long strides, he pushed through the swinging door with me in his arms. Here, there, anywhere I could have him, I wanted him. Inside the kitchen that looked cleaner than any I'd ever seen, he went straight to the butcher-block prep table and set me on it.

"Here looks good," he said.

His hands diving into my hair, he cradled my head and silenced my protest with a searing kiss. My hands went under his shirt, my fingers tracing contoured muscles and smoothing over his velvety skin.

"You're so beautiful," he said, his voice ragged.

Breaking the kiss, Bryan stared at me. His gaze was hot enough to incinerate my clothing, but instead he grabbed the plunging neckline of my dress and tugged. Hard. The knot that tied the dress together at my waist gave way. The two opposing sides unraveled, and so did I when he put his mouth on me.

He kissed me hard and deep, setting me on fire. Ripping his mouth from mine, he rained kisses down my neck and then lower still, shaping my swollen breasts in his talented hands while I praised him for his efforts.

"That feels so good." My fingers tangled in his hair as he sucked one nipple until it throbbed, and then the other.

"You're my every fantasy fulfilled," he said when he eased back.

I didn't doubt his claim, even though I was perched on a bakery counter, my dress open, the wet lace of my bra stretched taut over my tits. Between my legs, behind another scrap of lace, I was wetter still and throbbing.

His gaze piercing, Bryan unbuckled his belt. I grabbed the hem of his black T-shirt and pulled it over his head. The ink of his tattoo sleeves glistened on his toned skin. Beneath the bright industrial lights, every defined muscle bulged.

"Did you get more buff while you were away?" I asked, staring at him with wide-eyed wonder.

"I worked out, or I played my guitar every time I thought of you." His gaze narrowed. "And I thought about you all the fucking time." Holding my gaze, he unbuttoned and ripped his jeans open.

"I thought about you all the time too," I said, and swallowed as he yanked the denim and his black boxers down his muscular thighs. His gorgeous cock sprang free.

Licking my lips, I lifted my gaze to see him stalking closer, his intention clear. He dipped his fingers in my lace thong and whipped it down my legs. My pussy and all the rest of me quivered. He placed his hands on my thighs and drew me toward him, spreading me open.

"I'm on the pill and clean," I said abruptly, wanting no delay in him taking me and nothing between us. "I was tested in the hospital and had to get retested before I signed with Black Cat."

"I had testing of my own for Black Cat." His eyes practically glowed with heat. "I'm clean too."

"All right then." When I reached for him, stroking his thick length with eager hands that trembled, he groaned and precum spurted from him. "I want—"

"Next time," he growled. "I have to be inside you now."

As he positioned himself, I watched . . . we both did. I moaned as he slid inside me, all the way to the hilt.

"You're so tight and wet," he said, grinning darkly.

"Because you're so hot."

"Because you are."

Grabbing my hips, he began to move. I planted my palms on the wood, trying to hold my position, but his thrusts were so powerful the table moved, the legs scraping across the floor with each thrust.

"Oh, Bry," I said, pulsing around him. Each time he stroked inside me, he made me hotter and wetter. My tits bounced. My body tightened. My breaths quickened. "I'm close," I said, panting as I warned him.

"Thank fuck." As he drove into me again and again, his expression was tight and his eyes wild. "Lace, babe, come," he growled.

I was already there. As he stiffened, I wrapped my legs and arms around him and held on tight. Flying with him, we went up and over the edge together. Hope, homecoming, and us combined.

Lace

Standing in the Sutton Place lobby, I watched Bryan leave the building with that loose-hipped saunter of his, and I trembled with the control it took not to chase after him.

What's going on?

What is he up to?

Why is he leaving?

I turned to Dizzy, the questions on my lips.

Reading my expression, my brother shook his head. "Huh-uh. I'm sworn to secrecy." He hugged me. "Bryan told you he has an elaborate surprise planned for you, so trust him. Don't look so worried."

I drew back and took in a deep breath.

"He's the one?" Justin hooked a thumb over his shoulder. "The guy you said you'd never get over?"

"Yes." I nodded, though I'd practically forgotten that he was even there.

Bryan had a way of eclipsing everything. He'd certainly changed everything with his return, saying the things he had, looking out for me from afar for weeks, and looking out for me on a much more intimate level just moments ago. He was going to have questions from his credit card company about the bill from that bakery, for sure.

"Looks to me like the feeling's entirely mutual." Justin shook his head with a smile and kissed my cheek. "Happy for you. Call me later, after the surprise. I'd like to hear about it."

"All right." I managed a small smile of my own before turning back to Dizzy. "That all your luggage?" I glanced at his guitar case and backpack.

He nodded. "All that's important, anyway. Me and my guitar."

"Okay."

I imagined Bryan probably traveled the same way. For as much success as the guys had had, they all still wore T-shirts and jeans. Making music was their motivation for their career choice. The money, the fame, and the rest were a distant consideration. Or at least that was the case for my brother and Bryan. We certainly weren't going to need a bellhop.

"I'm on this side." I gestured.

Dizzy grabbed his bags and followed me down the corridor. We passed the tiny gift shop, and I led him to a narrow hallway that had two small elevators.

"How are King and Sager doing?" I asked, needing a distraction. What I really wanted to do was grill my brother about Bryan and his mysterious surprise.

"They're good," Dizzy said as the elevator arrived. "Usual K&S routine on the plane ride, both of them cutting up and trying to get a cell number from the first-class flight attendant." He shrugged as I pushed the button for my floor. "Without Bryan to help me keep them in line, it was tough."

I let him off the hook and didn't question him further until I had him inside the apartment. But once there, I pounced.

"Dizzy Lowell. Tell me right now what you know."

"No." Grinning, my brother set down his things and pulled an embossed vellum envelope out of his leather jacket pocket. My name was scrawled on the front in Bryan's handwriting. "You'll find out yourself in a couple of hours."

chapter

45

Lace

I clutched the invitation in my hands and glanced down at my formal gown. The light pink silk dress was a 1965 vintage Oleg Cassini, strapless and gathered in an elegant rhinestone-encrusted bow beneath my breasts. It was a real find, very Jackie O. The dress and matching shoes had been delivered to my apartment moments after Dizzy and I'd entered.

My palms were sweaty as I waited in the lobby for Bryan to pick me up. I didn't know what to expect tonight. The invitation just said dinner and dancing, and was signed, "Love, Bryan."

I loved that, and was mulling over the possibilities of what he might have planned for tonight when a limo pulled into the front circle. I knew it was for me when it parked beside the clipped topiaries adorned with twinkling white lights. Keeping with the sixties theme—Bryan certainly knew it was my favorite design era—the car was a 1968 cream-colored Mercedes Benz.

Wow. This was quite the elaborate setup.

I pulled the matching silk wrap around my shoulder. It didn't do much to ward off the damp, chilly Vancouver night air, but it gave me something to do with my hands. My legs were another story. My silver heels felt as shaky and fragile as glass slippers as I walked out to meet him.

A uniformed driver popped out of the vehicle and scurried to open the back door for me. I thanked him as I ducked inside. Expecting to see Bryan, I was disappointed to discover that he wasn't there.

The driver folded himself into the front seat and tipped his cap to me in the rearview mirror. "Mr. Jackson said to tell you that you look beautiful, miss."

I smirked. I couldn't help it. How could he know how I looked?

"He also said to tell you that he's waiting for you at the restaurant. It's only a short drive from here."

I nodded and settled into the seat, trying to relax, taking in the scenery as he drove. The lights of downtown sparkled in the light evening mist. I noticed we were driving downhill toward the waterfront.

After a short ten-minute drive, the driver pulled up in front of a tall glass building, turned off the engine, and came around to open the door for me. He waited as I smoothed out the ankle-length skirt before offering me his arm.

"I'm to escort you to him," he said.

I nodded, and we rode the elevator up to the thirty-fifth floor in silence. I found myself more and more curious as to what was coming next. When the door slid open, I gasped. I didn't even remember stepping off the elevator or the driver leaving. I just stood there in complete awe.

The restaurant was deserted, but all around me, candles flickered atop white linen tables sprinkled with red rose petals. Out the windows and beyond the water, the lights of West Vancouver sparkled elegantly in the distance.

The invitation, the gown, the car, and now this. I was overwhelmed with the emotions that swirled around inside me. Bryan had gone to an awful lot of trouble. No one had ever done anything so special for me.

Tears filled my eyes, and then he appeared, stepping out from behind a column to greet me.

"When a Man Loves a Woman" began to play over the sound system, but my eyes, my heart, my soul, and all the rest of me were focused on Bryan. He had never looked so handsome or so serious.

Silky layers of brown hair rested lightly against his furrowed brow. A black tuxedo jacket hugged his broad shoulders, a crisp white shirt and a shiny black silk tie underneath. His black trousers moved fluidly against his muscular thighs as he walked toward me, his hand outstretched, his gray-green eyes beckoning with deep emotion.

"You look wonderful, Lace," he said, low and soft.

"You look wonderful too." I put my hand in his, a surge of warmth hitting my cheeks as soon as we touched.

Bryan led me out to the middle of the dance floor. Moving into his arms, I inhaled deeply, my senses flooded with the familiar pine scent of him. I licked my suddenly dry lips.

His presence, his hands on my bare skin, the strength of his shoulders beneath my fingertips, the evening, the way I felt about him—all of it made me sway a bit as if I were a little tipsy.

I drew in a shaky breath and gazed up at him. His eyes were heavy lidded, his face drawn tight with desire that I was sure matched mine.

He came closer, and I didn't resist. The time for caution was over. This man had me from the moment he'd made that first silly face at me when I was five years old. I'd only gotten a tiny glimpse of his tender heart back then, but it had been more than enough to completely rock my world.

Bryan Jackson was the constant in my life, my irresistible refrain. I could no more keep myself from needing, wanting, or returning to him than I could keep myself from breathing. It was always going to be him.

Our bodies brushed together, hard against soft, the silk of my dress rustling between us. I felt a shudder run through him. His warm hands made me shiver as they slid down my arms and came to rest on the small of my back. His eyes burned into mine as he held me close.

"Lace, I made a mistake on prom night." His voice was deep and thick with regret. "I should have claimed you back then."

I shook my head. "There was a lot going on back then, Bry. With you. With the band. I had stuff of my own to work through."

"Maybe, but it was still a mistake. You're my love, my one and only one. I'm claiming you now."

I held on to his forearms to steady myself, just as I'd done that day on the beach when he'd first kissed me. My head spun as if I'd just gotten off the Tilt-A-Whirl ride.

"What exactly are you saying?" I whispered.

He blew out a ragged breath. "I had it all planned out, but I'm finding it fucking difficult to think straight, let alone make the kind of speech you deserve when I've got you in my arms like this."

Bryan took a step back, not much, about an inch, but enough that I felt bereft without the delicious warmth of his body pressed against me. He reached in his jacket pocket, and I held my breath, my eyes filling instantly when I saw what he held.

"Oh my God." My wide eyes met his. "Is that what I think it is?"

He nodded, and I stared at him in dazed wonder.

It was the ribbon I'd worn around my neck on prom night.

"Lace Lowell, I love you. You're the most beautiful woman I've ever known, the most incredible one, and I want you to know that I've always had faith in you, even when you lost your way. I know that you're no weak-minded princess in need of rescue, and that's okay because I'm not a real prince. And it's really me who needs the rescue, from a life that means absolutely nothing to me if you're not in it."

His hands moved softly through my hair, and he scanned my features as if he was committing them to memory.

"I love you, Bryan Jackson. Your strength. Your loyalty. Your kind and valiant heart. You're a true prince to me."

"What I believe in most is us," he said softly. "You and I are better than any fairy tale. And if you want me to wait for a day, or a month, or a year for you, until you're ready for us to begin our life together, I'll do it. But just like I've been doing for the past several weeks, I'm gonna do it right here in Vancouver, where I can watch over you." His eyes blazed with intensity. "You know me. I take care of and protect what's mine."

Holy shit.

I didn't say that out loud. *Hello.* I have much more princess class than that.

I didn't need any more time to think it over. Bryan was right. I could take care of myself; I knew that now. That impediment to our being together was out of the way.

I didn't need fairy godmothers, or enchanted coaches, or even glass slippers. I just needed him. *Bryan.* His faith in me was all the magic I would ever need.

"I'm ready now, Bry." I took the ribbon from him, holding it across my neck, and turned around. Bowing my head, I offered him the loose ends to tie.

He breathed my name across my neck, and his rough fingertips trembled as they brushed across my bare skin. The silk ribbon was cool as he fastened it around my neck. Once his task was complete, he placed a soft kiss on the delicate skin between my neck and shoulder.

Bryan turned me around to face him. His dark, possessive gaze swept warmth over me before his lips claimed mine in a deep, hot, wet kiss.

Bleep. The sound of an incoming text.

"I think that's your phone," I whispered breathlessly as he rained passionate kisses up and down the column of my throat.

"Mmm." Bryan groaned without pausing from his tender assault on my fevered skin. "Forget it. Tonight's just for us."

He hauled me closer, slid the cell from his pocket, and tossed it on a nearby table without reading the message.

MARY TIMMONS: Meeting reminder: My office. Nine a.m. Tempest has a new lead singer.

Thank you!

Thanks so much for *reading Irresistible Refrain* . . . I certainly enjoyed writing it. If you would like a little more of Bryan and Lace, a bonus extended epilogue available to read for free, you can link to it here (https://dl.bookfunnel.com/drbgruc4ur).

Wondering what to read next? Check out the other Tempest novels. It's a complete series with six books ready to binge, one book for each member of Tempest. Audio add-on is offered for each book, and a steeply discounted box set is also available.

If you're in the mood to fall in love with a rock star, I have several other completed series. The Rock Stars, Surf, and Second Chances series has a box set available. And the Rock F*ck Club series has been compiled into a box set as well.

For short release texts for my new releases or sales, text ROCK BOOK to 33777.

Sign up for my newsletter for exclusive chapter reveals at http://eepurl.com/Lvgzf.

Stay in touch by joining my reader group. We have a lot of fun, and I sometimes offer advance review copies here: https://www.facebook.com/groups/1673519816224970/.

HEROIN FACTS PROVIDED BY THE NATIONAL INSTITUTE ON DRUG ABUSE

Heroin is an opioid drug that is synthesized from morphine, a naturally occurring substance extracted from the seed pod of the Asian opium poppy plant. Heroin usually appears as a white or brown powder or as a black sticky substance, known as "black tar heroin."

In 2011, 4.2 million Americans aged 12 or older (or 1.6 percent) had used heroin at least once in their lives. It is estimated that about 23 percent of individuals who use heroin become dependent on it.

How Is Heroin Used?

Heroin can be injected, inhaled by snorting or sniffing, or smoked. All three routes of administration deliver the drug to the brain very rapidly, which contributes to its health risks and to its high risk for addiction, which is a chronic relapsing disease caused by changes in the brain and characterized by uncontrollable drug-seeking no matter the consequences.

How Does Heroin Affect the Brain?

When it enters the brain, heroin is converted back into morphine, which binds to molecules on cells known as opioid receptors. These receptors are located in many areas of the brain (and in the body), especially those involved in the perception of pain and in reward. Opioid receptors are also located in the brain stem, which controls automatic processes critical for life, such as blood pressure, arousal, and respiration. Heroin overdoses frequently involve a suppression of breathing, which can be fatal.

After an intravenous injection of heroin, users report feeling a surge of euphoria ("rush") accompanied by dry mouth, a warm flushing of the skin, heaviness of the extremities, and clouded mental functioning. Following this initial euphoria, the user goes "on the nod," an alternately wakeful and drowsy state. Users who do not inject the drug may not experience the initial rush, but other effects are the same.

Regular heroin use changes the functioning of the brain. One result is tolerance, in which more of the drug is needed to achieve the same intensity of effect. Another result is dependence, characterized by the need to continue use of the drug to avoid withdrawal symptoms.

Injection Drug Use and HIV and HCV Infection

People who inject drugs are at high risk of contracting HIV and hepatitis C (HCV). This is because these diseases are transmitted through contact with blood or other bodily fluids, which can occur when sharing needles or other injection drug use equipment. (HCV is the most common blood-borne infection in the Unites States.) HIV (and less often HCV) can also be contracted during unprotected sex, which drug use makes more likely.

Because of the strong link between drug abuse and the spread of infectious disease, drug abuse treatment can be an effective way to prevent the latter. People in drug abuse treatment, which often includes risk reduction counseling, stop or reduce their drug use and related risk behaviors, including risky injection practices and unsafe sex. (See box, **"Treating Heroin Addiction."**)

What Are the Other Health Effects of Heroin?

Heroin abuse is associated with a number of serious health conditions, including fatal overdose, spontaneous abortion, and infectious diseases like hepatitis and HIV (see box, "Injection Drug Use and HIV and HCV Infection").

Chronic users may develop collapsed veins, infection of the heart lining and valves, abscesses, constipation and gastrointestinal cramping, and liver or kidney disease. Pulmonary complications, including various types of pneumonia, may result from the poor health of the user as well as from heroin's effects on breathing.

In addition to the effects of the drug itself, street heroin often contains toxic contaminants or additives that can clog blood vessels leading to the lungs, liver, kidneys, or brain, causing permanent damage to vital organs.

Treating Heroin Addiction

A range of treatments including behavioral therapies and medications are effective at helping patients stop using heroin and return to stable and productive lives.

Medications include buprenorphine and methadone, both of which work by binding to the same cell receptors as heroin but more weakly, helping a person wean off the drug and reduce craving; and naltrexone, which blocks opioid receptors and prevents the drug from having an effect (patients sometimes have trouble complying with naltrexone treatment, but a new long-acting version given by injection in a doctor's office may increase this treatment's efficacy). Another drug called naloxone is sometimes used as an emergency treatment to counteract the effects of heroin overdose.

For more information, see NIDA's handbook, Principles of Drug Addiction Treatment (http://www.drugabuse.gov/publications/principles-drug-addiction-treatment).

Chronic use of heroin leads to physical dependence, a state in which the body has adapted to the presence of the drug. If a dependent user reduces or stops use of the drug abruptly, he or she may experience severe symptoms of withdrawal. These symptoms—which can begin as early as a few hours after the last drug administration—can include restlessness, muscle and bone pain, insomnia, diarrhea and vomiting, cold flashes with goose bumps ("cold turkey"), and kicking movements ("kicking the habit"). Users also experience severe craving for the drug during withdrawal, which can precipitate continued abuse and/or relapse.

Besides the risk of spontaneous abortion, heroin abuse during pregnancy (together with related factors like poor nutrition and inadequate prenatal care) is also associated with low birth weight, an important risk factor for later delays in development. Additionally, if the mother is regularly abusing the drug, the infant may be born physically dependent on heroin and could suffer from neonatal abstinence syndrome (NAS), a drug withdrawal syndrome in infants that requires hospitalization. According to a recent study, treating opioid-addicted pregnant mothers with buprenorphine (a medication for opioid dependence) can reduce NAS symptoms in babies and shorten their hospital stays

There are real life heroes, and there is hope and help.
http://www.abovetheinfluence.com/
Go to the website. Make a difference
by supporting the cause.
Do better. Be better.

"I'm going to take that chance and I'm going to do better. I'm tired of the roller coaster I've been on. I'm tired of all the lies, especially the ones I've been telling myself. I really thought I could quit whenever I decided. I realize now that's not true." – Lace Lowell

ABOUT THE AUTHOR

Michelle Mankin is the New York Times bestselling author of the Black Cat Records series of novels.

Fall in love with a rock star.

Love Evolution, Love Revolution, and Love Resolution are a **BRUTAL STRENGTH** centered trilogy, combining the plot underpinnings of Shakespeare with the drama, excitement, and indisputable sexiness of the rock 'n roll industry.

Things take a bit of an edgier, once upon a time turn with the **TEMPEST** series. These pierced, tatted, and troubled Seattle rockers are young and on the cusp of making it big, but with serious obstacles to overcome that may prevent them from ever getting there.

Rock stars, myths, and legends collide with paranormal romance in a totally mesmerizing way in the **MAGIC** series.

Romance and self-discovery, the **FINDING ME** series is a Tempest spin off with a more experienced but familiar cast of characters.

The **ROCK F*CK CLUB** series is a girl-power fueled reality show with the girls ranking the rock stars.

The **Once Upon A Rock Star** series is sexy modern-day fairytale retellings.

When Michelle is not prowling the streets of her Texas town listening to her rock or NOLA funk music much too loud, she is putting her daydreams down on paper or traveling the world with her family and friends, sometimes for real, and sometimes just for pretend.

BRUTAL STRENGTH series:
Love Evolution
Love Revolution
Love Resolution
Love Rock'ollection

TEMPEST series (also available in audio):
SOUTHSIDE HIGH
Irresistible Refrain
Enticing Interlude
Captivating Bridge
Relentless Rhythm
Tempest Raging
Tempting Tempo
Scandalous Beat
The Complete Tempest Rock Star Series, Books 1-6

The MAGIC series (also available in audio):
Strange Magic
Dream Magic
Twisted Magic

ROCK STARS, SURF AND SECOND CHANCES series
(also available in audio):
Outside
Riptide
Oceanside
High Tide
Island Side
The Complete Rock Stars, Surf and Second Chances Series,
Books 1-5

FINDING ME series (also available in audio):
Find Me
Remember Me
Keep Me

Girls Ranking the Rock Stars series
(also available in audio):
ROCK F*CK CLUB (Girls Ranking the Rock Stars, Book 1)
ROCK F*CK CLUB (Girls Ranking the Rock Stars, Book 2)
ROCK F*CK CLUB (Girls Ranking the Rock Stars, Book 3)
ROCK F*CK CLUB (Girls Ranking the Rock Stars, Book 4)
ROCK F*CK CLUB (Girls Ranking the Rock Stars, Book 5)
ROCK F*CK CLUB BOX SET BOOKS 1-5
ROCK F*CK CLUB (Girls Ranking the Rock Stars, Book 6)

ONCE UPON A ROCK STAR series
The Right Man
The Right Wish
The Right Wrong

The Music and Art of Black Cat Records
For cover reveal, flash sale, and release alerts:
Text ROCK BOOK to 33777 (US only)
For release alerts, follow the author on Bookbub:
https://www.bookbub.com/authors/michelle-mankin
Receive exclusive content in the Black Cat Records
newsletter: http://eepurl.com/Lvgzf
Hang out with me in my reader group. Join the Rock All
Stars. Be an Author Michelle Mankin VIP.
Find the author on Instagram:
https://instagram.com/michellemankin/
Facebook: https://www.facebook.com/pages/
Author-Michelle-Mankin/233503403414065
Twitter: https://twitter.com/MichelleMankin
Her website: http://www.michellemankin.com/

Made in United States
North Haven, CT
08 May 2023

36392173R00174